He's in hiding... until her.

FALCON

Kindred Book Five

SCARLETT FINN

Also by Scarlett Finn

GO NOVELS
GO WITH IT
GO IT ALONE
GO ALL OUT
GO ALL IN
GO FULL CIRCLE

EXILE
HIDE & SEEK
KISS CHASE

WRECK & RUIN
RUIN ME
RUIN HIM

THE BRANDED SERIES
BRANDED
SCARRED
MARKED

FORBIDDEN PREQUEL DUET
ALL. ONLY.
ONLY YOURS

NOTHING TO...
NOTHING TO HIDE
NOTHING TO LOSE
NOTHING IN BETWEEN: ONE
NOTHING TO DECLARE
NOTHING TO US
NOTHING IN BETWEEN: TWO
NOTHING TO SAY
NOTHING TO GAIN
NOTHING IN BETWEEN: THREE
NOTHING TO YOU
NOTHING TO THIS PREQUEL: ONE WILD NIGHT
NOTHING TO THIS
NOTHING IN BETWEEN: FOUR
NOTHING TO DO
NOTHING TO FEAR
NOTHING IN BETWEEN: FIVE
NOTHING TO DENY

THE FORBIDDEN NOVELS
FORBIDDEN DESIRE
FORBIDDEN WANT
FORBIDDEN WISH
FORBIDDEN NEED
FORBIDDEN BOND

TO DIE FOR...
TO DIE FOR TRUTH
TO DIE FOR HONOR
TO DIE FOR VIRTUE
TO DIE FOR DUTY
TO DIE FOR LOVE

LOVE AGAINST THE ODDS STANDALONE COLLECTION
SWEET SEAS
HEIR'S AFFAIR
RESCUED
MAESTRO'S MUSE
GETTING TRICKY
THIRTEEN
REMEMBER WHEN...
RELUCTANT SUSPICION
XY FACTOR

KINDRED SERIES
RAVEN
SWALLOW
CUCKOO
SWIFT
FALCON
FINCH

THE EXPLICIT SERIES
EXPLICIT INSTRUCTION
EXPLICIT DETAIL
EXPLICIT MEMORY

MISTAKE DUET
MISTAKE ME NOT
SLEIGHT MISTAKE

RISQUÉ & HARROW INTERTWINED
TAKE A RISK
FIGHTING FATE
RISK IT ALL
FIGHTING BACK
GAME OF RISK

LOST & FOUND
LOST
FOUND

ONE

DARKNESS. The only certainty Devon had was that she would spend each day in darkness.

Most of the time she was gagged and attached to the metal wall by cuffs and heavy chains at the small of her back. Her only reprieve from those binds came when she was taken to the dank bathroom once or twice a day.

During those times, she wasn't relieved of her gag or blindfold, not that it mattered because the internal room had no light or window. So even when she tried to take off the blindfold, she was greeted by darkness.

Today was Saturday. Her Spanish was pretty good, so she could pick out most of the words her captors exchanged. Those words were few because they weren't often nearby, but when they were, she listened closely. At first, she'd been intent on their conversations because she wanted to know where she was and what was going on. After that, there was simply nothing better to do than follow along with what she heard.

The fast Mexican drawl wasn't the only sound. She also heard the voices of terrified women, often American and young, pleading for mercy. Screams of torture and tears of agony gave Devon a clue about her fate.

The small cell she occupied wasn't much more than a

four-foot square. She couldn't lie down or sit up straight, as the bolt that was welded to the wall where she was chained protruded into her spine. Devon could slouch and stretch her leg to touch the other three walls around her, so she knew she was shut in tight even though she had no visibility. From the close quarters, she had to assume that wherever they were, space was at a premium, meaning her captors endeavored to maximize it by packing their victims in tight.

For hours at a time, all she heard was the clang of metal and the shuffle of bodies. In her first days here, she hadn't tried to call out for help; the other women who arrived at the same time did too much shouting for her to be heard. But when she did gather the courage to question the men who came to her, they beat and gagged her.

When new girls came, they called out but received no reply. The resident girls were either gagged or knew better than to engage in dialogue. Devon listened as other women were beaten and threatened by the men who referred to them as 'cattle' or 'heifers.'

After enduring the onslaught of regular assaults, the women learned to be silent. It didn't help that they weren't fed much, meaning their strength was quickly sapped. Even crying became exhausting when you were surviving on an ounce or two of dirty water and table scraps every few days.

Sometimes a real fighter came along, but those girls didn't last long. Their screams faded into the distance as they were dragged away, never to be heard from again.

Devon didn't know how many women were caged here, it could be five, it could be fifty. Just as she didn't know how many men ran this racket. She wasn't even sure how long she'd been here. The first few days had been a blur of crying, screaming, and beatings, then in her period of despair when she'd come to accept her helplessness, she became so numb that she didn't even bother to open her eyes, let alone register how many days passed.

At night it got cold. She hadn't been given a blanket, so her only protection against the plummeting temperature was the blue dress she'd been wearing when she was snatched. Given the darkness that she existed in, surrounded by the smell of rusted metal, foul sweat, and stale urine, the temperature was the only way she could tell when one sun set or another rose.

In her head, she sang and imagined the vivid landscapes she'd painted. She tried to conjure memories of the long brushes in her fingers and the scrape of pencil lead on weighty paper. Art was her greatest love. She'd made some money with her creations but always had to work other jobs to make ends meet.

This existence wasn't living, but there was no escape and no explanations. She had to have hope, to believe she'd get out of this predicament, but she had no idea how it would happen while she was locked in irons and sealed in this metal box. The heat became unbearable at times, and she'd discovered there had to be holes somewhere above her because sometimes she'd feel a welcome breeze, though that could just be a delusion brought on by her seclusion. She often felt she was losing her grip on reality.

Sliding from asleep to awake, she'd stopped feeling the pain of her restraints and expected this day to be like any other. Footsteps came first and she piqued, expecting to be treated to the sound of voices.

Much as she hated these men for what they were doing to her and the other women, hearing them talk, sometimes about current events or the weather, was the only normal human contact she experienced, even if it was by proxy. For those few minutes while she listened to them, she could pretend that she was eavesdropping on a conversation in a coffee shop rather than in her prison.

There were several people in the hallway outside her cell, she could hear them moving around, but they weren't talking. A door was opened, movement followed, and then the cell slammed shut and the noise ebbed away.

Trying to figure out what the men out there were up to was futile; she'd stopped even trying. So when calm returned, she let her eyes close and tried to grab some elusive sleep. But just when she was drifting off, the noise came again, closer this time. Metal rattled, and the scrape of rust intensified the oxidized odor.

A rush of air came as the heavy door to her cell was opened. Two men spoke in Spanish, but their words were so fast that she struggled to compute what they were saying. She was only escorted to the bathroom once or twice a day, and until now it had always been by a single man who took her into the blackened hallway.

This time, a shotgun barrel touched her neck. A heavy male body crouched to muscle her aside, then Devon was being unshackled. Hauled to her feet, the gun moved and she was shoved out of the cell into the corridor where there were half a dozen new voices all commenting on how little time they had or what she looked like. Never had so many men been around when she'd been taken for a quick bathroom visit.

Shoved forward, Devon was forced down the hall into a room at the far end. Not all the voices followed her, only one figure came in behind her to slam the door, sealing them alone inside.

Although she was able to stand, she still couldn't see. Sound had been her greatest ally and worst enemy while she was here. The pant of breath behind her made her edgy, and the rush of water in front of her sounded almost like a shower, but there was no heat.

Her legs struggled when they were given control of her body again after being cramped for such long periods. Their numbness became a painful tingle, and she shifted to try and relieve her discomfort. Their usual bathroom consisted of a toilet and didn't contain so much as a sink. If there was a shower in here, this room was new to her.

"You shower," the voice behind her said, then he whipped off her blindfold.

A blade touched her neck and in time with her gasp, he sliced through the fabric of her dress and underwear, slashing her skin in the process and leaving her nude. Without her blindfold, she could see that there was no light invading this space. These men had to be paranoid about the women escaping or outside observers because Devon had never seen a window.

In the darkness, her modesty came second to the

sting on her hip caused by his blade. She had no way to know how deep the cut was, because her hands were still connected to each other at the small of her back. From the intensity of the pain, she feared it went through to the bone, but her defenses were low and her equilibrium shot, so it could easily have been nothing more than a scratch.

The offending knife came around her throat, so close to her skin that a deep breath could have caused him to cut her.

The man behind her was large and smelled of sweat, but when he unlocked her hands from each other, she was grateful to him for a moment. Mobility was bliss, but Devon couldn't fully embrace it, as she was forced forward into the gush of lukewarm water and reality impacted her in a blink.

A bar of slippery soap was thrust into her hand. "You shower," he commanded again.

The space in the shower stall was so small that when she lifted her hands to run them through her hair, her elbows hit the side walls. Devon tried to step out of the stream of water and was prodded in the back with the blade. Tiled walls on three sides hemmed her in, fighting would achieve nothing and there wasn't a better place for him to stab her to death and wash away the evidence if she tested his patience.

He wanted her to shower and she wanted to be clean, for now their wants segued. She lathered the soap and cleaned her body, avoiding the open wound on her hip and the one on her back. The suds still made them sting, but they weren't agonizing, so she took that as a good sign.

"Hurry now," he said, fumbling for her hands to snatch the soap. It clattered to the floor and she tensed in preparation for his wrath at her clumsiness. Except it wasn't clumsiness, she'd been revolted at the feel of his hands on hers and had reacted by trying to get away.

Bracing her hands on the walls, she couldn't see a thing and had no idea what fate these monsters had for her. The heat of the stranger came closer to her naked form, and she held her breath, expecting the worst. Icy liquid seeped onto the top of her head compelling her to gasp.

"Wash your hair," he commanded.

The scent of shampoo began to permeate as the thick goo spread on her crown, so she did as she was told.

Once the last of the shampoo had run away, she was pulled from the spray and pushed face first against a dry wall. Fearful of what this possible ogre could do to her, she swallowed her parched terror and clenched her fists, ready to fight if she had to.

A warm metal cuff closed around her wrist. Once it was secure, he wrenched her arm to her lower back and forced the other down to be locked in a second thick cuff. The knife he'd used to keep her obedient wasn't in his hand anymore and the shotgun was gone too. His size made it unlikely she'd triumph in a fight, so if she wanted to win, she'd need the weapon.

Using the dark to do more than disorient her, he'd ensured she couldn't seize a weapon she couldn't see. With all his pulling and shoving, her sense of direction was lost, too, so despite her assumption that this room was small, she still wouldn't be able to find the exit.

She had tried pleading with her captors before and it had never worked, but she wasn't ready to surrender yet. "Why are you doing this? Please let me go," she said.

The man backed away, and she stalled her breathing, hoping beyond expectation that he might listen or that maybe this shower had been a prelude to release all along.

"I'm not allowed to mark your body today, but if you do not sell tonight, my boss will let us have you." The tone of menace in his unmoved voice made her already frigid body chill.

Sell? Sell what? If the alternative was being handed over to this oaf and his buddies, then she'd sell sand in the desert. There was no time for her to try and figure out what he meant. Something dug into her hair and pulled down, and it took her a second to realize that he was combing her wet hair.

When it stuck in her locks, he cursed but carried on until it was combed, ignoring her yelps of pain when the comb snagged. After it left her hair for the last time, she stayed pressed to the wall, listening to the deep pants coming from her assailant.

Devon wanted to ask what was going to happen to her. But she was terrified that he might give her an honest answer and she wasn't prepared for what he might say.

Having endured so much sensory deprivation, her sight was useless, but her hearing was heightened. His breathing became so magnified that the burn of tears she'd thought were long dried up streaked her face again.

"Please let me go," she whimpered, resting her forehead on the wall, but he said nothing. "Déjame ir, por favor."

Her energy was gone and her legs gave out, sending her to the floor. There was nothing left to fight for. It was hopeless. At first her cell was a prison, but now it was a sanctuary for her. Out here was unknown, in her cell she listened, tried to sleep, and had her hands released during the times they served the slop they gave her for food. Here in this hell, that was the happiest her life could be.

Women were treated as animals, beaten for misbehaving, and when they left, they never came back. Since she'd been here, they'd hosed her down in her cell twice, but they'd never given her a shower or let her shampoo her hair. Much as she wanted to believe her luck was turning, she was too realistic to think this situation could ever culminate in a positive experience.

Grabbing hold of her arm, he pulled her up, and raised a knee to drive it against her spine. When he covered her eyes again, he didn't use the standard dirty rag blindfold. The fabric was softer, and it had a band of elastic that went over her ears to hold it around her head. Lace scratched her cheeks and she figured it out, it was a sleep mask.

The cuffs weren't the same restraints she'd worn before the shower either. The new ones were looser and gave her more latitude to separate her hands because there was a foot of chain between them. Devon still couldn't get out of the shackles, but the changes were noteworthy because to her they meant one thing: she wasn't going back into that cell.

While she figured all of this out, something was put around her neck. Warm and smooth, she smelled leather and heard him fasten a buckle that constricted her throat as it tightened. Devon had worn her share of chokers, but she had never worn a collar.

Her neck was pulled forward and the door opened. The collar had to have a leash because she was tugged forward again, but no one was touching her. Stumbling along the corridor, she had no idea where they were going, except this walk was longer than any she'd had since she'd been here.

Voices returned and were joined by some jeering wolf whistles. They stopped and her heart was beating so hard that she could feel each pulse in her ears. Metal scraped and squeaked, a door maybe, then they were walking again.

Through the sleep mask, she could see glimmers of light but couldn't pick out figures to go with the speakers who seemed to be moving with them. Becoming aware that she was still naked and now in a place with illumination, the crowds of voices belonged to men who could see every inch of her.

Being tugged and yanked was making the back of her neck hurt, but not as much as the flesh at the edge of the collar that was cutting in and chaffing every time he pulled it.

Another door was opened and the voices around her came to an abrupt silence. Susurration in the new space piqued her interest until she was yanked forth into the familiar atmosphere of an air-conditioned room. All this time she'd been close to home comforts and they'd been denied to her. Maybe this was where the cool air she'd felt in her cell had come from.

Until they were taken away, she hadn't realized how she relished life's little luxuries. If she got out of here, she vowed to never take what she had for granted again.

She was led out about eight feet and halted when the tugging stopped. At the same time, the murmurs that emanated from one direction, ceased.

"Here we have the final lot of the night, our most premium specimen. An unblemished brunette, a petite model, delicate at five foot four and now less than a hundred pounds. She is an English-speaking American. I'll remind all participants that bids are in United States dollars. She comes with new ID papers and a corresponding passport. I'll start the bidding at ten thousand dollars."

Bids. The masculine voice who had declared the terms was a native English speaker, a confident one without compunction. The bidders had to be using paddles or something because they were silent, but the auctioneer was talking faster and faster as the bids grew.

Like cattle, she was being sold. Everything slotted into place and panic seized her. Reeling from this development, and on instinct, she pulled away from the leash and because her captor wasn't expecting her resistance, she got away from him. The blindfold was restricting and with her hands cuffed behind her back, she wouldn't be able to pull it. Still, launching herself forward, she ran until she hit a wall. Using her body, Devon tried to find a doorway, but she'd struggle to open it with her hands where they were. Something burned her waist and she screamed, but her body spasmed and hit the floor, then everything went black.

TWO

DEVON FELT LIKE she was floating. Her whole body was warm and so relaxed that she thought she might be resting in a nest of s'mores.

The sweet scent of vanilla made her smile and stretch. And that was when she became aware of the knots in her muscles and the aches in her bones. The pleasure of the moment disintegrated and she sat up.

She was in a bed. A large bed. Except the last thing she remembered was…

Holding the white bedsheet to her chest, she tried to figure out where she might be. A bedspread was folded the width of the bottom of the bed. Intricately embroidered, it matched the canopy on the regal mahogany four-poster bed she sat in the center of.

Looking from one side of the bed to the other, she registered that there were two doors, one in the far corner, beside heavy, drawn drapes that had to cover a window and another larger one to the left of the bed. Nightstands flanked the bed, simple tables without drawers, and there was no other furniture in the rectangular room.

Although there was no imminent danger or weapons trained on her, she wasn't ready to breathe in relief yet. Intent on checking out what was behind the doors, Devon tossed back the covers and jumped out of the bed. Sidetracked by her need to see some natural light, she seized the drapes and yanked them open.

Except she was disappointed. Pressing her hand to the glass, she could see light, but there was no view, just fogged glass that distorted the landscape so much there was nothing to see but a vague white glow.

With hopes for a moment of happiness dashed, Devon became more determined to find a weapon or a way to escape. Heading for the humble, secondary corner door near the window, she opened it to find a sleek, modern bathroom containing a double wide shower and what a surprise… no window.

Back in the bedroom, she tried the larger door, but it was locked, confirming her worst fear: she was a prisoner again. Detailed memories of her previous captivity came back to her, and she went to sit on the bed.

Letting her head fall into her hands, she recalled the auction. The panic. Her attempt to flee. It hadn't mattered. She had been sold. She could be anywhere in the world, in the home of a pervert who may have plans to do anything to her.

All her life she'd avoided being bad. Her roots were humble and most of her family members had spent some time in jail, but she'd always been good and had worked hard to earn an honest living. How could her life end in this way? Devon couldn't understand how fate could lay this destiny on her when she'd never hurt anyone in her life.

Wallowing wasn't going to get her anywhere, so she took a deep breath and straightened up. At the auction, she'd been naked. Now she was wearing a white, cotton nightgown with wide straps. Just as she registered that, the large door opened.

Devon leaped to her feet and prepared to fight, but she came up short when a middle-aged woman came in wearing a smile and carrying a tray. The woman kicked the door closed with her heel and came deep into the room.

"I'm pleased you're awake, I was beginning to worry," she said, putting the tray on the nightstand. "I have bottled water for you."

The woman sat near the pillows on the bed, took a branded bottle from the tray, and held it toward her. Though the woman still wore a polite smile, had a plump waistline, and projected a calm benevolent air, which was completely unthreatening, Devon was reluctant to trust her.

"I'm Bess," the woman said. "What's your name?"

Devon wasn't going to fall for any act that might make her feel secure. For all she knew, this was what got her boss off. He could be watching this pleasant conversation. She knew nothing of who had been at that auction.

This Bess woman sounded American, but that didn't mean they were in the States. The person who had purchased her could be related or married to this woman pretending to be her friend. If they wanted to hurt and humiliate her, she wasn't going to trot along like the lamb to the slaughter. Maybe Bess was testing her naivety. Could they want a sweet little virgin who they could corrupt and destroy? If they did, she didn't have to play to that.

She'd learned about her captors during her last captivity by pushing them, getting as near to their boundaries as she could. Granted, they didn't have a high threshold for sass, but maybe this new environment was different.

Devon couldn't hope to find a way out if she didn't test what her new hosts would let her get away with. Information was going to be the key to her freedom, that and taking every opportunity, but while they kept her locked in here, she wasn't going anywhere.

"The traffickers didn't tell your boss?" Devon sneered but angled her anger at the bottle because she feared too direct a confrontation. Despite being benign, Bess could be a cobra waiting to snap. Devon didn't know and she didn't trust her own judgment so soon after waking up here. "Didn't they say I come with papers like a Kennel Club mutt?"

"Forged papers meant to get you in and out of countries as necessary. We want your real name, if you're willing to give it."

"Devon," she said, seeing no way her first name could

be used as a weapon against her. Taking the water bottle, she checked that the seal was intact before she opened and began to gulp. If they meant to poison or drug her, she'd have to give in to that reality. Weakening herself by refusing water or food wouldn't serve her purpose.

"Take your time, dearie," Bess said and touched Devon's knee.

The unexpected contact made Devon recoil, and the open water bottle dropped out of her hand to glug the remainder of its contents onto the thick carpet. The stain spread fast, and Devon was taken back to a place of anxiety. Being clumsy, making a mess, meant punishment.

Bess went to the floor to pick up the bottle and plucked a cloth from her pocket to begin blotting the carpet.

"I'm sorry," Devon said, dropping to her knees opposite Bess, though there was little she could do to help clean up.

"Don't you worry," Bess said. "It's my fault, I've always been tactile like that. The boys always remind me to be reserved, especially in the early days."

No punishment? Falling back from her knees onto her butt, she examined the woman who was focused on the stain, completely unguarded, and paying no heed to Devon, who could launch an attack if she wanted to. Beating Bess wouldn't get her far because she didn't know if the door to the room was even unlocked, and if someone was watching, she doubted they'd forgo punishment after an escape attempt.

Still, Devon couldn't figure out why this woman was so nonplussed by her bad behavior. Accidental though it was, Devon had just given Bess the excuse to show her true nature and dish out a taste of the limits in this place. Yet there had been no reprisal. "I don't… I don't understand," Devon said.

Bess continued to mop. "I'm not surprised that you're disorientated. The cartel insists on strong sedatives so that the women can't identify them or where they are. They're particular about concealing their identity and location. I'm sure the sedative on top of the taser blast must have thrown you for a loop."

This was all so much for Devon to take in. Bess was

being… nice. Too exhausted to try and figure out the plot behind this act, Devon suppressed her exhaustion and sat up on her heels, reminding herself to be vigilant. "Where are we?"

Bess finished up and put the damp cloth back in the pocket of her apron. "You're safe here, Devon, completely safe."

Tempted to believe the kindly woman, Devon let herself be gathered up by Bess and placed back on the bed beside her. "Then when am I locked up? Why can't I see out of the window?"

Becoming contrite, Bess patted her hand. "Unfortunately, we have to be careful about revealing our location and identities too."

Devon was sure she knew why that was and shifted up the bed away from Bess. "Because your boss enjoys raping women? Torturing them?" If a man wanted to abuse a woman, it would stand to reason that he didn't want that woman to have any sense of control. Concealing even the view constrained her. Despite not being in chains, she was still a prisoner at their mercy. "What am I to expect? What's my fate going to be? What will he do to me?"

Bess reached out, but Devon wouldn't let herself be touched. She didn't want to be touched. She was tired of being touched and contorted by others without them needing to have any consideration for her wants.

"He is a good man. But you don't have to worry about facing him. You will never see the man who purchased you," Bess said, further confusing Devon. What was the point of buying her if she was never going to see him? More questions arose in Devon's mind after Bess' next statement. "A doctor will come to you later. You shouldn't fear him; he'll visit you in a professional capacity." Bess rose. "There is soup in the bowl, try your best to eat something."

Removing the soup bowl from the tray, Bess put it on the nightstand and took the tray with her as she went in the direction of the door.

Unsatisfied, afraid of the unknown, and reluctant to lose the only direct female or kind contact she'd had in a long time—even if Bess' behavior was a ruse—Devon began to panic. "Wait," Devon said, leaping up. "I don't understand. What happens next?"

"Next we fix you up," Bess said, her smile returned. "You can drink the water in the bathroom, refill your bottle as much as you like. You can shower if you want to as well. But I'd advise you to eat and rest first. You're skin on bone, dearie. You need to get your strength back. You can take all the time you need."

Returning to her former self was unlikely, she would never be the same after this experience. Her health might improve, but she'd never be the same inside. Spending another minute here, anywhere where she was out of control, would lead to more anxiety. Devon couldn't take living in this fraught state any longer. "Will you let me leave here? I want to leave."

Tears of frustration, anger, and devastation threatened to spring, but she sealed her lips, determined not to break in front of this stranger.

Softening, like she could tell Devon was right on the edge, Bess' chosen tone was meant to soothe. "The doctor will check you out before we think about that. We'll get you better, back to full strength, and then we'll get you back to your family, don't worry."

Bess pressed her thumb to an illuminated blue circle in the middle of the doorknob, and it flashed. That had to be the key to getting out of here, fingerprint recognition. Great, Devon had no chance of disabling that. After Bess was gone, there was no sound of a key on the other side of the door.

Devon waited a few seconds then darted over to check the door again, just in case Bess had neglected to secure it. But it was locked, making Devon assume it was an automatic bolt.

Going back to the bed, she sipped from the remnants of her water. The bowl of soup was thick and warm, steam rose from the shining surface. Dipping the tip of her finger in the warm liquid, it wasn't scalding, the temperature was just right.

Licking her finger clean, she was struck by the potency of the flavors that burst in her mouth. Unable to resist the temptation, she snatched up the bowl to begin slurping. It didn't matter that no spoon had been provided; she didn't need one. She was famished and hadn't had real food in what felt like months.

When the soup was finished, she drank more water and flopped onto her back. Whether she was safe or not, this was a real bed and she needed to sleep. So she let her eyes close and hoped to have more strength when she woke.

***

STIRRING FROM HER sleep, Devon sensed that someone was close by. But when she opened her eyes, the last thing she expected to see was a man sitting on the edge of her bed.

Scrambling to a seated position, she took in his features: handsome, maybe mid-thirties, clear blue eyes and a faint smile on his lips.

"What are you doing here?" she asked, clutching the sheet to her chest although she still wore the cotton nightgown beneath. "Are you him…? The guy who's going to…"

"I'm the doctor, Bess told you I was coming."

When he scooted closer, she scooted away toward the other side of the bed. It was downright creepy that he'd been sitting there, watching her sleep. He couldn't be one of the men who'd told Bess not to touch because he clearly had no concept of decency himself.

"I don't need a doctor," she said. "I just want to leave."

The strength of his brow and narrowness of his eyes was peculiar. "We're here to help you," he said. "There's a nasty gash on your hip and your back was bleeding at the auction. The taser can have after-effects too."

Ah-ha! She'd caught them in a lie. "You were at the auction? Bess said I would never meet the man who purchased me. So she's a liar, that nice lady thing was all an act? I don't know what kind of operation you're running, but if you think I'll be charmed by some soup and a fancy bed then you're wrong." Tossing the sheet away, she climbed out of the bed on the opposite side from the one he was sitting on. "If you want to help me, let me go."

Wobbling on her feet, Devon felt light-headed and grabbed for the post at the foot of the bed.

"Let's take a step back," he said, rising from the bed, but his tone didn't come across to her as calming. It was condescending, coming from a know-it-all doctor, and it only succeeded in raising her hackles. Except, she had to keep blinking because her eyes were blurring and couldn't maintain focus. "I'm an MD, an emergency room resident. You can call me Wren."

She didn't want his name or his help. "Good for you, Wren, let me go."

"Bess didn't lie to you. I wasn't present at the auction, and I wasn't the one who paid for you. I got a report about it from my colleague," he said, ignoring her plea for freedom.

Closing her arms around the post, she began to regain her balance. "That's convenient, is that the same ghost colleague Bess referred to? The one I'll never meet?"

"Yes," he said.

Nothing made sense. If she'd been sold to these people for sex, why wasn't she being subjected to assault? Why wasn't she forced to be naked? Why were these people being nice to her and why was this purchaser even at an auction if he had no intention of ever meeting her? "Why? Why can't I meet this phantom?"

"There's no need for you to meet him," Wren said. "Bess will provide all the meals you need. I'll tend to your injuries. I want to take some blood and run some tests—"

"Why would I let you stick me with a needle?" she said and let go of the post only to grab for it again when invisible heat rushed north. "Why would I show you my body and let you examine me?"

"I'm a doctor."

According to him he was. Just like with Bess, this guy acted like he was entitled to do whatever he wanted. He might be telling her that it was for her own good, but that was her decision. If she wanted help, she was capable of finding a hospital on her own. "How do I know that? Am I supposed to trust you because you show up with a couple of Band-Aids?"

"I… I'm telling you that I'm a doctor, and yes, you should trust us because we saved you from that place. Would you sit down, please? You're running a fever."

"I am not," she objected but twisted to collapse on the bed, twining her arm around the post and resting her face against it. "What's wrong with me? Did you drug me? What was in that soup?"

"You weren't drugged," he said. "We want you well and strong, Devon. No one will hurt you here, you have to trust us."

They weren't being upfront about what had gone on or their plans for her. Knowing that she couldn't let her guard down, she did what she could to maintain it, despite encroaching dizziness. "You demand my trust," Devon said. "But you don't trust me."

"We don't—"

"You say you rescued me, but you've locked me in here. You want me to trust that you're a doctor here to care for me? But you won't tell me where we are. Get real. And what's with the mysterious guy, the one who purchased me? Is he the wizard behind the curtain? Something doesn't add up. No, I—"

"We have to protect ourselves. You could endanger what we do if you reveal our details. We're withholding to protect others."

He came into view in front of her, and she pulled her legs onto the bed to scramble back. "Admitting that you're not telling me everything doesn't help you. I won't give you my trust until you give me yours. I don't want you to touch me! I don't want anyone to touch me!"

With a step backwards, he seemed stunned, and for a man who apparently made snap life and death decisions, that was suspicious. She had no doubt in her statement.

"You won't let me treat you?"

Yeah, he had it now. Why should she trust this stranger to stick her with a needle? Devon felt sick and crawled back up the bed, closing her eyes to try and quell her nausea. "You don't trust me, and that gives me no reason to trust you. I won't be a part of your sordid experiment. Prove to me you mean well and let me go."

She couldn't say any more, now it was up to him. All decisions were his now. He could do as she asked, or he could disprove his claims by forcing her to submit against her will. Whatever he did next would prove his morals.

To his credit, he didn't leap onto the bed and attack her, but he didn't toss her a key for the front door either. After a few seconds of gaping, Doctor Wren went around the bed and bent to pick up a plastic medic case from the floor that she hadn't previously seen.

Turning over, she watched him leave in the same way Bess had. There wasn't enough energy left in her reserves to let her move to check the door again, and she couldn't handle having her hopes dashed again anyway.

She would love a shower and a drink of fresh, cool water, but she couldn't be sure they weren't watching her, and until she had proof of their intentions Devon couldn't accept any more of their aid.

THREE

"IF SHE REFUSES treatment, there's nothing I can do."

Devon could hear the voices, but they were faded and fuzzy. She'd been vaguely aware of them for maybe a minute or two, though her sense of time was off. She felt detached from her own body, like her mind was swimming somewhere else while her figure felt heavy and weak.

Immobile in what she assumed was the bed she'd woken up in when she first arrived here, Devon could barely open her eyes, so she gave up trying. Her mouth was dry, and when she parted her lips, something plastic squeezed between them. It took her a moment to figure out that it was a straw.

"Go on, dearie, drink," came a female voice and on instinct Devon sucked the cool liquid that was being offered.

"Don't let her drink too fast," a male said.

Devon released the straw and opened her eyes enough to see Wren at the end of the bed. Bess was seated beside her. While she did see these images, it still felt as though she were watching the scene rather than existing in the same moment with them.

"Look at her," Bess said. "She's burning up." Bess reached over to shift a wet weight on Devon's head that was neither hot nor cold. "You have to do something."

"If she refuses treatment, I can't touch her."

Bess scoffed, losing patience. "Boy, don't give me your ethics now, this poor girl needs help."

"It's illegal," he said. "It's assault."

Another sound of impatience left Bess' lips before she got up from the bed to join the doctor. "Don't give me that," she said. "Tell me it's illegal? How did this girl get here? Of all the things you all do—"

"I don't break the law, I just… tag along."

Devon's eyes closed because it was too much effort to keep them open, and her vision was blurred anyway. She tried her best to focus on sound instead, feeling that it was important to hold on to one point to steady her sanity. Although as the seconds ticked by, she felt more and more like she was sinking.

"You're going to help that girl. She needs it. Don't you give me, 'Do no harm' and then watch her wither away. There's something about mental competence, isn't there? She's delusional. She's not in her right mind. If you get her better, she'll thank you. You don't have a choice."

They were talking about her, yet she was too foggy to contribute. "She'll let me treat her if she meets him," Wren said. "She said if we showed trust—"

"He won't come," Bess said. "You know him better than to expect that. Most of the time it's a struggle to get him to talk to us. He won't come."

"Not even to prevent her death?"

"He won't come up here, he'll never lay eyes on her again."

"I'm supposed to compromise my moral code by forcing treatment on a patient who doesn't want it."

"She's not a standard patient," Bess said. "You get stubborn about all the wrong things, my boy. He is the way he is."

"Maybe I'm sick of giving him dispensation for that."

"Look at all he does for us," Bess said. "Your issues with your cousin are your own. Would you let an innocent woman die just to prove a point to him?"

Wren didn't respond. Or maybe he did and Devon

didn't hear it. What she did hear was the word "cousin," so they were related. The man who'd purchased her was the doctor's cousin. Holding on to that one small revelation, something she probably wasn't supposed to have heard.

She opened her lips again, but whatever she meant to say was lost. The heaviness in her body began to consume her mind. Speckles of light became dark; dizziness made her head feel like it was spinning despite her never moving an inch.

Whatever these people had done to her, whatever they planned to do, she was weak and powerless. This could be how they wanted her, but there was genuine worry in their voices. The trouble was, she didn't know what reality was and what was a dream because nothing seemed tangible anymore, she barely remembered who she was, what she wanted from life. Her dreams and ambitions were gone; surviving had become her primary objective, and today it seemed she was going to fail in that accomplishment.

***

THE NEXT SPELL of her life was nothing but mottled images, pieces of words and statements intermingled with images of everything and nothing. Devon's awareness faded in and out. Sometimes she was lucid and remembered exactly what had happened to her. Other times, she struggled to remember her name. Sometimes Bess came with food that she refused, and whenever she was with-it enough, she refused all of Doctor Wren's treatment.

More time went by and the heaviness faded. One day, morning, noon, or night later, Devon lay in bed wrapped in the thick bedspread and began to speculate about what the lack of sound meant.

All alone in this room, for the first time she felt that her fingers and toes were completely under her control. Seeking water, she found a bottle on the bedside. When she sat up, her body screamed, each joint ached, her muscles were stiff. But she had no idea how long she'd been confined in this room, because she'd been fading in and out of consciousness while she struggled to regain her health.

She was sipping the water when the door opened and Bess came in. The beaming grin on the woman's face was almost enough to make Devon smile. Except her throat still scratched and still ached, she wasn't quite herself yet.

"Good morning," Bess said, full of joy as she came over to smooth the bedspread that was so large it still covered the bed despite being wrapped around Devon. "Did you sleep well?"

"I think so," Devon said, pushing her hair away before she leaned to the side to put the bottle back on the nightstand. Dragging her fingers through her greasy hair, she craved the comfort and refreshment of a shower but feared how she might handle life outside this bed. "What happened to me? I can't remember exactly what…" Trying to put the pieces together was too difficult.

"You had a fever," Bess said. "It's no surprise. We worried that you might have a parasite or an infection. Wren has chased it away now."

"A parasite? From where?"

"You didn't have one, Wren ran tests just to be sure. We have all types of state-of-the-art medical equipment here. You might not remember, but we have been looking after you."

"I told him not to treat me," Devon said, only partially aware of the conversation she'd had with the doctor, though she did remember feeling unwell during it, feeling dizzy and struggling to stay upright. "How do I know you didn't infect me with something?"

"We've given you good food and clean water," Bess said. "I doubt those you were staying with before were so kind."

That was the truth, and although she still wasn't at full strength, Devon could tell she was healthier. "Thank you," she said, because it felt like the right thing to say. "For looking after me. You didn't have to do that."

"No," Bess said, folding her arms. "We didn't have to do that. We don't have to do any of this. I told you that you were safe here. We told you that you could trust us. I'll bring you up some breakfast. I have already put fresh towels and toiletries into the bathroom. So whenever you're ready, you can feel free to eat something and to bathe, although we wouldn't advise you to do too much too quickly.

"Did he come here?" Devon asked. "The man who purchased me?"

"No," Bess said. "You were told that you never have to worry about that."

Yet part of her wanted to see this man. Maybe it was the mystery that allured her. Maybe she hoped that by looking into his face that everything would fall into place, that she would suddenly understand why these people would buy her like a pet, keep her locked up and do nothing but feed and care for her.

They could've abused her while she was ill, but no intimate part of her body felt as though it had been violated.

"I'll get your breakfast," Bess said. "Wren will come to see you too. We will have to keep an eye on you."

"There aren't cameras in here, are there?" Devon asked, wondering how they always knew when she awoke. If she was going to shower, she didn't want them to watch her struggle with something as simple as washing her body.

"For a man so particular about his privacy, the owner of the house wouldn't offer his guests anything less than his own standards."

More cryptic comments that increased her curiosity. "No one has explained why I'm locked up," she said, pushing away the blankets that were constricting her. "Are you afraid I'll escape? I've been too ill to leave this bed."

Bess paused before she replied, her smile faltered for just a second, but she quickly pasted it back on. "Information unlocks all secrets," Bess said. "There are things in this house which can reveal more about who we are."

"And you need anonymity to do what you do," she said. Devon didn't like being locked up, but she could understand their need to protect themselves, at least until they knew who they had in their home.

She could be a killer or a thief, and if they unlocked their home to her, she could hurt them. Except given her current state, that seemed like a ridiculous concern for them to have.

"Everything will be explained to you," Bess said. "For now, we just want you to be well. You sit there and get your bearings." She retreated to the door. "I'll come back with your breakfast, and then we'll leave you alone for a while."

Devon could do with the chance to center herself. Bess did as she said and came back with some food, some toast, some coffee, some milk, some juice. They seemed determined to replenish her liquids and didn't provide anything that would be too taxing on her stomach.

She hadn't eaten properly in a long time. Devon did exactly as Bess said and took her time to eat her breakfast, which filled her up after just a few bites, and she was almost ready to sleep again. Except, after delivering the breakfast tray, Bess had turned on the shower in preparation for her. The bellowing steam that poured out of the bathroom created such an enticing mist that she couldn't resist.

Luxuriating in the hot jets of water that came at her from every angle, Devon washed and conditioned her hair, twice. She exfoliated using all the products and accessories that Bess had laid out and took her time while shaving so as to smooth every spot.

The experience of grooming took her a long time, and she was grateful for the built-in, tiled seat in the corner that allowed her to sit and catch her breath when she tired. After she was out, she combed her hair and donned the new nightgown that Bess had put onto the vanity for her.

Having taken her time in the bathroom, she'd filled a vast portion of her day. It wasn't like she had anywhere else to be or anything better to do. Going through the motions of doing something so ordinary was a comfort.

It was probably the normalcy of grooming that made her take advantage of every tool available to her. Usually, she'd have done these things every day. Having the free rein to do them again, and to take as long as she wanted in the bathroom, helped her to regain some of her identity.

It was only when she exited the bathroom that she paused, because there was Wren, sitting on the bed.

He leaped up and smiled. "Hello," he declared. "How

are you feeling today?"

Suspicious of him and how long he might have been there waiting for her, she felt uneasy standing red-skinned and damp-haired in front of a man who had treated her, which meant he could have seen every part of her body and examined it in detail.

"Much better," she said because if he was the one responsible for ridding her of her illness, she should be grateful instead of hostile. "Thank you."

Wren went around the bed to the other side and picked up his first-aid box to hold it aloft. "Can I check you out?"

Fighting him, after all he'd already seen, was a battle she didn't have the energy for. Giving in, she tossed her damp towel and previous nightgown to the corner of the room.

Devon went over to the bed to sit. "What do you want to do?" she asked.

"Just a few routine checks," he said and put the case on the end of the bed to open it. On the nightstand was a clipboard, and as he went through a basic check-up routine, he noted his findings.

"How are your other wounds?" he asked, examining the bruising on her wrists.

"The one on my hip itches a bit, but it's okay."

"Can I see it?" he asked, and he didn't seem as condescending this time.

Leaning back, she gathered up the gown. Keeping her intimacy covered, she took the fabric up over the wound to allow him to take a closer look.

He touched the edge and she flinched. Examining it closely, he then leaned back to retrieve something from his box. "Yes, there was a bit of an infection in it," he said. "It's cleared up for the most part and you've cleaned it already today, which is good. I'll apply some antiseptic and dress it, and then we'll give you some antibiotics, okay?"

She nodded at his smile and let him do his work because he carried an air of professionalism now. Acting detached from her, yet caring, he was thorough but not overbearing. If she'd come across him in a normal doctor's office or hospital, she'd probably be quite impressed.

As it stood, she didn't know exactly what to think about a man who was good at his caregiving job but chose to spend his free time at human slave auctions. "How do you hold down a job if you're always here?" she asked.

Her shower had made her feel more human, and bonding with her captors could be important. If she could cultivate a connection with them, they may be more inclined to let her go or at least may think twice before hurting her.

"I'm not always here," he said. "This isn't my house. This house belongs to my colleague."

"Your cousin?" His attention leaped from her wound. "I heard you and Bess talking, just bits and pieces," she said. "Your secret is safe."

Although it took him another moment, he did go back to his work. Examining the moldings and white walls, she tried to block out what he was doing. It wasn't like there was anyone around here she could tell. Even if she wanted to scream his secrets out loud, no one would be able to hear her, no one except those who already knew them.

When it became obvious that he wasn't going to say anything in response, she continued. "So where do you live?" she asked.

It might seem as though this was a typical doctor-patient conversation and that couldn't be further from the truth. But the more she could find out, the better her chances of finding some kind of weakness.

"You ask a lot of questions," he said.

"Valid questions I think," she said, sensing his barriers going up. "I don't mean you and your friends any harm. Isn't that what you keep saying to me? Isn't that what's meant to make me feel better? So shouldn't it make you feel better too? What could I possibly do to hurt you even if I wanted to? You have all the power."

He finished taping the dressing onto her hip and sat up on the bed beside her, keeping a respectful distance. "I'll give you some salve for the wounds on your wrist. Can I see the injury on your back?"

His expectation created anxiety, and this moment was

a crossroads in their relationship. She had to give trust in order to gain it, so she flipped onto her front and folded her arms under her head. Closing her eyes, Devon tried not to think about her ass being out there on show for him after she pulled up her gown.

"How long have you been practicing medicine?" she asked, trying to hold onto the normality.

"All my adult life," he said, tracing his fingers down her vertebrae. "Have you had any pain in your joints or difficulty with movement today?"

"I've been a bit stiff," she said. "My shoulders ache, but I figured that's what comes from being restrained in a confined space for so long."

"A massage might help," he said, checking the bones and muscles in her shoulders, arms, and neck. "I don't see redness or swelling. I've been keeping an eye on it. We'll check your range of movement once I've finished with the wound on your back." He went to work on it. "You're lucky, they don't appear to have beaten you as often as others. Not to diminish what you went through, it was horrific, but we have seen worse."

"I learned to keep my mouth shut," she said. "And one of the guards said something on my last day there about not being allowed to mark my body. They sold me as unblemished, I guess that was important."

Although he'd managed to slash her hip and injure her back. Maybe that was standard breakage factored into the trade. Even if her body had been unmarked, her soul was certainly tarnished.

"Were you sexually assaulted?" he asked, in that doctor voice of his.

Tensing, she was pleased when his hands withdrew but because she couldn't see him, she didn't know exactly what he was doing. "Not me, but others were. That's the reason I kept quiet. I heard what was done to them, what the men threatened. Some of the girls didn't come back after annoying the guards, and the men would boast about what they put those poor women through. To hear their stories was torture enough."

Devon noted that his hands didn't return to work on her, so she assumed he was finished. Turning her cheek onto her forearm, she opened her eyes to try to see him. "Wren?"

"You speak Spanish?" he asked in a rush of breath.

"Yes."

A kind of hope and happiness merged in his voice, and it perplexed her. His next words flowed fast out of him. "Did they know that?"

Rolling over onto her back, she pulled down her gown and sat up. "No, they didn't engage me in much direct conversation. Why?"

His wide eyes and frozen forehead made her frown. He licked his lips and swallowed, trying hard to pace his words as though this wasn't a major deal. But she could tell from the way he'd reacted already that it was.

"Did you hear them talking to each other?"

Well obviously, she thought to herself, because the only words the women spoke in Spanish, English or any other language were the same pleadings for life as they begged for mercy in their desperation for liberation. Devon didn't have to speak every one of their languages to know that's what the women wanted.

"Yes," she said. "The men hung out in the hallways during and after their rounds. They talked to each other when they fed us. It was as if we weren't there. I wanted to stay alive, so I didn't interrupt them. I kept my mouth shut."

At the time, it had been a great idea to stay quiet, under the radar, and out of the way. But since she'd been here, Devon had been dealing with her own type of survivor's guilt.

While she'd been in the shower, trying to relax her weary self, she'd experienced gratitude for the fresh, clean water coating her body, washing away her woes. The fight mode she'd been in since waking here was fading. More at ease now that she could feel the sickness slipping from her, she was rested and clean, and that made a huge amount of difference to her mood. It was then she began to put herself together again.

The negative side of that was embracing the reality that some of the other girls who were sold on the same night as her were probably dead or being abused and tortured. Devon didn't know what was going on here. She was still suspicious, so she would keep her guard up. But after living in a metal box for months, this place was like a palace.

Whatever these people wanted from her, Devon would make no promises to them. But she'd learned not to take even one minute of peace for granted. She wasn't shackled, there was food and clean water, giving her little to complain about, even if she was still under lock and key.

Wren began to toss his things into the first-aid box, without much thought for where they landed. He sealed it up and surged to his feet. "I'll come back for the blood in a minute," he said, whipping off his latex gloves and balling them into his pocket as he dashed for the door.

"Wait, what did I say?" she asked because his entire demeanor was different, his mood had changed in an instant and she wasn't sure of the significance of what she'd said.

"I'll be back, Devon, just… just wait here."

Wren darted out and the door slammed. Rolling her eyes left and right, she took a minute to herself then exhaled. "Hmm," she said. "Okay."

There was nowhere she could go, so she'd just have to hope that Wren came back to explain himself soon.

FOUR

WHETHER IT WAS soon or not, she had no idea. It seemed like it took a long time for her to see another soul, but she was grateful for it. Her shower had sapped some of her energy, and although adrenaline kept her on her feet for a while, Devon eventually had to take a nap.

Upon waking, she didn't feel the need to lie in bed as she had for the past undefined period. Devon had to start building her body back up again. Tedious though it was, she began to pace the room, just to give herself something to do and to remind herself what it was to stand and walk upright. She would pace for as long as she could, varying the speed and length of her strides, then she would sit, have some water, stare at the canopy over her bed for a while and ponder who these people might be.

Wren was odd in that he seemed genuine in what he did. He was knowledgeable in the way he acted. He was deft and skilled with the medical supplies, knew the procedures and performed them while holding a conversation without giving much thought to what his hands were doing, suggesting to her that he was indeed a medical doctor of some variety, just as he'd claimed to be.

Bess, she liked the best because the woman had zero

expectations. Bess brought her food and water, she provided her with clothes and toiletries and seemed more intent on looking after her than asking her for anything.

Because Devon had no idea where they were, they could be in a house with a hundred rooms or this could be a single unit trussed up to look like an upper-class building. There could be a thousand people, another hundred women like her, or she could be all alone. Wren said he didn't live here full-time, and that was an interesting fact. It might be difficult to find out when he came and when he left, but if she could make a break for freedom while he wasn't here, the only people she may have to contend with were Bess and this enigmatic man she'd never met: the buyer.

She was slowing her pace and considering going back to bed when the door opened again. This time Bess came in with Wren. After they closed the door, they stood together in front of it.

"We'd like to ask you some questions," Wren said.

Devon had stopped in front of the window. She folded her arms as she scrutinized them both. Maybe it was the invigoration of exercise or that she was finally feeling fully rested, but not only did she crack a smile, she laughed.

"You're kidding," Devon said. "You want to ask me questions?"

"Yes," Wren said. "It could be important. If you sit on the bed—"

"I don't think so," she said. "I appreciate that you gave me medical care, I don't know if you plan to slap me with a bill, whatever. I've asked for two things since I got here, neither of which I've gotten. So, unless your questions are A) which airports I'd like to fly from and to, and B) how much monetary compensation you can offer for keeping me hostage, I'm not going to answer a single thing."

Devon didn't remember ever being so confrontational or so sassy. She had a sense of humor, but she'd never been one to mock or ridicule with sarcasm.

"You don't understand," Wren said. "What we do is help people, women like you. Can't you see that?"

"All I see is that your boss bought me at an auction,

like I was some eBay listing. He brought me back here, and by the way," she said, turning around to grab the curtains and thrust them open as far as she could reach. "I still don't even know where here is! You've kept me locked in this room without answering any questions. I don't even know what day of the week it is, what month of the year it is, I don't know how long I've been here, I don't know how long I was there. All I want to do is go home."

"What do you think is waiting at home for you?" Wren asked. "I'll tell you what's waiting at home. Nothing. You've been gone for so long, I bet even your landlord has rented your apartment again."

Bess slapped his arm and move forward. "Don't listen to him, dearie," she said. "This is difficult for you and you must be frustrated, especially now that you're starting to feel human again, and here we are making demands."

"It does seem a bit rich," Devon agreed and allowed Bess to link their arms to lead them over to the bed where they sat down.

"You must be confused and hurt."

"We don't have time for this," Wren said.

"You hush," Bess chastised him. "You should never have let Raven coach you before you came in here. You treat this girl like a human being, not like a walking reference manual."

"It's because I understood them," Devon said. She might still be groggy and Bess was right that she was confused, but she hadn't missed how Wren had run out of here when he learned that she'd eavesdropped on her captors' conversations. "I could have valuable information, but I have no reason to share it with you."

"Why would you protect them?" Wren asked, marching over to stand in front of the women, who were still seated on the bed.

"I don't know who you are," Devon said. "You could be a rival gang, grooming vulnerable women like me. You say you want to help people, and I agree that you've treated me well while I've been here, despite keeping me confined. But you don't trust me and you don't treat me with respect. You said that you wouldn't let me go until I was back to full strength, but look at me, I'm healthy."

"You have a long way to go," Bess said. "We have to get you eating properly and build up some of those muscles. You're still weak."

"I'm alive," Devon said. "And I bet not every girl who was in that place when I was can say that. Can you imagine for a second what they must be going through? And I still don't know why I'm here, can't you understand how that unnerves me? You tell me I'll never see this man who bought me. But I can't begin to understand why that is and that terrifies me. Who is he? What's he hiding?"

"He won't come," Bess said, seeming upset while delivering a non-apology apology.

"But why?" Devon begged. "The information I have, I can take to authorities, and maybe they can take these people down."

"That's what we do," Wren said. "That's what he does. That's why you can't see his face."

Devon didn't accept that. "I don't hang out with these bastards. Just because I see the buyer's face doesn't mean I'd know who he was or that I'd be able to share his identity with anyone."

Bess and Wren exchanged a look. "We can't take that chance."

"You can't or he can't?" Devon asked. "He's comfortable around the scum of the earth but won't talk to one solitary woman? Telling you everything that I know gives you an advantage that you could exploit. Either you tell your boss to come here and face me like a man, or you let me go."

"He won't come," Bess said, but she was talking to Wren. "I've tried."

Wren rubbed the back of his neck. "We've all tried. He's not built for this and doesn't know how to handle it. He won't even talk to Swallow. Hell, he won't even talk to me."

What was it about this guy? Devon didn't understand why he was so determined to shut himself off. She didn't know who Swallow was or what significance the person had, but at least Devon wasn't alone in being excluded from this man's company.

"If he's so desperate to know what I know," Devon said. "He can ask me his questions himself. I'm not telling you guys squat. So if he won't face me, you can let me go, and I'll tell everything I know to the authorities."

"You can't go to the authorities. You can't tell them about this, about us."

Another demand, these people had some nerve. "So I'm supposed to pretend I wasn't abducted and held against my will? You want me to forgive the men who did this to me?"

"No," Bess said and stood up. "There is one person he'll listen to. We have to try again."

Bess and Wren went out of the room together. Lying on her back, Devon rested her hands on her upper chest as she contemplated the future. These people were now claiming they deliberately rescued her, like they were some kind of vigilantes. If that was the case, then they did need to protect their identities, like all good vigilantes did.

But it wasn't enough for her. If they wanted something from her, she had to know more about them because if she relied on her assumptions and they turned out to be wrong, more innocent women could be hurt.

***

HOURS PASSED, she knew it because the fuzzy light faded from behind the fogged glass until it became black. Bess came in with food, which Devon refused, much to Bess' surprise. She was sick of the games, sick of the waiting, sick of being controlled by everyone else. She demanded that Bess take the food away and reiterated what she'd said: either she was let go or the man pulling the strings came to tell her exactly what the hell was going on.

More time went by, all the light faded and she was left in the pitch black. Devon lay down in bed, ready for another night of sleep in this place that was nothing more than a gilded cage. Thinking about what the lack of artificial light outside the obscured window could mean when she married it with the silence she'd monitored, Devon didn't reach many conclusions.

When Wren and Bess weren't here, she heard nothing. Either this place had the best soundproofing on the face of the Earth or they were far from civilization and any kind of external noises like traffic and other people.

No artificial light meant no headlights, no passing cars, no streetlights. While putting all of these pieces together, her eyes grew heavy until sleep threatened. Just as she was about to lose herself to it, she heard a click and the sound of a door opening.

A sliver of light appeared on the opposite wall, and she pulled her blankets higher over her chest. It grew wider and then was filled by a looming silhouette that she saw only a flash of before it grew so large it blocked all of the light.

When she sat up, Devon registered the tiniest strip of muted light seeping underneath the now closed door that definitely hadn't been there before. It let in just enough illumination for Devon to decipher the tall, broad shape standing at the end of her bed.

"You're him, aren't you?"

"Yeah," he said. His deep voice had the impact of a gut punch. A low rumble, the single syllable seemed to shake the whole room. "You're trying to regain control."

There was so little emotion in his voice that she couldn't tell if he was angry or upset or if he was just trying to condescend her as his doctor buddy had done when he came in here the first time.

"You don't have to patronize me. You need me."

Her strength was bravado. Demanding to see this man had been a way of trying to regain control, to show these people how unfair it was to try to force someone into doing something that they didn't want to do.

And yet, he'd chosen to come to her at the worst time because while she was in the dark it was like being back in her metal cage. Although the ground was soft here and she had space to stretch and walk, the memories were vivid and still raw, making it difficult to tether her emotions to something solid.

"You're a pain in the ass."

So far she'd deduced that he didn't say much, but when he did speak, he was honest. "Why are you holding me prisoner? Why don't you let me go?"

"You can go."

Just like that, did he have that much power, could he allow her to just walk out? If that was the case, she was right, he was the one pulling the strings. Something told her that it wasn't going to be quite that easy.

"But?"

"It's the middle of the night. It's cold out."

"I'll get a cab."

"We're on a private island."

An island. That idea hadn't occurred to her. It explained so much, such as their confidence that they wouldn't be caught holding a woman captive and the lack of sound or artificial lights.

"Who are you?" she asked, the words coming out of her of their own volition because of her innate need to know who this enigmatic man was.

"Names don't matter."

"You have a private island. Does it belong to you? If you have enough money to splurge on buying a person, then I guess it stands to reason that you'd have enough to buy an island. Is it a tropical island?"

"We're in the Pacific Northwest, Devon, prepare to freeze your ass off if you go out there in a nightdress."

Okay, so she accepted that leaving this minute wasn't a good idea. "How do I get off the island?"

"You don't. Not until you tell us what we need to know." A threat. These people weren't as benevolent as they made out. "You do that and we'll take you back to the mainland."

"You can't—"

"You wanted to meet me, here I am," he said, becoming stern. "Tomorrow, Bess and Wren will introduce you to some new people. Answer their questions."

"And you?"

"Forget me," he said. "Sleep, 'cause tomorrow you better be ready to talk."

In less than two strides, he was at the door, and he was out before she could voice any objections. The light beneath the door vanished and she was alone again, blinking into darkness. That brief encounter could have been a dream, something her mind made up, or maybe they'd just conceded.

Devon didn't know who these new people were or what they would ask. But she'd made progress by forcing the buyer to come here against his will. Although her victory was tiny, she slept easier because of it.

FIVE

BESS HAD PUT a small nail file and tweezer set in the bathroom with the other supplies she'd left. Devon had finished plucking her eyebrows and was giving herself a manicure when there was a tap on the ajar bathroom door. Whirling around, Bess was there with a pile of clothes in her hands.

"Would you like to get dressed?"

Devon wouldn't say no to that offer. Wearing anything but this shapeless nightgown would be an improvement. Bess came over and laid the clothes on the vanity. "Come into the bedroom when you're ready, dearie."

Bess went out allowing Devon to see what clothes were there. New underwear with the tags on was a relief, so she quickly put that on then looked at the other choices. There were two dresses to choose from, a blue one or a purple. Devon doubted she would want to ever wear blue again, so she chose the purple. It was long sleeved with a scoop neck, but the loose skirt went to her knee and didn't disturb any of her wound dressings.

Being in new, clean clothes gave her a surprising boost of energy. This day had revived her; she felt like a new woman. Since her conversation with the stranger last night, her burden had lightened and she could feel pride in herself for standing her ground and achieving something.

Departing the bathroom, Devon was going to ask for some books or some paper, because if she was going to be stuck in this room, she'd need more to entertain her than pacing between the walls. But she didn't get the chance to open her mouth. To her surprise, the door to the hallway was open. Beyond her room was a wide corridor with a hardwood floor and a red carpet runner.

Bess stood at the end of the bed and gestured to the open door. "Would you like to eat lunch with us?"

Devon didn't have a clue what to say. More must have happened last night than she realized, somehow in those few minutes of conversation, she'd made a breakthrough. "I can leave?"

"Come with me," Bess said.

Linking arms, Bess took her out of the room into the hall, which had crisp pale walls and a window at the end of the corridor behind them, flooding the space with brilliant day light.

Turning right at the end of the corridor, they descended a double-wide stairway with a grand gothic banister. At the bottom was a large, square hallway. Various doors led away from it, and Devon waited for Bess to direct her.

Going through one of those doors, they carried on along another internal hallway. At the end were double doors that took them into a massive triple-story space. An even more immense gothic stairway was central. High above was a vaulted ceiling, and Devon had to stop and gaze upward at the breath-taking sight.

"This is incredible."

The massive pointed arch door to her right had ornate stonework around it. Above it were many skinny arched windows which filled the cavernous foyer with rays of light that shot out in stripes, highlighting the stairs. Around the perimeter of the room were carved stone arches shielding open corridors where there were further doors.

"You like the architecture?" Bess grinned.

"It's beautiful."

"Let's get to the dining room."

Bess took Devon's arm and began to lead her away, but she couldn't stop gaping at the ceiling. Bess laughed as she pulled her under an arch and into another room. This one had a long table in the middle, which was covered with food. But Devon ignored the food and ran to the double window inset in another large stone gothic archway. The small panes of glass were different textures, and that made it impossible for her to get a wide view which frustrated her.

"Come and eat," Bess said, filling a plate, which she put at one of the chairs then pulled out the seat. "Come on, come and sit."

Giving up at the window, Devon went to the table and began to pick at the food while Bess filled her own plate. Except the woman didn't sit with it, she put the plate at one place and then went to work filling a third plate.

Touching the edge of her plate, such an amount of food was a wonder. "What's the special occasion?" Devon asked. "Why am I allowed out now?"

"Eat and enjoy," Bess said. "The boys will be along once they've finished arguing."

Devon was startled. "The boys? The buyer came to me last night saying I'd meet new people today. Is that what this is about? Are they here?"

"Yes," Bess said, putting the plate at the head of the table then retrieving another to put some food on it.

A door at the end of the room opened and Devon stopped picking at her food to watch Wren come in, but he was alone.

"Settle your differences?" Bess asked, sitting beside Devon.

"Do we ever?" Wren asked, striding across the room to sit opposite Bess. "He'll be along in a minute."

A stranger in this house, Devon was trying to get her bearings. "Will someone talk to me?" she asked. "Will I be allowed to go home today?"

"Usually after my assessment we decide how long a girl will need to recover," Wren said, digging into his food.

"Then before we send her home, we give her the lecture."

"The lecture?" Devon asked.

"About what she should tell police about her ordeal and about us. We impress upon her how important our anonymity is."

"So I'm getting the lecture today?" Devon asked.

"You're not getting the lecture," Bess said. "The boys think you might have some valuable information."

"We're going to ease her into it, Mom. Don't just lay it on her like that."

Another surprise. "Mom?" Devon asked.

So Bess was Wren's mother. Could she be the mother of both men she'd met?

"Well done," Bess laughed. "Anonymity is important, we don't give out last names or relationships, and now you're one for two."

The door at the head of the room opened, and this time a familiar stranger entered. Tall like the silhouette she'd seen last night, Devon assumed this was the man who had visited her. Although she hadn't picked out the specifics of his features last night in the dark, he carried the same air around him.

This had to be the other man Bess had referred to, the one Wren bickered with. Devon presumed their party was complete. Except the stranger who'd just come in waited at the door, and she didn't have to ask why when a smiling woman emerged.

The woman's sleek, black hair was loose around her narrow shoulders, and she seemed to effervesce with zeal. As the male stranger closed the door, the female one came to the table.

"Devon," the woman said, coming over to sit beside her. "It's wonderful to meet you."

Glancing back at Bess, Devon wasn't surprised to see her smiling, just as Wren was too. "You have Swallow here to thank for your liberation," Bess said. "The woman can get the boys to do just about anything, you've never seen anything like it."

"She's the demi-chief," Wren said and took a big bite

from his sandwich.

The male stranger came over and sat at the head of the table. Swallow left Devon's side to go to his. And instead of being enlightened, she was more confused.

"He's the man who came to me last night?" Devon said, preferring to direct her question at Swallow.

"Yes, skulking around in the dark, freaking women out, is his specialty," Swallow said, standing up to assemble some food on a plate. "This is Raven."

"Raven?" Devon asked. "So you're Swallow, he's Raven, he's Wren… you guys have a thing for birds?"

Bess was the one to answer. "Like we said before it's protection." The kind woman reached over to pat her hand.

"You're not a bird," Devon said to her.

"No," Bess said with a smile and a shake of her head. "They tried to give me one of their codenames, but it never sticks. I'm not out there. I'm here. I'm safe. I feel silly when they try to include me as Kindred. I'm just here to look after them, that's all."

"Kindred?" Devon asked, looking at all the faces again.

"Way to go, Mom," Wren said. "Guess I know where I get my loose tongue from."

Swallow picked up a cherry tomato and popped it between her lips. "Mom?" Swallow said. "You guys weren't this open when I joined the team."

"How did she find that out?" Raven asked, his tone cold and irritated as he fixated on the doctor.

"It just slipped out," Wren said. "We don't usually have the Liberated down here."

So she wasn't the first. "The Liberated" that suggested that there had been others before her, just like they'd said. "You rescue women?" Devon asked. "Like me, you go in and buy them from these men and then bring them back here to patch them up?"

Looking from one face to the next, she expected an answer from Bess. But Bess was looking at Wren, who fixated on his plate until he glanced up to look at Raven, who definitely had more authority than the others in the room.

Except Raven was more interested in the woman at his side.

"Answer her question," Swallow said. "You can't expect her to tell us what we want to know if we're not willing to be honest with her... our professional relationship got much easier after I knew who you were, didn't it?"

"Easier? We fucked before you knew who I was," Raven said. "Doesn't get much easier than that."

Swallow hit his shoulder, but he picked up another tomato, bit it in two and slid the extra half between Swallow's lips. Their intense eye contact made Devon blush and avert her eyes to Bess's end of the table.

"Swallow is the best thing that ever happened to the team," Bess said, and the normally happy woman was positively overjoyed.

Swallow seemed normal, she was beautiful, sophisticated in her own way. She sat straight and proud, managing to lean in to the man at her side without being obvious about their sexual connection. Their attraction was undeniable, it zipped between them even when they weren't looking at each other.

Before in her room when Bess had insisted that the buyer wouldn't come to her, Wren had said the buyer didn't talk to Swallow. Bess had said only one person had his ear. Devon wondered now who that was. If Swallow had so much power that she could secure Devon's liberation from that room, how could it be said that Raven didn't speak to her?

"We know where the auctions happen," Wren said. "We've spent a lot of years building up a network, we're on the inside, we've made them believe that we want to buy these women for perverted reasons and they believe us."

"They? You consort with these cartels?" Devon asked, disgusted by the idea. "The money that you give them, it fuels what they do."

"We know," Wren said. "And that's why we go after them in other ways too. Each member of the Kindred has their own special skillset. Every penny that we give them is siphoned off somewhere else. We have a man who can access any computer system in the world and he's drained more than one criminal's bank account, believe me. We work hard to stay covert and—"

"Enough," Raven said. "Stop running your mouth, Wren. She doesn't need to know all the details."

"She does," Devon said but immediately shrank when Raven's glare shot to her.

Formidable and oppressive, she was mentally impacted by his displeasure. With dark eyes and a darker demeanor, he grew as he became angry and his expression tightened. Swallow placed a hand over his and somehow that released the pressure and Devon watched him deflate, the anger seeping out of him.

"We have to be careful," Swallow said to Devon while interlinking her fingers with Raven's.

"I know, I've been given the spiel about protecting yourself and anonymity. But you all know who I am, you know my real name."

They knew her first name at least, not her last, although Wren had said something which made her think they knew more than they were letting on. He'd referenced what was waiting for her back home like he actually knew.

Maybe her apartment had been rented out from under her, and she would be disappointed to lose her possessions, her sketches and her work. But more important to her was her brother. They didn't see each other often, but he cared for her when she was in trouble and checked in on a regular basis to make sure she was okay.

If she had been under lock and key all this time, he would've noticed that she was gone. The problem with her big brother was, he was up to his eyeballs in his own messes. Going to the cops wouldn't have been an option because he had no friends in the authorities. It was as likely they would blame him, find a way to contort the evidence to implicate him. At least, that would be his fear. Her brother had never met a cop that he trusted, and while he'd never been explicit about what he did or how he earned his money, she knew he was far from squeaky clean.

"To take them down, we need to know how they select their women. We need to know who's in charge and how high up it goes. Did you hear any of these things?"

Swallow asked.

"She is still weak," Bess said. "You're asking her to relive a horrific experience. We can't ask too much of her too soon."

"Maybe not, but we don't have forever," Raven said. "There will be another auction in a few weeks, and they'll be collecting girls for it as we speak."

It was starting all over again, like a cycle, and never had a single thought made her feel so sick. Right now, there were women walking from their homes to their cars, going from coffee shops to newsstands, feeling safe, oblivious to the fact that they were about to be abducted.

"Do you know how you were selected?" Swallow asked and Devon shook her head, not because she didn't want to answer, but because reliving that moment of her life was too traumatic for her to face. "Can you tell us about your abduction?"

Shaking her head faster, Devon pushed her chair from the table and stood up. "I just want to go home. Why won't you let me go home?"

"You're right," Swallow said. "This is too soon. We'll give her some more time."

It was when Swallow stood that the men did too. "We have our own shit—" Swallow touched three fingers to Raven's lips to silence him and moved her body against his.

"It will keep," Swallow murmured. "You made me a promise, come on. Time to pay up."

Saying nothing else, the couple left the room hand-in-hand, and she wondered about the kind of woman Swallow was. As normal as she may seem, Swallow was with a man who bought women. Just imagining how he viewed them, the things he had to say and hear and see at those horrific auctions, it was difficult to imagine how any woman could lie down with a man after that.

"She's protective of you," Bess said, getting up and going over to clear Raven and Swallow's places at the table.

"Protective?" Devon asked.

"Swallow is the heart of the couple," Wren said. "Raven likes to take action, likes to be in control. But Swallow sees things from a perspective that he doesn't. She'll buy you the time you need, but you will have to tell us what we need to know eventually."

Devon wasn't sure she was ready to put all those pieces together. She wasn't sure she could. Confronting her own abduction wasn't something she'd attempted, not even while she lived in her metal box.

Something began to beep and Wren stood up. He grabbed a phone from his pocket, made eye contact with Bess and then left the room.

Bess offered no explanation for his departure. "I hope you feel more comfortable, now that you know we're here to help," Bess said, taking the plates she'd gathered toward a door on the far side of the room. "I'll be back in a few minutes, try to eat something."

Being alone in such a vast space, Devon didn't know what to do with herself for a few seconds and felt an initial surge of motivation to flee. Then she recalled what she'd been told last night, that they were on a private island. Even if she lost herself in this house, ran away from these people, and managed to get outside, she wouldn't be able to get to freedom. Unless perhaps it was a lie.

Despite knowing she wouldn't see much through it, she headed for the narrow window and lifted the latch. It only gave her a foot-wide view, and the space wasn't large enough for her to climb out. But it was enough to confirm there was sea outside.

Assaulted by thick, salty air, it hit her skin, her mouth, her nose. The blessed sensation made her gasp in the natural aroma. The sound of the waves was loud, louder than she could've imagined having not heard anything while in her room. They crashed against the shore she hadn't yet seen. A single gull called out, and a sound she may have once considered intrusive became part of a symphony of pure, natural reality. Eager to embrace this new environment, she leaned forward.

Opening her eyes as she pushed her head out the window, Devon couldn't stop her grin from splitting her face. The sky was overcast, the thick, gray clouds mirrored an angry gray-blue sea that was rough and filled with scattered white horses. There may have been mists in the distance, but all she could see was the unbroken horizon, which revealed no blip of land.

From this position, she had a descending view toward a rocky outcrop that blended into a pebble beach that stretched to the end of her view where the land disappeared in a curve around the other side of the house. Pushing herself out further, she wanted to know how far she could see. The beach disappeared into a group of rocks in the distance. Still, she saw no land on the sea, no boats, no lighthouse or markers to suggest anyone was anywhere within rescuing distance.

It made sense for her to retreat back into the room to hide what she'd done by snooping out here. Opening this window had been a risk, looking outside was a risk. If Bess caught her, or Wren, or God-forbid, Raven, she could anger them and their kindness may only stretch so far.

But the salt in the sea air was too alluring for her to want to cut herself off from it again. She'd never realized what liberation was until this moment. It didn't matter that she was confined in these walls, she would go back to stressing about that later. In this single moment, standing here in this place, breathing in this pure, pungent air, she realized liberation was a state of mind as well as a physical situation.

It was about spirit, it was about holding on, it was about knowing yourself and your strengths and believing that you would make it through, no matter what you faced. Devon didn't want to give up this moment. She wanted to go out there, to sit on those rocks, and stare at that sea to remind herself that she was alive.

It couldn't last forever and she didn't want to be restricted from doing this again if she got the chance. So she took hold of the latch and was about to close the window until, in the distance beneath her from behind the shielding window, a figure came into view from the direction opposite to the one she'd been staring in.

A man with jet black hair. He was running along a path cut in the windswept grass above the rocks and beach. Wearing a black tee shirt and shorts, he was fast, zipping along the shore like it was nothing. Despite the vast distance in front of him, he was not fazed, he kept going. His long legs cut down the distance with every sure stride.

He slowed. He was too far away for her to make out specific features, but she'd guess he had to be fit given the distance she'd seen him cover in such a short time. He stretched and she was transfixed. Even the gull and the sea became silent to her ears. Sight was her primary sense again.

He picked up his tee shirt to wipe his face, turning into the wind as he did, giving her a view of a tanned, toned torso that was more than just fit, it was sculpted. For a moment, she was inspired to adjust her artistic medium just for that perfect form.

Fearful that he may catch her staring, despite the distance between them, she pulled the window as closed as she could while still managing to peek out with one eye. He dropped his tee shirt and turned to the sea, pulling a handheld device of some kind from his back pocket. Standing where he was for a moment, he admired the stretch of water she'd been admiring before he came into her eye line. Now it was invisible to her because she was too busy trying to peer closer at this stranger's muscular calves trained for exercise.

He began to work on the device and it took all of his attention. Wandering from the trodden path, he moved to the rock edge and she held her breath. For half a second, she feared he might keep going as he was too engrossed in his device to be paying close attention to what his feet were doing. His hair was long enough for a woman to tunnel her fingers through and it was beaten by the wind, telling her that that position, so near to such a precarious edge, couldn't be safe. But he stayed there, right at the precipice, working on his device.

Who was he? Why was he here? Was it possible that they weren't on a private island at all and he was just a citizen? Should she call out and beg for freedom? Except this house was clearly vast, Bess had brought her from one side to the other and Devon was already lost. She would never be able to find her way back the way they'd come. She probably wouldn't even be able to find the grand entryway that still distracted her thoughts.

The whole building was amazing and her fingers itched to embrace its lines, curves, and angles and to commit those sleek shapes to paper with her delicate lead. But right now, her artist's eye was focused on something else, a solitary figure, on a wild shore. Alone. Like she craved to be.

She wanted to know more of who he was. Even if she was to call out, the wind would carry her voice away from him and may take it to the ears of those who kept her captive. Maybe he was an employee here, someone who tended the grounds, if there were any. Or maybe there was more going on here than she'd been led to believe and these people didn't trust her as much as they were trying to convince her they did.

Before Devon was ready to bid farewell to her view, he put the device back in his pocket and took a few backward steps to return to his path, then he was running again. His legs moved slowly in long, easy strides, and then he was gone, out of view. He disappeared around the farthest corner she could see and once again, she was desolate.

SIX

PULLING THE WINDOW closed, Devon latched it and ran her fingers through her hair. Spinning around, she wanted to seek out Bess, who hadn't returned. Making a beeline for the door Bess had used, Devon was determined to get answers. Finding the door open an inch, she wondered if the wind had pushed it open or if Bess had left it that way.

But when she got to it, she discovered why Bess and Wren hadn't come back. They were occupying each other. Their engaged voices made Devon stop. They weren't right on the other side of the door because their voices were quiet. But wherever they were, they believed themselves to be alone.

Devon wasn't going to pass up this chance to collect more information, so she put her own curiosity about the external stranger out of her mind and craned to hear everything that she could.

"I don't like it," Bess said. "I know the Kindred has to do things in certain ways. But Art wouldn't like it either."

"Don't invoke our deceased chief, please," Wren said. "It wasn't my decision. You know how this works, I follow orders. I don't make decisions. I only get called on when someone needs patched up. Nothing else is my business."

"You're as much a part of this as anyone, you're the

reason Zave does this. It's only because of you that he got involved at all." Zave. Devon folded her arms, that was a name she hadn't heard before and it wasn't a bird alias either. "You have every right to tell him how you feel. This is one of those strategies that Brodie and Zave come up with together and the rest of you go along with it because you believe they know best."

"They do know best," Wren said. "They put their asses on the line more than the rest of us do."

Bess wasn't taking any excuses. "Not more than Zara. That girl's been involved in every mission since her life was consumed by the Kindred."

"So why aren't you talking to her?" Wren asked.

Devon didn't like the whiney, petulant tone in his voice. It was like he was a teenager being blamed for something he insisted wasn't his fault. Bess was his mother, so maybe this was the way he always spoke to her.

Devon preferred a person to take ownership, for men to be stronger and more decisive. Wren was a doctor; he should have all the confidence in the world because he made life and death decisions all the time.

But he wasn't taking responsibility for whatever Bess was talking about. "You know sometimes they need their heads knocked together," Bess said. "Art isn't here to do that. Zara tries her best, but Zave is still wary with her, you know how he is with women."

Devon didn't know who Zave was, she didn't recognize any of the names that Bess was using and she assumed they were the real names of the people she'd met at the lunch table. Given that they'd admitted to using aliases, it made sense.

"You tried to get him to go to Devon's room," Wren said. "Zave wouldn't do it. You told Devon there was only one person that Zave would listen to and we both know that's Brodie."

"And even Brodie couldn't get through to him," Bess said.

"But they came up with a plan, and that was why Brodie went to Devon last night, to make her believe that he was the buyer."

"But he wasn't," Bess insisted. Devon had never heard her voice so strained. "That's what I have a problem with. You're lying to that girl and she's been through enough."

"What was the alternative?" Wren asked. "If we didn't let her meet the buyer, she wouldn't tell us what she knows. Now she thinks she's met the buyer, she'll tell us the truth. She's honest—"

"But we're not?" Bess asked. "I don't like lying."

"I know you don't, Mom. But we do this for a reason, we got involved for a reason, we save these women for a reason."

"I know, son, because of Bronwyn," Bess said, and she became soft and soothing. "I know, Thad, sweetheart, and I'm sorry. I don't have a problem with what you do. I don't have a problem with what any of you do. You know how proud I am of you all. You put yourselves in danger time and time again and you never ask for thanks or gratitude."

"You lost your brother," Thad said. "We've all made sacrifices."

"And Zara lost her life too," Bess said. "If it wasn't for you, she wouldn't be here, and that's what gives you the right to stand up and tell them that they have to be honest with Devon."

"I can shout it out. Zara can, too, and she can work on Brodie. But when Brodie and Zave get together they're like an iron wall, they don't bend, I've never seen loyalty like it. They stand together; they would do anything for each other. Brodie would never risk Zara's life, he loves her too much, but anything else can be sacrificed. He'd do anything to defend Zave too. They're closer than brothers."

"They both lost their parents in the same way," Bess said. "Their bond is deep. But you have to tell Devon the truth. If she finds it out later—"

"What do you want me to do?" Wren asked, exasperated. "I can march out there and tell her the truth. Will Zara stand behind me? Probably, because she's too nice not to. But Brodie, he'll go ballistic and when Zave hears about it… that's it, he'll shut down, he'll go back to how he was before."

"You don't know that," Bess said. "He's come so far in these past few years. If we just push a little more…"

"Then yeah, we could make progress, or he could regress," Wren said.

"I don't think so." There was a curiosity in Bess' voice, which made Devon lean in closer. "Did you see how he was with her on the trip here? I only saw them when they arrived, but I've never seen him with any other girls the way he was with Devon. He carried her all the way up to that room in his arms and laid her on that bed like she was precious. I watched the way he stroked her hair—"

"I know," Wren said. "It was different. I don't understand it but it was. From the minute he brought her out of there, I knew there was something different about her for him."

"Do you think that's why he's being so stubborn?" Bess asked. "That he knows she's different? That for some reason, he cares about her in a special way?"

"And he's worried about getting too close?" Wren asked. "It's a possibility. But I don't see him sacrificing the mission for that, he's bullheaded. I've never seen him go gaga for a girl, not even when we were kids and there were dozens of them in his life. There was never one that stood out."

"He's older now and been through a lot," Bess said.

All of this was fascinating for Devon and several facts had become clear from this short spell of listening in. First off, the guy who had come to visit her last night, Raven, also known as Brodie, wasn't the man who'd bought her at all. Swallow, who had to be Zara, as it had been stated she and Raven were in love, wasn't ignored by her Brodie, she was ignored by this Zave character who they were talking about.

Zave was the man who had bought her, he had to be. Wren, who she now knew was called Thad, just said Zave had brought her out of the auction. By themselves, these facts were interesting, and it was startling to learn that while Devon thought she was making progress in receiving honesty, she was actually being drawn further into a pit of lies.

But this man, Zave, she'd made an impression on

him. Although she didn't know how she'd done it. Why was she different? Why had he carried her so carefully to the room and stroked her hair in a gesture which suggested affection? Devon couldn't be flattered.

Hearing a noise from beyond the door, she worried they might be coming. Stumbling back a few steps, she fled back to the table and her previous seat. Did this Zave person keep his distance because he cared for her? But how could he? They didn't know each other. She couldn't get the notion from her head that it was unsettling for him to be stroking her hair. A man she had never seen had had his hands on her, even in such a benign way, not only without her permission, but without her knowledge, too.

Picking up a stick of celery, she took a bite for no other reason than it would look good for her to be eating if someone was to come in. She thought about the man on the shore. Could that be him? The man they were talking about? He'd made an impression on her, for sure. He was the only person she'd seen who didn't have a name. It had to be him.

She couldn't be here anymore, she couldn't be honest with people who lied to her, but she couldn't decide how to tackle the situation in a way that would earn her freedom. If she told the truth about overhearing the conversation, it might prompt them to be honest with her or they could get mad.

Bess came back in. "Have you had something to eat?"

Devon was amazed at how quickly she'd gone from having a fraught conversation with her son to having a pleasant, breezy tone as she addressed the prisoner.

"Yes," Devon said, dropping her celery onto her plate and standing up. "Thank you."

"I can take you back to your room—"

"No. If you want to prove you trust me, I want a different room, one without a lock on the door, in this part of the house." Bess was startled. "You can talk to your family about it, but I don't want to be in that room anymore. If you want me to share with you, then you'll share with me, and that starts by giving me some freedom. If this house is truly on an island, I can't go anywhere, can I? Even if I wanted to run, I wouldn't get far. Your friend Raven told me last night, it's cold here, and I'd only be punishing myself."

Bess nodded. "I don't know if the boys will agree to that."

The hierarchy here, whether official or not, would dictate that Bess wasn't a decision maker, she'd said as much herself. Her hesitancy wasn't a surprise, but Devon wasn't going to back down just because she liked this woman's nature.

"I can tell you who they fear, who's in charge. I can tell you when he visits and what their vulnerabilities might be. I can even tell you about an aborted mutiny that they're desperate to keep quiet. News of that would probably get them all killed if word about the top guy is true. Now you guys can come together and decide if that information's worth having. You'll only get it if you let me see what's going on here. Are you actually vigilantes intent on helping people or are you nothing but a bunch of liars and criminals? Or you can let me go and I'll tell everything I know to the cops."

"I'll talk to them."

"Okay," Devon said, sitting herself back down. "I'll wait right here for your answer."

SEVEN

DEVON GOT HER way. After waiting for an inordinate amount of time, she was shown to a bedroom on the floor above the dining room, which had the same view, suggesting to her that they didn't want her to see more than she had to.

But it had a view and that was a step up from where she'd been before—she'd learned to be thankful for life's small graces. While the furniture was sparse, she had a bed and a chair and a TV. Before this ordeal, she had never been one to watch a lot of TV, but when she found it was tuned to the movie channels, she enjoyed losing herself in fantasy for a couple of hours.

The bathroom attached to this room was larger than the last one and had a full bath. Throughout her day, she kept one eye on the door. After Bess had shown her the room, Devon checked that the door wasn't locked. She'd been overjoyed to find it wasn't, more so than any person should be about an opening door. The blue circle was present on the doorknob, but it must have been disabled because every time she checked the door it would open.

She never got much beyond opening it a couple of inches. Her room led to a mezzanine floor that overlooked the grand entryway. Either they'd put her here to taunt her with the possibility of an easy escape or those doors were unlocked and she could make a break for it. Maybe that was what they were waiting for and if they'd been truthful about where they were, they could use her attempt at escape to return her to her previous digs.

Whether they were expecting her to try to run or not, she couldn't ignore the chance. She made a conscious choice to wait until nightfall, when it would be easier to hide from them outside, if she got that far, and it turned out that they weren't isolated.

Devon had only the dress that Bess had given her and a nightgown like the one she'd had in her previous room. If rescuing women was something they did on a regular basis, she presumed they bought the basic cotton, oversized gowns in bulk.

Neither item of apparel was warm and she didn't have shoes either. If she got lost outside then Raven was probably right that she'd freeze to death. All of this would be moot if she couldn't find a way out of the building. So far all of the windows she'd seen were tall and narrow, at most only a foot or two wide. Her view also told her that this side of the house was raised. If she had to climb out of a window, she couldn't do it here or she'd hit rocks.

The narrow strip of grass she'd seen the mysterious man running on earlier was thirty feet below her bedroom and only a few feet wide. She'd never be able to jump and aim for there, beyond were more rocks then the waves. No, she'd need a better plan than kamikazeing herself just to make a point.

Anxiety reined as she formed her plan. No one came back into her bedroom, not even to offer her food, and she wondered at the plans they might be cooking up. Except Devon had to focus on herself.

Without a clock in the room, she couldn't be exactly sure what time it was, so she waited until darkness fell and tried to occupy herself, hopefully giving the rest of the house time to drift off to sleep.

When she couldn't take the waiting anymore, she tiptoed toward the door, telling herself that even if she didn't get out tonight, she could gather valuable intelligence about where she was.

Turning the handle, so as not to make a sound, she pulled open the door just enough to allow herself to slip out. Taking one careful step out of the room, she hoped that the thump of her heart wouldn't alert her captors to what she was doing. Looking left and then right, she checked for observers or flashing lights that might indicate she was being watched.

"Need something?"

The voice came from nowhere and she stumbled back, clambering to catch the thick doorframe that her back struck. Frantic in her search for the source of the voice, she couldn't decipher any person until, to the left, in the shadow cast by one of the repeating arches that showcased the grand entryway below, a figure stepped out.

He didn't come near enough to remove the darkness from his face, but she knew this wasn't Raven, and Wren didn't have the same formidable stature.

"Zave," she whispered, unsure if it was a question or a statement.

"You were watching me."

The only time she'd ever laid eyes on him was at lunch when she'd seen him outside. She didn't know how he could have seen her. "And now you're watching me," she said. "What are you doing out here?"

"I live here."

Stoic, the lack of intonation in his deep voice didn't help her figure this man out. So intrigued by who he was and what motivated him, she forgot about her own escape plans for a minute. "That doesn't explain what you're doing standing outside my bedroom. Your aunt and your cousin think you have some kind of special interest in me." Maybe saying something that might upset his equilibrium would help to put them on equal footing because her heart hadn't slowed, in fact it was speeding up.

"Idle speculation entertains them," he said. "Go to bed, Devon."

When he slunk back into the darkness, she leaped forward. "Wait," she said. "Why won't you talk to me?"

He paused. "We each have our roles. Mine is to purchase. Conversation isn't in my repertoire."

Yet he was clearly intelligent and not intimidated by her, so that wasn't entirely true. "You've purchased other women before?"

His response didn't come right away, but she waited. It wasn't like she had anywhere else to be. This conversation could take all night if that was what it took, but she would make progress with the man she believed had to be in charge. "Yes," he said.

At least he wasn't going to embarrass them both with denials. "But you have never spoken to one of them?"

"No."

Knowing that this was a first for him made her a little more comfortable about being so out of her element. "Then why are you talking to me now?"

"Everyone else is asleep."

Implying that this was a hardship didn't wash, he had to be curious about her or he wouldn't be here. Waking one of his houseguests if he wanted company wasn't beyond him, not if he was happy to mislead her about who bought her, proving that he had no shame.

Now it was time to test if he'd defend that lie or admit it. "Why did you buy me? Why were you at the auction?"

"Women purchased at those auctions don't last long, as most buyers are rich and depraved men who torture, rape, and kill. I saved you from that fate."

He had a way of answering her questions without actually answering them, which infuriated her. "And now I'm supposed to be grateful? So grateful that what? I should drop to my knees for you?"

Nothing shocked this man or invoked much of a reaction at all. "If you hadn't thrown your fit, you and I would never have met. I'm not interested in your gratitude, your knees, or any other part of you."

Then this whole mess made even less sense to her than it had before. "So what do you want from me? What's your motive for doing this? Do you think you're some kind of hero?"

"No. My motive is complicated and personal."

There would be no other reason for him to be involved except if it was personal. Devon still wanted to know more. "I don't understand any of this... How can I be sure you will let me go? I could go to the cops, get you into trouble—"

"We know who you are. We know we can trust you. We're careful, Von, if we set the wrong woman loose, our mission could implode."

Von. Why would he call her that? "Only my brother calls me that."

The satisfaction in his response was dry. "I know."

Oh, her stupid, ignorant, always-on-the-wrong-side-of-the-law brother knew these people. "You know him?"

"Raven does."

"Did he send you after me?"

"We're done."

He thought he'd reassured her enough that he could go, but she wasn't willing to let him turn his back on her yet. "What is your mission?"

"To take these people down."

Admirable, but she still didn't understand. "Why do you keep your identity secret?"

"You ask a lot of questions for a woman who won't answer any."

Devon didn't understand the setup, but she was more confident that the situation wasn't sinister. She might not be able to see this man, but he came across as sincere and that raised more questions for her, especially since she knew now that he knew her brother.

"By going to those auctions, you're endangering yourself," she said. "Do you understand how dangerous those men are?"

"I understand," he said.

Choosing to walk into that scenario proved he had courage. "Why take the risk?"

"Someone has to."

As simple as that? It couldn't be. "So you do want to be a hero?"

"They trade in human flesh. What their victims go through is sickening."

And from the way he spat out the words, she was convinced of his disgust. But again, he hadn't answered her question, which forced her to speculate further. "You lost someone to them, didn't you?" He didn't respond. "It's the only explanation for your conviction and why you take the risk to do what you do."

"She wasn't mine to lose," he said.

Maybe it was because of the dark, or because she'd spent so long in an endless night that her other senses were keen, but she could read raw emotion in his tone even though his intonation didn't change.

Intrigued, she stepped toward him, but that caused him to descend deeper into the darkness. "What are you hiding?"

"What does it matter?"

A hint of anger in his voice could have signaled his discomfort, but she chose not to be discouraged. "Just trying to figure you out."

"Why?

It shouldn't matter who he was or why he did this, but people fascinated her, and she wanted to understand what drove such an enigmatic figure so intent on secluding himself. "Bess is personable, she seems to like being social. Wren is a doctor; he spends his life helping people. But you…"

"What?"

Though he'd tried to back away before, he was staying put now, and his prompting questions made her wonder if he wanted her to figure him out. He could tell her to shut up, mind her own business, and then lock her up in the bedroom. But he didn't, he encouraged her to keep talking by asking these open questions.

"You're obviously the money, you carry some sense of personal guilt or responsibility, which is why you do this. But you take no glory, you admitted to never having had a conversation with the women you help, so I think you're right. I don't think you do want their gratitude."

"What does that say about me?" he asked.

"Not as much as you coming to me in the dead of night while everyone else is asleep does."

"I'm a night owl."

Whether that was true or not, it wasn't why he was here. "Is that it? Or are you using the night to keep hiding from me? Why would you do that? Will I recognize you? Or are you just that insecure that you can't let me look you in the eye?"

"Being anonymous is in the nature of what I do."

"And what is that?" He didn't say anything, but she could sense him deliberating over his possible response. "Rescuing women from sick pigs like the cartels has to be a hobby, there's no money in it and you need money to make the purchases, don't you? So it has to come from somewhere, you have to have a day job and a lucrative one too. Those guys don't just let any john walk in off the street."

"Auctions are by invitation only."

Folding her arms, she tried to figure out how someone like Zave, who kept himself locked up all the time, would find himself invited to such a place. "So what do you do?"

"I build hardware innovations."

Good. That was a direct answer and one she interpreted to mean that he was an inventor, which could be a solitary profession after all. "Alone at night in a small, dark room?" she asked. "You don't like people?"

"I don't understand them. Tech is easy, it's clean and has rhythm that makes sense to me. People are a host of contradictions. I like sense and order, one and one should always equal two."

This was the most he'd said since their conversation began. He loved what he did, even if he didn't let it trickle into his tone or demeanor. He enjoyed thinking about it, speaking about it, creating was his passion.

"My great passion is art," she said, giving him some space but moving across to lean on the solid stone banister at the edge of the view below. "Pencil, pastel, paint, I love them all. I don't need order. Often when I sit down at my easel, I don't know exactly where the colors will end up on the canvas.

There's nothing I enjoy more than spending time alone with my pencils and sketch books."

"Then you can identify."

To a degree, she could understand why he was so happy to live his life alone. Loving what he did meant he was always occupied and happy even when there was no one else around. "Unlike you, I like light. I'm captivated by how the angles and brilliance can alter the mood of a piece, just as it can alter the mood of a moment."

"Like this one?"

"You came to me in the night to try and hide who you are."

"I like the night. It's quiet and calm."

"But you ran during the day, when the sea was wild." And anything but calm. "The view is inspiring."

"Sometimes I run at night."

His movements had put him back into the blackness that filled the enclosed hallway that this covered mezzanine led to. She could be hallucinating and talking to herself, anyone watching might think that she was, but she knew it was no delusion, this man was real, she could feel his presence, actually feel it, even though there was a wide space between them.

"If that's true then please, don't go near the edge like you did today. My heart was in my throat when you went so close to the rocks."

"If I fell, maybe you'd have had your freedom."

"Maybe," she said, moving forward to lean on one of the arch's vertical posts. "Or maybe there would've been nobody around to authorize my release."

"We make decisions by committee around here. If you think that manipulating me—"

"If I wanted to manipulate any man, I'd choose Wren. He'd be easier to get close to, wouldn't he?" she asked.

Raven would be off-limits because for one thing, he seemed a bit unhinged, and the second reason was Swallow. She wouldn't like another woman cozying up to her man. Bess and Wren had referenced Swallow's involvement in Kindred missions, too, so it probably wouldn't be smart to mess with her.

"All Kindred men have women issues," he said.

Although it wasn't guaranteed, that might have been a joke or at least as close to light-hearted as he got. "Is that a pre-requisite?" A laugh was too much to expect. "I think there's hope for you. Granted, I don't know much about your normal behavior, but already you've broken your mold for me, haven't you?"

"You've put up more of a fight than the other girls. Most are just grateful to be free of where they were, so they don't question our motives or question our trust."

"How many times have you done this?"

"Enough."

The war would continue. Ending human trafficking hadn't been achieved by even the furthest-reaching law enforcement agencies in the world. One small band of men couldn't hope to make much of a dent, but that didn't seem to matter, they just kept on plugging away. "You're a dedicated bunch. How did your group get involved in crime fighting?"

"How about you tell me how you ended up in Mexico."

"Mexico, is that where I was?" She'd suspected as much. South America was her assumed location, but she hadn't had it confirmed until now.

"The Mexican mafia is becoming the largest, most widespread organized crime disease in the country, and they're not as ethical as the Italian mafia were back in the day."

Her assumption that he was intelligent was right; he was clear and articulate when he wanted to be. "You know a lot about it."

"Information's easy to gather."

They had to be practiced if they could be so nonchalant about wandering into danger, and she'd been told that the Kindred had various skills, including their computer whiz, who must be able to access whatever files they needed to put knowledge together. Except she doubted the Mexican cartels kept up-to-date employee records and informative calendars for the Kindred to hack, which might be why Zave's cryptic comment felt frustrated.

Devon heard what he didn't say. "But there's more that you want to know?"

"I want to know what made you so suspicious of people."

So that was how she'd gotten his attention, by question everything that was done to her here, and everything that was said, though that didn't explain why he'd been so gentle with her after the auction.

"I am proud of that suspicion and would advise everyone to have it," she said. "Shouldn't you feel the same given your hobby?"

"Yes," he said. "But my experience has made me this way. What made *you* this way?"

He emerged from the darkness, just enough for her to make out his outline again, and she tried not to overreact. Like he was an animal she could spook if she reacted to strongly, she tried to maintain the same posture and tone.

"I lost my parents young," she said. "My brother looked out for me. But I was always independent, we butted heads all the time. I thought I knew best, so I jumped in without looking because I was sure I could handle anything."

"And you couldn't?"

"As it turned out, I couldn't," she said. Their trust might be building, but she wasn't going to reveal all of her humiliations at once. "Tell me about the woman that got you involved with this."

He shook his head, proving that he was coming out of his shell, and the triumph over the challenge he posed made her more determined to extract more from him, to get closer, maybe close enough to touch.

"That's not my story to tell," he said after a pause. "She is why we do this. But she wasn't mine."

Something profound and almost romantic about that statement drew her closer to him, and this time he didn't back away. "Did you want her to be?"

"Women," he said with a light-hearted dismissiveness. "Why do you have to make everything about love?"

Was that another different experience that had

brought him to that conclusion? "Love is the most effective motivator."

The philosophy of relationships wasn't something she shied away from discussing. "Some would say that love is merely an extension of sex."

As soon as the words came out of his mouth, strong but said without thought, she wished he could take it back. He made no physical indication that the word had impacted him, but for some reason, hearing the word aloud in the company of this man, standing alone in the dark, made her nipples peak. Her chin fell to allow her hair to hide her face, and the thumping of her heart fell to her gut.

Backtracking the topic that she hadn't even opened up, she tried to quell her inappropriate awareness. "Not all love is linked to sex," she mumbled. "There's parental love, sibling love, friendship love."

"You're embarrassed."

The volume of his word made her gasp and look up, and sure enough, there he was, right in front of her. Intent black eyes fixated on her with an intense curiosity that made her even more self-conscious. "I'm not," she said, and when she tried to withdraw, he caught her shoulder. Although she gasped, she didn't resist.

His head tilted. "Sex," he murmured and her insides quaked. If she looked at him now, she might combust, but he got even closer, so close that she couldn't breathe. "Did they touch you, shy?"

"Wren already asked me that," she whispered.

One finger curled under her chin and when he urged her head back, Devon was forced to make the eye contact she'd avoided. "Now I'm asking you."

"Why would I lie to Wren, but tell you the truth?"

"Because you are special," he said even though she could tell from the way his eyes tapered he'd rather not have to confess that truth.

"Why?"

"I don't have a fucking clue," he said, and then he lowered his mouth onto hers.

This kiss wasn't like any other she'd ever had. Sensing

his patience, she guessed it was for her benefit because he didn't strike her as the restrained type, not if he was stalking her bedroom and kissing her in hallways.

But from the moment she'd watched him run along that shore, she'd known he wasn't like any other man on Earth. Something about the way he moved, his confidence, his enduring pace, it displayed a resolve that was proven in what he did by rescuing women like her.

Opening her lips, she tried to tease his tongue, but he withdrew, dropping his hand from her face and taking a step back. "They didn't touch me," she said and tried to narrow the space, but he retreated, maintaining the distance between them. "I can't tell if you're afraid of me or afraid of what will happen if you let someone in."

Moving away again, he didn't give her the courtesy of a response. "Take care of yourself, Devon," he said.

But she couldn't let him walk away from her. In an estate this large, she may never see him again. "I'll work with you, not with them."

He stopped. "What? Why?"

"I think you've isolated yourself for too long," she said. "I think your aunt and cousin want you to do more than just exist. You do what's expected of you and not an iota more. All the money in the world can't save you, Zave, you need to live your life."

"You don't know what you're talking about."

"You've spoken more to me tonight than you have to any other girl you've pulled out of that hell. From the way Bess and Wren speak, you've said more to me than you have to them for a long time. I don't know what it is, but you do feel connected to me whether you like it or not."

"If that's true, then we stay the hell away from each other."

"I disagree," she said and went toward him, slowly again, so as not to scare him away. "What I went through… I can't share that experience with just anyone. I have to trust you."

The humiliation, the pain, the sorrow, it all came together sometimes to leave her devastated and she'd never tried to just talk about it, to tell the story. Somehow, she knew that she wouldn't be able to tell Bess. She'd worry that the woman would be overwhelmed with pity and her own distress at the tale.

Wren was a doctor and had probably heard all sorts of tragedies throughout his career, but there was something too casual about him, something that made her fear he wouldn't understand the gravity of what she'd endured.

Anything she told to Raven would be told to Swallow and vice versa. She didn't know the couple half as well as she knew Bess and Wren, but Devon already knew she'd never be comfortable enough to confide in them. Their bond with each other was too great; she'd feel like an interloper if she tried to insinuate herself into their lives with accounts of her own experience.

Maybe that was what bonded her to Zave. Whatever had gone on in that auction hall, he'd been the one to pull her out and bring her here to safety. His serious nature gave her confidence that he'd find her statements as profound to himself as they were to her.

His exhale was slow but unimpressed. "You're not shy about making demands."

Usually she would be, but she had to assert herself or the Kindred would own her. "Sleep on it. Figure out if the mission is more important than your seclusion."

Returning to her room, Devon closed the door and went to bed. Tucking her feet back under the sheet, she halved her body to pull the bedspread too. Adjusting her pillow, she relaxed to let her eyes close. Now that she knew who was behind this and where she was, it was much easier to surrender to sleep.

EIGHT

"YOU MADE AN impression."

Devon had her head turned down against a towel and was trying to shake water from her ear when she came out of her bathroom the next morning to find Bess standing at the end of her bed. "Have you guys ever thought about knocking?" Devon asked.

Bess made a dismissive hiss. "You don't have anything Swallow and I haven't seen before and Wren is a doctor, he doesn't care about naked bodies."

"And Raven?" she asked, hooking the hand towel around her neck.

Devon had been using it to dry her hair and had a bath towel wrapped around her body. It wasn't likely that she'd be walking around naked anywhere, but that wasn't exactly her point.

"He wouldn't let it distract him," Bess said and propped a hip on the end of the bed. "What about Falcon? Are you okay with him walking in on you naked?"

"Falcon?" she asked, that was a name she hadn't heard yet.

"Zave," Bess said. "He told us that you know his real name."

If Devon had been paying attention, she might have heard the twinge of innuendo in Bess' voice. All Devon could think about was the word "sex" on his lips. She hadn't handled that murmur. If he walked in and saw her nude, she'd probably burst into flames.

Zave handled himself with such composure. But maybe walking in on her while she was naked and damp from the shower, he might not find it so easy to hold himself aloof. And that kiss, if it was just the slightest hint of what he was capable of doing to a woman, Devon wouldn't stand a chance if he made a serious advance on her.

"I caught him spying on me," Devon said when she caught the suspicious glint in Bess' gaze.

"When you were sneaking out at two in the morning?" Bess said. "This estate is his, he can wander where he likes, when he likes."

She wouldn't suggest otherwise. "Whatever he was doing, I'm glad that I got to meet him."

"Sounds like you did more than that," Bess said.

Squirming at the scrutiny of this curious woman, Devon didn't like the idea that Zave had shared the news of their kiss. She believed some things should stay private, and their impromptu first kiss lost some of its magic now that she knew everyone in the building was aware of it.

"Why do you say that?" Devon asked. Although she kept her head up, she let her eyes drift down.

"Because of this," Bess said.

In her peripheral vision, she saw Bess hold something up and had to see what it was. The black device was lit and a shot of energy made Devon leap forward. "A cellphone!"

"It's encoded to call only one number, and after the call, I have to take it back," Bess said. "We need you, and Zave wants your trust... Call your brother. I'll come back when you're done."

Bess put the phone on the bed and left with a smile on her face. Devon opened the dresser drawer to look for the dress she'd put in there last night. Except it wasn't there. The drawers were all empty, and she spun on the spot desperate for something to wear. She couldn't exist in the towels she'd found stacked in the bathroom.

That was when she saw it, the door in the corner—which had previously been locked—was open. Dashing over, she poked her head past the frame and was stunned again. Rows and rows of brand new clothes hung on the rails of the walk-in closet. Grabbing open the drawers, she found underwear, accessories, makeup, everything a woman could want.

Had this been here all the time or had Zave set it up after their kiss? She didn't want to be seduced by the material, but it had been a long time since she'd had choices and that was what thrilled her, not the high-quality of the garments or the sparkle of the jewelry, but the idea that she could make her own decision about what she could put on her body.

The various styles made her head spin, and it took her some time to remember how to be decisive or even which of the clothes were her type. Trying on a few things, she got to check out her reflection in the vast mirror on the far wall, and although she didn't usually wear much, she put on some makeup just because she could. She got so caught up in the enjoyment of playing with these frivolous things that she almost forgot about her brother.

Talking to him could lead to so many answers, so as soon as she tied her hair back, she went back to the bedroom, climbed onto the bed and pressed call on the device that was displaying her brother's number.

"Who is this?" came a stern voice on the other end of the line.

Suppressing the urge to weep, she yelped, she'd never been so pleased to hear her brother's voice in all her life. Cursing all those times in their childhood when she'd fought with him, run away from him, or made his life hell, Devon never wanted to be away from his voice for this long again.

"Rig!" she said, meaning the word to sound strong, but it came out as more of a whimper.

"Jesus, fuck! Von! Rave said you were calling ten minutes ago, where the fuck have you been?"

She hadn't been told that he was sitting by the phone waiting for it to ring. "I'm sorry," she said.

The men were in contact. That was encouraging. It suggested more than a loose association and hinted at mutual respect. Much as she didn't like to be discussed behind her back, her brother cared about her and if these people were willing to be forthcoming with him then they would rise in her estimations.

"Sorry? What the fuck."

Drawing up her knees, she hugged them with one arm. "I'm sorry, I got carried away with something else. Oh, God, it's so good to hear your voice."

"Do you know what the fuck I've been through? What the fuck happened to you? I was so fucking worried!"

His urgency and panic betrayed that he had been through an ordeal of his own, maybe not as horrific as hers, but he'd felt her absence. "I'm okay now. I'm safe."

He scoffed. "Yeah, well, I know that," he said as if it was the most obvious thing in the world.

There was no concern in his voice, no worry, all she sensed was relief "You know where I am? Can you come and see me? I'd feel better if you were here."

"I can't come there."

If they were in such a remote place, that made sense because her brother couldn't fly a plane or sail a boat. Also, if they were in the Pacific Northwest, her brother was all the way back in New York, which was too far for a quick daytrip.

"I'll come to you," she said. "I'll find a way. I've been trying to get them to let me go, but they just won't and—"

"Rave says you can help," Rig said. "That true?"

Her exuberance reduced at his new neutrality. "Maybe."

"Don't be in any rush to leave there. It's the safest fucking place on earth."

"So you do know where I am?" Because she would feel better if he had her exact GPS coordinates as opposed to a vague inkling that she was still on Planet Earth.

"No, not really, just that you're with the Kindred, and when Rave's around—"

"I'm not at Rave's house," she said, assuming he meant Raven. "I mean he is here, or he was yesterday, but—"

"He's still there," Rig said. "I know you're confused. I know this is messed up and you've been through some shit. If I could bring you here and keep you safe, I'd do it. When it's time, I will, I'll figure something out for you. But those guys saw me good, they got me set up, and we've seen some shit together."

"You trust them?" she asked the most important question.

"Yes, I trust them, Von. I wouldn't be telling you to stay there if I didn't."

Her brother was a shady character who surrounded himself with men she'd cross the street to avoid. But when it came to her, his heart was pure. "Are you trying to keep me safe, or are you involved in something you don't want me to see?" she asked.

"I'm always involved in shit I don't want you to see," he said as if it was a joke, but there was too much truth in the statement for her to laugh. "When you went missing, Von, I was so worried, and I couldn't do shit about it. There's only one guy you call when you need a desperate situation sorted, you know? Tracking people down isn't his gig, but, like I said, we've seen some shit together. Those guys you're out there with, they're the real good guys, better than me that's for fucking sure. And they've got skills, proper skills to keep you safe."

Her eyes were wet, in part because she wanted to be with him, as it would make them both feel better. Also because he was sacrificing his own ego by admitting he didn't have the ability to keep her as safe as these people did.

Rig had a healthy ego, so healthy that his pigheaded confidence often got him into trouble. Apparently, he drew the line at taking risks with her safety.

"They kept me locked up," she said. "For days after I got here, weeks maybe, I don't know."

"Rave told me when they had you, told me you were sick. They've got a guy, he patched you up, right? Rave kept me in the loop."

All along her brother had known exactly what was happening to her, and she'd been oblivious to his involvement. "Why didn't you come? Why didn't you call? If I had known you were friends with these people…"

"Because they like to keep their shit low-key. They did this for me as a personal favor. Rave said he had a guy already on the inside, didn't surprise me, Rave always knows somebody who knows somebody, you get me? But you were never supposed to see their faces, never supposed to know who they were, that was the deal. They got you out, they got you better, and they got you back to me. You were never supposed to know fuck all about them."

"But that changed when they found out I had information?" she asked, not sure if she should be grateful or offended. "So now that they can use me…"

"You can be pissed if you want," Rig said. "Put up all those barriers, hide behind that meek little personality of yours, be the gal who can't stand up for herself."

With a growling expression, she pushed back against her brother's impatient taunting. "I'm not meek," she asserted.

"Sure you are, ninety percent of the time, and then it's like you bottle it all up and it blasts out in one short burst of rage or sarcasm. And then it's as if you're so mortified by the fact you showed an emotion, that you actually reacted to something, that you shut the fuck up for like six weeks. Are you that scared of losing people, Von, that you keep your mouth shut and just hope to blend in?"

"Please don't," she said, swiping tears from her cheeks. "I really don't need to hear about my flaws."

"It's not a flaw, it's who you are and I love you, sis. It's better than my personality. I just keep spouting shit, blowing hot air. I make a lot of noise, but don't say shit."

She laughed, the only time he was self-deprecating was in front of her and when there was no one within earshot. "I am grateful for what they did. If they hadn't gotten me out…"

And that was the thought she'd tried not to confront because for whatever reason, Zave was there, he made the purchase, and brought her to his cloistered home. That act had saved her life, had saved her from a horrific fate.

She'd thought about the women who'd been in those metal boxes with her, terrified of the fates that laid in their futures. Those women were tied to beds and floors, or maybe they were chained to walls or trees, God only knew where they were and what they were enduring. They were being subjected to appalling treatment; she knew it because the type of men who would buy another human being weren't the type who would have a strict moral code. Except Zave. Except the Kindred.

It would be a nice fairy tale fantasy to believe that every woman was rescued by their own knight in shining armor and that they were all staying in houses like this on remote islands, discovering closets full of clothes, bathing in luxurious bathrooms, and being brought food and clean water while being treated like a decent human being.

But it was just that, a fairy tale, there was no way it could be true.

"You should be grateful. I'm grateful," Rig said. "And I've made it damn clear to Rave that I'll do whatever the fuck he wants. My ass belongs to him for this."

Concern shook loose her melancholy thoughts. "Will he call that in? What favor will he want?" Hoping that her brother hadn't sold his soul, or whatever soul he had left, she didn't want him to be roped into anything negative just because he cared for her enough to barter himself for her safety. Whatever they asked him to do could be a thousand times worse than the fate he'd saved her from.

"He'll call it in," Rig said. "When the time is right. But he only calls in favors when he needs them; the Kindred keep as much in-house as they can. He'll keep it real. It won't be shady. Well, it's always shady." She could hear his smile radiating down the phone line. "But it won't be any kinky shit, and I won't be asked to take the fall."

Rig seemed to have it so under control. He was calm and she didn't know how he could be so together when he'd just admitted owing such an intense man a favor. "I owe Rave from way back," Rig carried on. "It kinda works on tit for tat, we end up even eventually."

"What about the rest of them?" she asked, since she

had the opportunity to find out what her brother knew. "The other people he works with, what do you know about them?"

"He works with his girl, Swallow, she's hot. That's about as much as I know about her. Rave's protective, seriously protective."

So Swallow was still a mystery. "What about the guy who patches them up?" she asked, referring to Wren as he had. "And…" As much as she trusted her brother, he'd made it clear the Kindred didn't want to be exposed and he hadn't mentioned Zave, so she didn't know if he knew him. Searching her recollection for what Bess had said, she elected to use his apparent alias as opposed to his real name, just in case. "Falcon, what do you know about them?"

"They call themselves the Kindred," he said. "Haven't met them all. I know Rave and Swift the best."

Swift was an unfamiliar name, and he wasn't here. Remembering what they'd said about their computer genius, about the man on their team who could hack any computer system, and she wondered if that was his name.

Torn between her instinct to flee and her desire to stay, she couldn't decipher what the right course of action was. "All I wanted to do was get out of here," she admitted. "But they've treated me so well and I didn't trust them. But now they need my help and if you're vouching for them… I suppose I should do what I can."

"There are worse groups to get involved with," he said. "You know how I feel about you messing with gangs or ex-cons or anyone like that." He'd always been adamant about her staying far away from criminality, and she'd never had a problem with that. "So it should tell you something about how decent these folks are that I'm not telling you to get your ass out of dodge."

That was a fair point, she thought, lying down on the bed and stretching her toes toward the end. After being stuck in that metal box where she couldn't even lie down, let alone stretch out, this was a luxury that she didn't want to take for granted.

"Those there are good people," Rig said. "They go about things in a… direct kinda way. But they'll protect you,

Von. Wherever the fuck they're keeping you, I guarantee no bullshit human traffickers will get their filthy hands on you there."

The Kindred needed her help now, but she couldn't live here forever. She would eventually have to venture back into the real world, onto the mainland of the United States, into a city somewhere, an apartment. She'd have to get a job; she'd have to use the subway and eat in diners and buy clothes. Devon couldn't stay locked in a fortress forever.

Sitting up to look toward the window on the left wall, past the end of the bed, she could see tiny segments of the ocean through the clear square panes of the mosaic window. Here was unknown. But it was safe. Out there was danger and when she had to face it, she would be alone. She wouldn't have anyone with her to watch out for her. There wouldn't be fingerprint locks to hide behind or Bess to bring her food and look after her. There would be no Wren to nurse her back to health and no Zave to make her blush.

"I'll help them," she said. "But when I leave here, can I come and stay with you for a bit? You said you had that big house now, there must be space for—"

"This isn't a place for you," he said. "You know I'd love to have you, and I'll never see you on the streets, but all my guys are here and I don't trust them. Shit goes down here that I don't want you involved in, you could get hurt."

"I understand," she said, nodding at no one. Devon picked at the cover she was sitting on.

This was her brother's usual rhetoric when she asked to be a part of his life. He would send her money without asking what it was for, he'd come and stay when she wanted to see him. But when she asked to be let into his world, he slammed the door in her face every time. He was trying to protect her, and she did appreciate that he cared so much to do that, but it often left her feeling alone in the world.

She had loose friendships with colleagues, but she changed workplaces so often that none of them ever stuck. Devon would say hello to neighbors but never formed a connection with them. Maybe Rig was right, maybe she was trying to keep everyone at arm's length because she was afraid to let them in. Because if she did that and then they rejected her, it would be a reflection on how poor her character was.

Her dad had died in prison, in a riot, when she was young. All through school she'd been told gruesome stories of the things he'd done. Some of them were true, some of them were fable. Rig would never confirm or deny which were which. Kids loved to taunt and for years called her "Con-Von" because her father was always in jail. Her classmates' treatment of her taught her to retreat, to hide in the corners, and not to put herself out there. On Daddy-Daughter Day, no one showed up to support her, she had no one to contribute on Career Day either.

Anyone who tried to approach her or bully her when Rig was around got dealt a swift blow. But when he hit his teenage years and got involved with his first crew, for a long time he seemed to be going down the same path as their father. Devon wasn't naïve, Rig could end up the same way.

And then there was the day she'd come home to find her mother dead with a needle in her arm. For years after that, she was numb, most of her teenage years were a blank. There were care homes that never stuck and foster parents who just wanted the income. Then Rig set her up in her own place, because even back then, his crew came first.

She worked hard to support herself and was proud of what she'd done. But what it had taught her was that she didn't need to rely on anyone because she could do everything herself as long as she kept her head down and her nose clean.

That might have worked when life was going along fine, but it meant that when she was in trouble, when she'd gone missing, there was no one to notice. She didn't ask Rig when he noticed something was wrong, whether it had taken him a day or a week or a month to realize that she wasn't where she was supposed to be.

They rung off with assurances that they would talk again, though she made it clear that she had no say, as Bess had advised she would be taking the phone away. Rig said he would talk to Raven and they'd figure something out. Then he made a comment about getting back to a scam he had running, and she knew his attention had moved on.

When his baby sister was in trouble, he mobilized and fixed it. Now she was out of that darkness, and he didn't need to be alert anymore. Promising him that she would do all she could for the Kindred, Devon couldn't tell him about her concerns. Rig wasn't much interested in the emotional side of their relationship.

He told her he loved her and proved by his actions that he did. But he wouldn't be interested in listening to her prattle on about how nervous she was at the idea of recounting her abduction experience or talking about her life in the metal box. Exposing her fears, her thoughts, and her plans while she'd existed in that hell.

There had been a time in that dark hole, when she'd craved death and considered how she might go about taking back control and ending her own suffering. Her whole body had ached, she'd been so weak, Devon just wanted to die. It must have been only a few weeks into her stay, just as the starvation started to kick in. A few scraps a day wasn't nearly enough to survive on. The amount got less and the frequency of feeding time became more erratic the longer she was there.

Devon had noticed in her last few days here that Bess was right about her being skin on bone. Devon would need to work hard to return to how she was, eating properly, exercising, taking care of herself. Just as she thought that Bess might be the best one to help her with that, Devon's bedroom door opened and her attention leaped up to the door, which was to the right, opposite the large window.

"All done?" Bess asked.

Something she'd always wondered about made her ask, "How do you know when I'm finished?" she asked, casting a look around the ceiling. "You told me there were no cameras, but how do you—"

"There are no cameras, not in this room," Bess said. "There are cameras in other parts of the house." She came over to the end of the bed. "But those are there to protect me."

Devon didn't follow how Bess could be at risk in this place that was apparently so safe. "Protect you?"

"When the boys are off doing their thing, Falcon and

Raven, they're often away. Raven can be gone for months at a time. Falcon's usually just a few days. But…" she said and her smile grew wide. "Those boys do like to fuss over me. And if one's not around, the other has to watch and check in on me. They tag each other in and out of babysitting old Bess."

"Does Raven live here? Raven and Swallow, full-time?"

Bess shook her head. "They have a house, identical to this one actually," she said, holding open her arms. "But it's on the East Coast."

"Identical?" That was a weird, but intriguing, idea. "Why would…?"

"It's a long story," Bess said. "And one I'm sure you'll hear from the horse's mouth."

A frisson of excitement sizzled within her hips. "Does he want to see me?" Bess could only be referring to Zave. Raven wasn't going to tell any stories, he shut Wren up at the lunch table and Zave was definitely in control here.

"Not yet," Bess said and came around to take the phone from Devon's two clutching hands. "He won't surface for a while."

"Surface? He's sleeping?"

Bess shrugged and rolled her eyes. "Who knows with that boy," she said, almost tutting as she smiled like a fed up but amused mother. "He locks himself up in his part of the house for days or weeks sometimes. He always comes out again in his own time. Knowing that you're waiting and that there's work to do, he'll be quick about it this time, I'm sure."

"His part of the house? He has his own part of the house?"

"Yes, he does. He always has, since he bought this place when he was a kid. But I shouldn't say too much about that," Bess said.

"Still secretive," she sighed. Every time she felt like she took a step forward, someone was there to pull her straight back.

"You've made amazing progress," Bess said, slipping the phone into her pocket to sit on the edge of the bed. "Zave has never spoken directly to any woman they've brought back from those places. And you say he was spying on you? If that's true, I'd take that as a compliment. He hasn't shown any interest in women in a long time."

Not saying too much only extended so far, because that was probably the most intriguing thing that Bess could've said. "How long?" she heard herself asking.

Flattening both hands on the bed between them, Bess covered Devon's hands when they were down. Her smile returned. "I just want you to know that you've gotten in, and we're grateful that you have. Just don't hurt him."

Devon wasn't sure that she would know how to hurt any man let alone a man as strong and stoic as Zave was. "Did he tell you what happened last night?" she asked, looking at their overlaying hands.

"No specifics, except that you'll be dealing directly with him when it comes to Kindred business. Don't be surprised if Raven and Swallow check out soon. They're sort of in the middle of their own adventure."

"Then why did they come here?"

"Because they're Kindred," Bess said. "They drop everything for each other when the need arises. Prioritizing is sort of Swallow's specialty, she'll let them know which case or mission is most pressing. Recently, that's been you."

It was probably meant to be a compliment, but Devon didn't like to think of herself as a case or as a mission. Certainly not as she pertained to Zave. "I deal with him directly?" she asked and Bess nodded.

"There's one more thing."

Devon didn't know what else there could be, but Bess got up from the bed and scurried out of the room. Sitting on her own, Devon wasn't sure if she was supposed to follow or if she was supposed to wait. She was usually given instructions when they wanted her to do something or not to do something. But before she could take action or call out, Bess came back in carrying a wooden box.

"What is that?" Devon asked when Bess set the large box over the footboard onto the end of the bed.

"Open it." Crawling to the end, she unhooked the small brass latch and made eye contact with an exuberant Bess before she lifted the hinged lid and looked down. "He said it was important to you."

The tiered box opened in three layers. The bottom section held a shining new sketch pad, in each of the other tiers were pencils and pastels. "Oh my God," Devon whispered.

"It's not a full set," Bess said. "He's working on that."

The tears that had dried after her call with her brother sprung out again. Running her fingers over the thick, premium paper, she wanted to use every pencil and pastel all at once.

"There isn't much to draw in here, but you can wander around the house. I wouldn't advise you to go outside, he doesn't want you to get lost. But the windows open and—"

"Thank you," Devon said, closing the box to lay her hands on it because she was just too overwhelmed to handle his generosity. "Tell him I say thank you."

"You can tell him yourself," Bess said. "He plans to meet with you as soon as he's finished whatever he's doing in his secret lair. Dinner I'd imagine, maybe breakfast, but he'll come for you soon."

Bess receded from the room. Alone with her gift, Devon was still high from her conversation with her brother. She almost couldn't believe this was the same house she'd been afraid of just a day or two ago. Now it seemed like a wondrous palace full of happiness and kindness, and she couldn't be afraid anymore.

Maybe if Rig hadn't given his seal of approval, she'd have been suspicious that these people were trying to buy her affection or her loyalty. But if Rig said she was safe here, she knew she was safe. She didn't know how she would begin to express to Zave how grateful she was for everything he'd done and for who he was.

Bess had told Devon not to hurt him and she still didn't know what that meant, but if things carried on the way they were at the moment, Devon feared she would be the one left devastated when she was forced to leave this place and return to reality.

NINE

A CLOCK WOULD be Devon's first request if she ever got the chance. Bess had told her that Zave may come to her tonight, and she had waited for him. Having her art supplies allowed the time to pass much more quickly. She got swept into what she was doing, and for the first time in a long time, Devon actually relaxed and enjoyed herself and forgot about all the horrific things that had happened to her.

But every time she paused and took her pencil from the paper, she thought about him, about his voice in the shadow, about the way he retreated from her, and how being close to him had felt profound.

And his kiss. When she closed her eyes, she could still feel his lips on hers. Throughout the day, she absently grazed her fingertips over the spot he'd stimulated, and as enticing as the experience had been, she speculated on why he had withdrawn so quickly and so completely.

He hadn't just stopped their kiss, he'd separated their bodies. Various reasons flitted through her mind for why this might be, and she wasn't sure she would have the courage to ask him for the truth, even if the opportunity to query it rose in conversation.

Devon had never had much luck with men. She'd

avoided them more than she'd embraced them. She'd never feared them, but she'd never understood them either. She never understood what it was they wanted her to be. Every man was different, every date meant a change of the rules, and she felt so off-balance each time she met a new man. Some wanted happy and bubbly, others wanted serious and demure.

A few years ago, she'd given up trying to mold herself into what they wanted her to be. Self-respect had been a struggle for her growing up and that carried forward into her dating life. It took a lot for her to assert her own personality and to stop prioritizing the wants of her potential mate in favor of heeding her own. When she was herself, they lost interest quickly.

Herself was calm and thoughtful. She didn't need to engage in small talk and she wasn't great at flirting and she was worse at innuendo. So the men invariably found a woman who would entice them instead of one who would rather debate the true meaning of life or discuss current events.

She liked to talk about things that mattered, knew nothing about sports, barely drank alcohol, and hated crowded parties. In short, she was the worst date ever.

Her thoughts returned to a timepiece because it was dark outside. Devon had opened the window to allow the crash of the waves to sound through her bedroom, and she loved the scent of the sea air. Something about it invigorated her and it made her want to go outside to run that same route she'd seen Zave on. Not that she'd ever been particularly athletic, but it seemed wild out there and it made her want to be wild too.

She couldn't tell if it was five p.m. or five a.m. She knew it hadn't been dark for long, but her internal chronometer wasn't accurate any longer, not that it ever had been. Devon didn't know if she should prepare for bed or if she should wait and hope that perhaps Zave did want to see her tonight. Bess hadn't come to feed her, but she had spent most of the day in the hallways.

She hadn't ventured far from this room, because whenever she tried to, Devon got herself lost. Most of the rooms off the hallway were fingerprint locked. She didn't press her fingerprint to any because Devon knew she wouldn't be authorized anywhere, but that didn't prevent her from rattling a few doorknobs, in hope of getting a different view of the ocean.

After sitting on the stairs in the grand entryway sketching for probably a few hours, she'd come to her room, stood at the open window, and using her pastel she'd crafted an image of the view. But it was awkward without an easel or a chair, and the angle limited the scope of what she could draw.

But she wouldn't complain, and she kept trying, even if it didn't end up being her best work. It was liberating to be once again consumed by her passion, when she once considered she would never get this chance again.

Putting away her pastels and pencils after the light faded and the ocean disappeared, Devon was fascinated by the sound of the water and could close her eyes to conjure the nighttime views. But she wished she could see the moonlight. From where she was in the house, she couldn't see the moon. She imagined it a brilliant white, reflecting a navy streak on the dark gray seas that would crash and thrash in white, foamy waves as the winds picked up carrying that salty scent through all of her senses.

Closing the window, despite her desire not to, she didn't want the room to get cold. The towering ceiling meant the heat would be captured far above, and Devon figured the temperature would drop in here quite fast.

Just as she fastened the latch, the door opened, and she whirled around, holding her breath, hoping to see Zave. But it was Bess who stood there.

"Are you hungry?" Bess asked. "You must be. You haven't eaten anything all day. I came to find you earlier, but you weren't here."

"I was drawing," she said. It was also a possibility that she'd been lost in one of the many hallways at the time. "I'm sorry, I suppose I lost track of time. I didn't feel hungry when I had my pencils in my hand."

"But you do now?" Bess asked, remaining in the doorway. "Come downstairs and eat."

Devon didn't know if that meant eating with Bess, in a group, or alone with Zave, but being invited downstairs was a step up from being relegated to her room at meal time. So she followed Bess out, along the mezzanine corridor and down the stairs to the left, onto the landing, and down again to get to the grand foyer on the lower floor.

"I can show you where the kitchen is," Bess said, over her shoulder. "That way you'll be able to help yourself. You can eat anything you want in there. There's a cellar and a cold store beneath it, so we're stocked up with enough supplies to see us through months. Just means you never have to worry about eating the last of something, there's always more."

"I suppose you'd have to be," Devon said, walking with Bess as she went through one of the pointed arches that held up the mezzanine above, where her bedroom was located.

Trying to leave mental breadcrumbs, Devon wasn't sure of their destination but wanted to try and remember how they got here in case she had to come back. Her sense of direction sucked, but she had to start trying to map the place if she was going to be staying here for a while.

Bess took her into the dining room. Devon recognized it as the same one she'd been in before, though the light was lower making the environment more sinister. The familiar room with its window on the opposite wall had a single door to the left, and another to the right.

The central table was dwarfed in the vast space, and she wondered why they didn't have a larger one when the space would accommodate it. If they were a small band of people, maybe they were happy with what they needed rather than the maximum they could have.

"There's plenty to eat," Bess said, pulling out a chair to the right of the head of the table.

Devon took the invitation to sit in it, and she appreciated being allowed to face the window. Although like hers upstairs, it was dark. Each different, textured pane showed the same ink of night beyond.

"Thank you," Devon said as Bess poured her water from a pitcher.

"Now, what would you like to eat? We have soup. I have a pot roast. There's pasta…" Bess went around to stand behind the chair opposite hers. "What are you in the mood for?"

"You made pot roast?" she asked. "Why would you make so many different things?"

Bess cocked a hip and a brow. "Because my boys are fussy. Because I never know when they'll want to eat or what they'll want to eat. Wren is in the kitchen trying to catch up with his patients' notes. So of course, he starts to eat and then he gets distracted. I tell you, it's like high school homework all over again. He gets distracted, and I point him back to what he's supposed to be doing. He starts talking, going off on tangents, I have to direct him back. It's a wonder he ever got through med school."

The affection in her voice was alien to Devon, as she'd never had that kind of maternal figure in her life. "Raven and Swallow, are they still here?" Devon asked, sipping her water.

"Yes, yes, but they're downstairs. When they're not in the gym, Zara's on the phone, and Brodie's playing with his hardware. All this space in their beautiful houses, and the lot of them are so predictable, they go to their same little rooms, their same niches, and use only a fraction of the space. They could own one house between the pair of them and never see each other, there's so much room."

Bess was in a chatty mood, which could mean Devon had the chance to fill in some of her blanks. "Who's Swift?" she asked.

Bess grew suspicious. "Where did you hear that name? Zave told us you overheard our conversation, but we weren't talking about Swift."

Torn between being impressed and being intimidated, she had to know how she was being monitored. "How could he know that?"

From how he'd reacted in the hallway, from the things he'd said, she knew he was aware of her eavesdropping, she just didn't know how he'd figured it out.

"There are motion and sound detectors throughout

the house," Bess said, waving her hands. "I don't know where they're all located. But they record and the boys can tell where people were in a room and what sound was picked up in certain spots. I suppose he knew you were near the door and that our voices carried. I'm sorry if we said anything that upset you."

Gobsmacked, Devon sank back in her chair. "You have technology like that?"

Bess laughed. "Oh, my dear, we have technology for everything. That's all Zave does, potter around, building different things. You can ask him for anything, anything at all. Tell him you've got a problem and he'll build a device that will fix it."

That was interesting. "You have these in my bedroom too?"

Bess nodded. "Yes, they don't record what's said and there's no camera giving anyone a visual." She wiggled her finger up and down. "It's just a little line that moves and spikes. They have different codes for different places and frequencies, I don't try to figure it out. Zave understands it, he can explain it… But, like I said, we weren't talking about Swift yesterday."

"No," she said. "Rig knows him."

"Ah, yes. How is our friend Rigor?"

"Better now that he knows I'm safe," she said. "He said that he knew Raven and Swift best but didn't elaborate."

"Swift is another Kindred member. He hasn't been here in a while. He's running things from Rave's manor with his girl."

Zave had said all Kindred men had women issues. "He has a girl too?"

"She's wonderful," Bess said. "The sweetest, most delightful person you'll ever meet in your life." That was unlikely. That Devon would meet the woman, not that she was a charming person. "So what would you like to eat? Pot roast?"

"No," Devon said. "It's sounds wonderful, but…" She put one hand on the table and the other on her stomach. "I want to take things easy. I'll need to build myself back up."

"It's good to hear you say that," Bess said. "You seem to be getting over your illness."

"I feel stronger today," Devon said. "I'm happier and more determined."

"All good things in this house," Bess said as she moved away toward the door she'd used the previous day. "I'll bring your food back in a minute."

And she did. She brought in pasta, salad, and garlic bread laden with cheese. Bess had agreed with Devon when she'd said she should take it easy and then produced all of this food.

Devon could tell that Bess was a woman who would go above and beyond for anyone. She had the best, kindest heart. Maybe it was what Devon had overheard the previous day, but she couldn't be wary of Bess. The woman had never made her feel unwelcome or like a burden.

Rig hadn't mentioned Bess at all and if she stayed here and was protected by the men, Devon's brother might not even know that Bess existed. Bess had been so good to her that Devon promised in that moment of fussing to never reveal the woman's identity to anyone no matter how her dealings with the Kindred turned out.

Bess was leaning on the chair back of the seat opposite hers, telling her about the food, as Devon twirled the tagliatelle around her fork. The sauce was thick and creamy, maybe more than she could handle. But it could be that her tastebuds had been on pause for so long that they would have to reacquaint themselves with what she liked and didn't like.

Bess didn't sit down and Devon wished she would, it would make her feel less like a burdensome guest. The woman could be eating with her instead of foregoing her own meal to make sure that Devon ate hers.

Assuming this was meal time for her alone, she didn't expect the door to her left to open, the same one that Brodie and Zara had emerged from the previous day. Except it wasn't the couple who came through it this time. It was the man whose company she'd craved all day, and she swallowed away her gasp.

TEN

"LEAVE DEVON and me alone," he said, laying his gaze on her.

Devon understood now why the illumination in the room wasn't as bright as it could be; he seemed happier to exist in the dark. Bess stretched her arms from the back of the chair and then followed his instruction. Scurrying away, Bess closed the right-hand door behind her, sealing Devon into this room with Zave.

Putting down her fork, Devon brought her napkin to her lips and wasn't sure of what would happen next. Waiting for him to guide her, she said nothing.

Sauntering toward the table with long, slow steps, his expression didn't give away much about his thoughts. "I should introduce myself," he said. An odd opening perhaps, given that they'd met, they'd kissed, but maybe that was why he felt the need to be more formal and to do things properly. It would keep her at a distance.

"I guess you should."

He kept going, walking the length of the table on the opposite side from the one she sat on. He was assured, with a confident posture and an athletic physique, and he didn't strike her as an anti-social recluse.

Turning, his stance was wide and he linked his hands at his back. "I'm Xavier Knight," he said. The name was familiar but didn't immediately conjure recognition, so she dismissed it and watched him stride back along the length of the table toward her.

Given that he knew her name, she couldn't respond in a traditional way. "I want to say thank you," she said. "For your gift today, it was thoughtful."

"No more than what you deserve, after all you've been through," he said, putting his hands on the back of the chair Bess had been leaning on to pull it out.

"And your house is beautiful. Thank you for letting me draw its lines and angles, it was a treat. Getting the chance to walk around was amazing, much better than being locked up."

"You're not a prisoner here," he said, seating himself opposite her and folding his forearms on the table. "This isn't our normal way of conducting business."

When his eyes met hers she almost choked on her own breath. They appeared as hollow points, drilling into her.

"Yes, I… I have guessed that," she said. After how the situation had been explained to her when she first got here and with all that Rig had told her about how these people were, she knew this wasn't "normal". The fact that she knew their names and relationships and that she had met Xavier and seen his house, all of this was unusual conduct for them.

"But last night," he said. "I have to apologize."

From such a formal conversation, she didn't expect anything personal. "For what?" she asked. "Standing outside my room? You're allowed. It's your house."

"No. For kissing you."

She didn't want him to apologize for that, she wanted him to do it again. But his detached expression didn't give her hope that that would be happening any time soon. "Don't apologize," she said. "I enjoyed it." Wanting to kick herself for making such a stupid statement, Devon was surprised that he didn't just laugh at her or sneer.

"It won't happen again," he said.

Disappointment hurt her more than it should after

such a short association, it wasn't like she had an emotional investment in their connection. But for some reason it hurt her to hear him dismiss any chance that they may explore the connection further.

"Why not?" she asked, not usually so bold.

Her time with him was precious and if she didn't take risks to utilize it to its maximum potential, she would have nothing but time in this place, and she'd wile it away with thoughts of things she should have done differently. Just like she'd done in that metal box. She didn't want to live like that anymore, she wanted to embrace life and that meant taking risks.

She would never know when life might be snatched away from her.

"Bess forges close relationships with the women we bring here," he said, and again she felt that twinge of intense hurt because he was ignoring her question and she was confused.

Did he not want to kiss her? Did he not enjoy it? Was he worried about what she'd been through and pushing her too far so soon after that ordeal? Did he want to avoid any appearance that he might be trying to manipulate her into favoring the Kindred?

Or did he maybe have a problem with her in principle? He had a large house, money, sophistication, a vast skillset, none of which she had. Devon was dirt poor and from the streets and scraped by living from paycheck to paycheck, often not making ends meet.

It had probably been easy for him to forget that in the night when they were just two human beings facing each other, exploring an attraction. But on reflection, he'd maybe decided that she wasn't good enough for him and she couldn't argue against that.

"Bess is a wonderful woman," she said. "She'd been good to me."

"She's good to everyone. It's her responsibility to talk to the women when they're healthy enough to leave here. She coaches them through every step of how to deal with their families and helps those who want to go to the cops to get their story straight."

The Kindred did offer a thorough service. "You advise them?"

"As you've been told several times, we do have interests to protect. Anonymity allows us to do what we do. We never discourage anyone from going to the authorities, we simply ask that they say they escaped those that purchased them and give no further details."

The strategy was smart. It allowed the Kindred to keep doing what they were doing without worrying about cops and other agencies chasing them. After being rescued and nursed back to health, it seemed like the least these women could do to simply say that they'd escaped their captors. They could say they'd been kept bound or gagged, blindfolded, that they knew nothing about where they'd been or who had bought them.

"Do you take them home?"

"We take them to various spots throughout the country so as not to raise suspicions or create a pattern, but we always let them go near a safe place. Those who don't want to go to authorities, we leave them near their homes."

"Meaning that even if the report gets back to the cartel that a girl has escaped and gone to cops, they don't suspect you?"

"Right," he said. "All transactions are final and there is no paperwork. The Mexicans don't worry too much about a girl's real identity. It's unlikely they would be able to trace her to a specific buyer. It would take a guy from the night of the auction remembering who she'd left with."

Both vendor and purchaser would want anonymity in the illegal transaction. His reminder of the night of the auction made her relive flashes of the experience, standing naked in that waterfall of light... Zave had been there waiting, he'd have seen her panic and try to bolt.

Rig had told her that she was rescued because of him, but Zave could've picked any girl that night and didn't have to limit himself to only her. Simply because she had a brother who knew someone with access, it didn't seem right that she was special. She wanted to ask him about what it was like from the other side of that beam of light but didn't want to remind him of her panic, of her naked body, of her vulnerability.

"Some women don't go to the cops?" she asked.

He took a long breath. "Not all the girls are on the right side of the law and some… well, premium girls mostly come from high society families who wouldn't want to admit the shame."

An explosion of anger made her bang a hand on the table. "It's not their fault," she said, defensive about the girls who endured the torture.

"You don't have to tell me that," he said, pushing one hand a few inches closer to her and then withdrawing it, keeping it flat on the table. "You're a real firecracker, Devon."

"I'm sorry," she said, embarrassed. She lowered her eyes and ran a hand through her hair. "My brother says I bottle things up until they burst out. I guess I'm nearing that point."

Until now, she'd been holding it together and she didn't want to lose it in front of Zave, not when she was trying to win his respect. "Don't apologize."

"What I wouldn't give for a strawberry and vanilla milkshake," she murmured. The cool mixture had a way of cooling down her emotions and comforting her at the same time. "I overreacted; I shouldn't have snapped."

"You've been full of fire since I first laid eyes on you," he said.

She didn't want to blush, but she was sure she did, so she focused on her food. So much for not reminding him of that night. It turned out he was thinking of it anyway. No one had ever called her a firecracker before. Rig accused her of trying to blend into the background, not of trying to stand out.

Being honest, her voice came out meek. "I didn't want to talk about that night."

"Good," he said. "Neither do I. I like logic, that means we start at the beginning. Tell me how you got there."

"I don't know," she said, and this was the moment she hadn't wanted to face—recounting her abduction. Not because she remembered so much about it and it was traumatizing, but because she remembered so little and it was unsettling to think of herself helpless. "I was leaving the gallery late and that's the last thing I remember."

"Chances are you were drugged. Sedatives protect their anonymity, they disorientate you and conceal their location, which is the same reason they use the drugs after sale when you're being transported to your owner's property."

"Okay," she said, trying not to read too much into that because if she thought too much about it she might cross that threshold and go into meltdown mode.

"Did you have a show on at the gallery? Is that why you were leaving so late?"

"Oh, no," she said, almost laughing, pleased by the way her mood lifted. "They let me use a space to work in. I live in a tiny studio apartment, there's hardly space for my bed. I do some cleaning and work reception for them on weekends and evenings when they need cover. In return, they let me paint there."

While she was happy talking about her work, something she'd said made Zave's expression grow curious. "You were in the premium auction," he muttered, like it was significant, although she didn't know the difference in the levels of auction.

"What does that mean?"

Although there was a plate in front of him and cutlery on either side of it, he hadn't paid any attention to the food or filled his empty glass with water, nor had he reached for the corked wine bottle further down in the spread. She'd like to think that he was enraptured by her, that she was all the sustenance he needed. But after vetoing the chance of their mouths ever getting close, she doubted that was his reason for flouting the meal.

"There are two types of trafficked women," he said. "Those who are sold at auction to high-end buyers, the men who want their own personal slave."

That was the type she frequently thought about. "And the second type?" she asked.

Scrutinizing his almost businesslike pose, his shoulders were square, his head level, and his expression unflinching. "What they would call wholesale merchandise. Women who are sold in batches, shipped to brothels all over the world."

Those were the type of women from her district, types who probably ended up in trouble and may even be groomed to end up in their own metal box by apparent choice, though they couldn't possibly comprehend the gravity of their fate.

Except now Devon understood his curiosity and had to ask, "Why was I in the premium auction rather than sent off to one of their brothels?"

Averting his eyes, it seemed he was still trying to come to a conclusion about that himself. "I don't know. The cartel you were with sells both types on the same night. There's one room filled with women batched into lots, they're bid upon like livestock. Once that part of the evening is over, the premium auction starts. Women like you are top of the bill."

She couldn't feel flattered, he didn't hint at gaining any enjoyment from being there, but he made it sound like an event. She wondered if they had a bar or a buffet, if canapes were passed around as buyers hobnobbed or if it was much less civilized with men skulking in corners, grunting to make their bids.

"I'd never thought about the details."

"There are several different gangs, who sell in different ways. We're invited to most of the auctions because we always buy. They assume I have... particular tastes that require me to need a constant supply of new women."

Disgust made her sneer, not because she believed he did have those tastes, but because the gang members revered him for being such an important repeat customer. "You risk your reputation going there," Devon said.

"We deal with a man called Carlos. He's not in charge, he's a go-between, he notifies contacts about the auctions."

Hearing the extent of his experience, she was both repulsed and sympathetic. "You've been there countless times, aren't you terrified that they'll find out what you do?"

"They kept you for months," he said, his voice descending into a growl. "Almost three in fact."

"What?" she asked, forgetting that he had dodged her

question. "A quarter of a year?"

"What I feel is insignificant," he said, and she realized that in an indirect way, he'd answered her question about his feelings on attending the auctions.

"If you were discovered, they would kill you."

"They might try. We've done this many times, and part of the reason I'm accepted is reputation. They won't hurt me."

He didn't elaborate, and she didn't know if he meant his Kindred reputation or some other rep. If those dregs of humanity knew about the goodness of his work, they would never allow him over the threshold.

"I don't understand any of this," she said, collapsing against the back of her chair and forgetting the manners she'd tried to fake.

It wasn't like she was raised to sit up straight at the table and keep her elbows off it. She'd seen sophistication in movies and read about it in books but had never been taught it growing up. Devon did her best to exude class, though it was likely she'd fail to convince him.

The harsh edge left his voice. "I know it must have been difficult for you. But it may work out in our favor that you were there for so long. There are only three or four premium auctions a year, hence why they held you for so long. They had to wait for the next auction to come up."

"How do you figure that it was good I was there for months?"

"That duration allowed you to be exposed to their conversations." Crossing his forearms, he leaned toward the center of the table. "You're the first woman we've had who speaks their language. You've lived on the inside, closer than we've ever gotten."

And so they'd returned to her usefulness, to how the Kindred needed her and how she could be of use to the women still trapped out there. Of course, she wanted to be a hero as much as anybody would. She would love to liberate every woman who was held against her will and to see these men brought to justice, but she still struggled with the motivations of this man and those around him.

"How did you get involved in this?" she asked, meeting his gaze with a frown. "I need to know why this is so important to you, why talking to you any different to me talking to the FBI?"

Rig had told her to cooperate and she would, but she needed to know why the Kindred would have more impact than those with a national reach.

"Law enforcement can't keep up. They have turf wars, agency conflicts, the process is far from smooth. We do have a contact in the FBI who we keep in the loop unofficially."

So the Kindred had some reach of their own and could either be tipped off or pass on information. Rig had implied that his relationship with Rave was sort of quid pro quo. If they worked the same way with the FBI maybe inadvertently, these men could be brought to official justice. Except, "That doesn't tell me why you're doing this. You said this started with a girl…"

Bess and Wren had referred to a woman, as well. Something had happened that had spurred them all into action. Of all the causes in all the world that these men could've taken on as their own, they'd chosen this and Devon had to know why.

"Bronwyn wasn't just any girl," he said. "She was Wren's girl. She was taken and she was dead before any of us knew what had happened." He slackened, like a daze passed over him. "I had the means to save her… if we'd known she was gone…"

From his reaction to the memory, Devon guessed this had happened quite recently. "Oh, God, I'm so sorry, that must have been awful for him… for you all."

Clearing his throat, Zave starched his posture again. "It took a long time for us to get here and hone our operation."

"And now you're dedicated to rescuing women?"

Despite it being a losing battle, because there would always be sick individuals stealing and enslaving others, it was noble of Zave and the Kindred to at least try to make a difference in a fraction of the women's lives.

"It didn't seem right to let women keep dying while we took their organization apart."

"That's a never-ending job with crooks like that," she said, sitting up to lean on the table again. "You take one out and two pop up."

"We'll take those two out, as well," he said and his determination was admirable. "We're coming at this from many different angles. We plan to be the thorn in their side for as long as we can… to explain it all in detail would take too much time. Suffice to say, we're all over it."

Fixating on his story of Bronwyn, she drifted in her thoughts. Wren had lost the woman he loved to these monsters. He'd called in his mother and cousin to get some justice for her or maybe it was revenge for what they'd done. Whatever it was, there were women saved, maybe not all of them, but for those the Kindred did pull out, it made all the difference in the world that they tried.

Zave was right that law enforcement would struggle to cripple such powerful cartels. They had their hands full combatting drug smuggling, racketeering, and money laundering. Layer upon layer of criminality that was almost impossible to pick apart.

Being a witness for the FBI would be so insignificant. She'd tell her stories, maybe shed a few tears, and they'd tell her they'd call, but she doubted they ever would. Who would they bring to justice? The men who'd snatched her from the street? She couldn't identify them. The men who'd kept her locked up? She'd never seen their faces in the dark either. The truth was those men were grunts who could be sacrificed. Pawns were expendable and losing one, ten, even a hundred of them, wouldn't slow down the kings, knights, and bishops at the top of the hierarchy.

Even if the Kindred weren't saving every woman, they were taking action and trying to make a difference. Sitting on her hands, ruing the world, and being terrified to set foot outside her apartment wouldn't help anyone, and Devon couldn't turn her back on this.

"Okay," she said, folding her arms as she made her decision. "I'm in."

For the first time, a flicker of surprise touched him and his chin tilted a fraction. "Excuse me?" he asked. "You're what?"

"You want intel," she said. "And I want to help, I don't want these bastards to keep getting away with what they're doing." Zave wasn't open to her suggestion. In fact, she'd say he prickled as he sat back. "I'm not asking for anything from you, I'm offering my assistance in your mission."

"You live in New York," he said, monotone in almost one syllable.

If that was his only argument, it was a weak one and she pulled her plate closer to slurp up some more pasta. "I have nothing to go back to, Zave," she admitted. "I won't even have a job if I've been gone for months."

"You're suggesting that you would relocate?"

If that was what it took then she would do it. Rig was her only tie to her previous state. "Yes," she said without flinching and wasn't sure if he could understand how her experience had affected her and her perspective. "Some events in life are defining. I can't go back to slogging my guts out for a paycheck, pretending this didn't happen. I want to get these bastards."

Rig had made it clear he'd do the barest minimum to keep her safe. She didn't have other family or a boyfriend to go rushing back to. There was no one she could share her ordeal with if she returned to New York to try to scrape her life back together. She'd have to pretend that this never happened and let these men keep doing what they were doing without consequence.

Suppressing her trauma would guarantee it ate her alive from the inside. Devon knew she would never be the same person that she'd been before this experience. But she couldn't be naïve and ignore the evil in the world. She had to do something to fight back. It was vital for her own self-respect and for her sanity.

Zave was shaking his head. "I can't let you do that," he said. "All we need from you is information."

"Information unlocks all secrets," she said as Bess

once had. "I need to know what happens to the information after I've given it to you." Even if she couldn't be a vital part in the practical aspects of the mission, she wanted to be a support, even just for a short while. "I can't leave and go back to the way things were. You weren't there, Zave… You weren't there." Suddenly the food became heavy in her stomach. Sitting with this spread of food, in the luxury of this house and the bedroom she'd slept in, she became disgusted with herself and pushed the food away. "I shouldn't be here."

"That's what I'm trying to say," he said, but it was her turn to shake her head.

Old insecurities and self-doubt rose within her. "No, you shouldn't have picked me."

"You think someone else was more worthy?" he asked, losing his defensive tone he became softer.

"No one would've missed me," she said, staring into her food. "Some of the girls there probably had parents or partners who are desperate for word on their loved ones, who'll never know the truth of what happened to them."

"That doesn't make you expendable. Someone had to catch you before you vanished."

"No one would've noticed," she murmured, reflecting on the sad commentary of her life.

Rig would've been pissed for a while, he'd have stomped about and punched things, but his life wouldn't have been any different without her in it. He'd kept her far enough away that she had no daily impact on his life.

"I would've noticed," he said, attracting her focus and once again, he was looking right through her. "I did notice you."

With their eyes locked, they both relived their own experience of the auction night and managed to share their perspectives without words. Her lack of apparel on that stage didn't make her self-conscious anymore. Somehow, she knew he saw beyond that.

Despite hearing a door opening, she couldn't tear her attention away from his. Bess was all the way at the side of the table before Devon or Zave broke their stare to look at her.

"Would either of you like a drink?" she asked.

Something about the glitter in her eyes above her wide smile intrigued Devon, but she didn't pursue that curiosity.

"No thanks," Devon said. "We were just in the middle of a disagreement."

Bess seemed engrossed in her own wonder and was examining both of them. "Doesn't look that way to me," Bess said, resting a hand onto Zave's shoulder to give him her weight. "What were you disagreeing on?"

Devon didn't want to lift her chin because she could feel his glare burning her skin. "I was just telling Devon why joining our operation would be a bad idea for her," Zave said, his voice was so stern that Devon almost felt like she was being given into trouble.

"Join us?" Bess shrieked and began to hurry around the table. Apparently Zave's harsh tone had no effect on the woman. "Thad!"

Zave straightened. "Why do we need Thad?" he asked.

Thad came in as Bess sat down beside Devon. "What is it?" Thad asked on his approach.

"Devon is coming to join us," Bess said, vibrating with glee, she made no attempt to disguise it.

Thad snapped out of his own distraction and seemed to perk up. "She is?" Thad asked, going to sit beside his mom.

Three on one side of the table and Zave on the other on his own. "That's not what I said," Zave said, pressing forward on his forearms again. "I told her no."

"Why?" Bess asked, snatching up Devon's hand.

"Because it's dangerous," Thad said.

"Yes," Zave agreed, jumping on his cousin's support.

Devon didn't know whether she had Thad's support or not. Bess was having none of it. "It's not dangerous for me," Bess said. "She could help from here."

Zave wasn't convinced. "What skills does she have that are of use to us?"

Bess gasped. "Shame on you, Xavier. What skills did I have?"

"You're family," Thad said.

Bess' happiness gave way to a more abrupt attitude.

"And you boys told me that Devon has little family of her own. What are we sending her back to if we dump her back where she was? Zara doesn't think Rigor will be much of a support for her. No, Devon should stay with us."

Thad laughed. "You just want company, Mom."

"And what's wrong with that? This place needs another female around to offset all the testosterone," Bess said, still clasping Devon's hand with hers while she waved the other.

Somewhere in this conversation, her meaning had been lost and assumptions were being made. "I didn't mean I would live here," Devon said, mortified at the idea they might think her so presumptuous.

"Why shouldn't you?" Bess asked. "We brought you here to care for you, so you're welcome to stay here for as long as you need. It's not like we don't have the space. Zave can find out what's going on with your property in New York, and we can have everything of yours shipped here. If it's been put into storage, we'll pay to have it released."

Devon's eyes flared because she couldn't ask anyone to take care of her personal business or pay her debts, and now she just felt like she was intruding in their family life.

"Can he?" Zave asked, showing more emotion in those two words than he had for the rest of the night.

Still, Bess dismissed him. "Oh, you already have and you know it," Bess clucked her tongue at her nephew then focused on Devon. "He likes to poke his nose in sometimes and he likes to think he's the most powerful man in the world."

Proving that she wasn't the only one he ignored, Zave didn't respond to his aunt. "Devon is trying to regain control," he said to his family members.

"It's Psyche 101 for trauma victims," Thad said and his position on the issue remained ambiguous.

"Don't dismiss her," Bess said. "If anyone should want to fight back against their aggressors, it's Devon, she's the victim."

"That's not what this is," Devon said, but the trio were more interested in each other than her.

It wasn't about hurting the cartel because they hurt her; it was about using her pain to ensure no one else had to endure it. "I have no objections," Thad said, with a shrug. "You're thorough, Zave, and I trust Swift. I have to."

Her own embarrassment was sidelined. "What does that mean?" Devon asked.

Bess swayed closer to explain. "Swift can find out anything and everything about a person. If you were a danger to us, we wouldn't have you here. I'm sorry to be blunt, but it's as simple as that."

She certainly wasn't a danger, and she appreciated Bess being upfront. "I can't start my own crusade," Devon said, comfortable about being honest with Bess. "If I go back to New York alone and try that, I'll either go crazy or get myself killed."

"No one would expect you to, dearie," Bess said, stroking her arm. "The other girls have had support networks to return to. We can't send you back to nothing."

"That doesn't mean we should adopt her," Zave said.

Like she was some kind of stray pet they'd found on the side of the road. "So what's your idea? Are you going to pay for therapists and security for Devon for the rest of her life? I thought shirking your responsibilities was a thing of the past, Xavier," Bess said with plenty of judgment in her tone.

Her comments only added to the layers of unknowns that Devon had in relation to this guy. Although she disagreed with Zave's position, she did have to highlight a point, which would be listed in his favor. "I'm not his responsibility," Devon said. "I've put the idea out there. I want to help, but I won't cause trouble. If there's no place for me here, I'll figure out another way that I can—"

"No," Zave said. "You're not taking on these guys by yourself. I told you, it's taken us years of work to get to this point as a team."

He had said that and she understood that not only did they have manpower, but they had resources that she could not even dream of. "Well then, I suppose it's settled. It looks like we have a new team member," Bess said and was grinning once again. "It's about time we shook things up."

"If Rave can adjust to a new person in his house, so can you," Thad said to Zave. "And I guess, nothing's permanent. We can take time to work it out."

Devon had gone from agreeing to give them information to promising Rig she would help him any way she could. And somehow through the course of this conversation, she'd become a troublesome roommate. Living in this house would be any person's dream but like Thad had said, nothing was permanent.

She couldn't get too comfortable, couldn't settle in and fall in love with the island because she wouldn't be here forever. But she'd won this battle because she did want to help in the fight against those who had hurt her. Devon wasn't ready to go back to her previous life. It was safe here.

Despite his assertion that they would never get close, she was eager to find out more about the man who held himself away from everyone else. Zave had rescued her from her isolation, she wanted to do her best to tempt him from his.

ELEVEN

DEVON WATCHED ZAVE leave the dining room not long after that conversation finished. He'd glanced back at her. In that half a beat of shared existence, she'd thought she heard his psychic plea for her to follow him. But he went out the door without a word, and she shirked that fantasy. Devon had never been allowed through that door; she didn't know what it led to. Whatever was behind it was private, but not private enough to warrant a fingerprint lock. Still, she was intrigued.

Bess had spoken for a while about how nice it would be to have a woman around the place. About giving her a proper tour. About arranging for her room to become permanent. The bedroom she was sleeping in at the moment was much better than the one she'd been in before. It seemed closer to the bosom of the family. But it was in a public space, leading off the mezzanine that overlooked the grand foyer.

It was a bedroom that she imagined would be given to visiting guests, if they ever had dinner parties or balls here. The building was vast and ornate, making it the perfect place to entertain.

Thad ate some of the food, and everything he said about her presence was positive. Except she couldn't help but feel he was holding something back. She'd eaten in small bites, and by the time her plate was empty, her body was rebelling to the quantity of carb-rich food. Devon excused herself and went to her bedroom and that was the last she saw anyone that night.

Zave may have been outside her room, and she hoped he wasn't expecting her to come to him again. The excitement of the day had left her so exhausted that she'd passed out before getting as far as changing into her nightwear.

She hadn't gotten around to closing the curtains in her bedroom either, but she wasn't woken by first light. By the time she opened her eyes, the sun was beaming through onto the floor, indicating it was high in the sky and nowhere near the horizon.

Pushing her hair out of her eyes, Devon brought her legs off the edge of the bed and yawned as she sloped toward the bathroom. After washing her face, brushing her teeth, and combing her hair, she came out to find Bess standing at the end of her bed.

Devon would've asked why the woman was there, except she was distracted by the sight of a tall glass sitting on her nightstand. Filled to the brim with pale pink liquid, the drink was topped with cream and right there at the peak of the white mountain was a glowing red cherry.

Such a delight was like a dream and out of place in this gothic house that she wasn't sure at first if she'd woken up and gotten out of bed at all. "What is that?" she asked, her finger floated toward the baby pink froth on the lip of the glass.

At some point she'd moved from the bathroom door to the bedside, and she coated the tip of her index finger with the thick foam.

"A strawberry and vanilla milkshake," Bess said, so proud of herself and so elated that Devon almost laughed.

"It's…" She'd asked for it in half a murmur yesterday and had completely forgotten that the request had come out of her mouth. She certainly hadn't expected this perfect and prompt gift.

"Straw?" Bess asked, coming over to take the paper-wrapped straw from the surface next to the glass.

Unwrapping it, Bess put it in the drink, poking a hole in the cream beside the cherry. It took its sweet time sinking into the sweet liquid, telling Devon that it was going to be thick, creamy, and decadent. Anticipation made her squeal and spring forward to hug Bess who whooped out a laugh but hugged her back.

Being so happy over something so simple was ridiculous. "I'm sorry," Devon said, tearing up. "I… It's just…"

It seemed so silly to cry over something like a milkshake, but streams of moisture skidded down her cheeks. Bess took her to the bed and held her close asking for no apology.

"You've been through so much," Bess said, soothing a hand down her back and reverting to her maternal role and giving up some of her own excitement. "It's okay to let it out."

Once she'd started, it was difficult to stop. Taking Bess' invitation to release the emotion was involuntary, but Bess held her and soothed her with reassuring words and a gentle hand. Such a warm, friendly gesture that was so accepting perplexed Devon because she'd never had someone care for her without expectation.

Calming herself down, Devon retreated from Bess' embrace to wipe her eyes with her hands. "I didn't know that was in there," Devon said, embarrassed enough that she would rather look at the carpet than at the woman who'd comforted her.

"You've been holding it in for too long," Bess said, taking Devon's damp hand to her lap. "You've been strong… We're going to work it all out with you, dearie, you're not alone anymore. We're going to help you."

The goal had been for Devon to help the Kindred, not the other way around. It seemed that all she did was take from these people who gave her shelter, food, and warmth. Now Bess was dealing with her emotional breakdown while Zave was showering her with gifts.

That reminder made Devon's focus float to the milkshake on the bedside. With another hand pat, Bess got up and retrieved the drink to bring it over to her. "Thank you," Devon said, feeling foolish yet calm.

"Try it," Bess said, sitting on the bed at her side.

As she'd said to Zave last night, the point of the milkshake was to make her feel better. But if Devon had needed the pick-me-up when she awoke, she needed it a hundred times more now that she'd just lost it in front of Bess.

Devon glanced at her, then caught the straw between her thumb and forefinger to direct it between her lips. She had to work hard to suck up the cold, thick shake. But it was worth it when the froth burst in her mouth. The icy liquid was so sweet and delicious that her eyes began to water again.

"Mm, it's amazing," Devon said with her eyes closed and her teeth gently clasping the straw.

Bess leaned in to stage whisper. "I make my own ice-cream and grow my own fruit."

"Is it strawberry season?" Devon asked, because she'd lost most of the year and was still trying to play catch up.

"We have a walk-in freezer where we store the fruit harvested in spring. Zave had a gothic-arch greenhouse built for me, too, so I can grow anything, at any time of year. It's all state of the art, of course."

Bess had mentioned the freezer before. This house was amazing and the more she heard, the more intrigued she became.

"You sit there and drink that," Bess said, patting her knee. "I'll put the shower on so it's nice and steamy in there for you before you get in. Thad will come up and see you in an hour, does that sound okay?"

"Thank you," Devon said. Bess was already on her way toward the bathroom.

The doctor hadn't been to examine her since she'd been in her new room. After their conversation last night, Devon would relish the opportunity to try and read more into his opinion on her hanging around for a while.

Taking another long drag on the straw, the glorious, thick liquid made her feel better, and she was glad that her weakness for sweet milkshake had slipped out. Every time she hinted at her likes in front of Zave, he went out of his way to fulfill her desire as quickly as possible.

The shower went on, and Bess fussed for a while before she came out. "We're having a family meal tonight," Bess said. "Everyone will be there."

"A family meal?" she asked. Did they mean biological family or Kindred family? "I'll make myself scarce."

"Oh no, you're the guest of honor! Our newest member needs a proper welcome. Brodie and Zara will be leaving afterwards," Bess said. "Thad will take them back to the mainland."

"At night? How will they get there?" It couldn't be safe out in the choppy seas she'd seen in the black night.

"He flies. We have a helicopter. Two actually."

The shake which she'd held in front of her chest lowered, and she rested it on her knee. "You have two helicopters?"

"I don't," she said, fussing with the curtains that were open anyway. Bess bent to gather up some of the art supplies that Devon had left scattered on the low window seat. "Zave does. He flies too. He was the one who taught Thad, he has his instructor's license."

That he could accomplish something so incredible wasn't a surprise, but that he had been patient and willing to teach Thad was a shock. "Zave?" she asked, putting the milkshake down after another drink. "Has he always been this way?"

Bess discarded the pencils to turn. "What way?" Bess asked.

"I don't know, he isolates himself."

"Yes, he does," Bess said.

Leaning back, Devon crossed her legs. "You told me not to hurt him, but I don't know why you would think I could."

"Bronwyn's death was horrendous for us all," Bess said. "If there was any silver lining, it was that it forced Zave out of his seclusion."

"Out?" she asked, assuming that was the kind of thing that would've pushed him in.

Bess took a long breath and came back toward her. "When he was a child, it was obvious he was brighter than everyone else. He graduated high school and got a college degree years ahead of his peers. Anything he wanted to accomplish, he could without effort. His knack for inventing made him a rich boy young, before he had the slightest clue what to do with that kind of wealth. Buying this house," Bess said, lifting her eyes to the rafters. "Was supposed to ground him. His uncle, Brodie's father, sold it to him after his grandmother died."

"This was Zave's grandmother's house?"

"Unofficially," Bess said. "When she died, the house lay empty most of the year. Zave liked the idea of having his own private island and being the king of the castle, so to speak." Bess sat down. Instead of exuding pride that Zave had achieved so much so young, her expression became almost pitying. "He was wild, incredibly wild. His parents couldn't control him. The only reason he got through high school at all was because it was so easy for him. Girls gravitated toward him. Seducing them was effortless, he was always a looker. It helped that he was raking in money faster than his friends could spend it. After Brodie's parents died, we discussed bringing Brodie to come and stay here, but the two of them together would've been too much."

"Brodie's parents died when he was a child?"

"A teenager," Bess said. "Guardianship was willed to my brother. It didn't take us long to see it would never work. I had Thad on my own, we weren't a part of Zave's circle then. We were common, decent folk. Zave was arrogant, ostentatious. He threw parties that lasted for days. Despite his parents' objections, he brought dozens of people to stay here. It's a wonder he got his company started at all."

His company? "But he did?"

"Mostly because of his father, who ring-fenced the money and restricted Zave to a generous allowance when he was a minor. Every time he threatened to sue for emancipation, they gave him a little more and then a little more. Owen Knight, Zave's father, worked hard to build up that company and to establish their impeccable reputation, despite their volatile moneymaker."

Zave didn't seem like the type to throw crazy parties or the type to be arrogant above his station either. Although she couldn't refute that he was educated and intelligent enough that a superiority complex could probably be warranted.

But he wasn't a crazy party animal now. "What changed?"

"The parties, the girls, the drugs, it got worse through his teenage years. But he kept inventing because it was his passion. I don't know how many of the early Knight Corp inventions were envisioned during the drug-fueled orgies that went on here. Even his parents moved out, no one could control him, then he started to get pissed off with the way his father was running the company and they had a falling out. Not enough to drive one or the other from the company, but it forced Zave to start showing up more than he had before."

Knight Corp, that was Zave's company. "So he straightened out?" Devon asked.

Bess sighed. "I wish it was that easy. Instead of being juvenile and throwing the equivalent of frat parties, his tastes became more glamorous. He threw exclusive, ostentatious events, like he was trying to shock his family and the press. There were costume events, he treated this place like a palace court, they got quite extreme and he became known for his fetish parties."

"Fetish?" Devon asked, and once again she felt heat burn beneath her face.

"The truth is, I don't know specifics of what happened here. All I know is the women he took to tropical islands on private planes were sleek and classy, and wrapped in designer gear. He was still as arrogant, he didn't reach out to the family. He held himself above everyone else, dismissed us, believed himself to be better and in a lot of ways, he was."

"Because he was making so much money from his inventions?"

Bess nodded. "It was effortless for him, it still is. Somehow when he sees a problem or has an idea, he can immediately put something together. He takes more time these days in his crafting because he's learned to appreciate the process. Back then, he could just close his eyes, imagine something, and soon after it would be in production. Success chased him, not the other way around. All he had to do was wish it and it came true. He didn't have to work hard or think about marketing, his father dealt with the practical aspects of the business."

So while the rest of the world had to work hard, Zave lived a life of privilege and ease. "What does he make?"

"Recreational technology mostly. In his younger years, the products were leisure items that he would invent and give out at parties. As he got older, he got more discerning and began to make products for private yachts and secluded villas, luxury technology, you know? Things that would make the lives of the rich easier than they already are. In his twenties, he put on a suit and walked the walk. The media hounded him, but he lapped up the attention back then."

The media? Could that be why he'd been nervous about revealing himself to her and why the name Xavier Knight had sparked recognition in her mind? He'd been worried she could recognize him.

Except Devon didn't pay much attention to the business pages. And the time Bess was talking about was ten years ago, maybe more, long before Devon would've had a smartphone with twenty-four-hour news pinging up at regular intervals.

In her early twenties, she didn't have a fridge, let alone a TV or phone. The only reason she had a phone before her abduction was because her brother paid the bill for her. She would never be able to afford such a luxury on her own.

"He wore the suit and had the fancy office," Bess said. "Women flocked around him. He was invited to every exclusive event and chose to only go to a handful ensuring his presence was notable every time he attended something. Being rich and handsome, he was everything a stereotypical eligible bachelor could be."

Devon struggled to imagine how he could go from that to what he was now. A man who didn't leave his island, who didn't want even her here and who chose to spend most of his life on his own.

What began to make sense was why the cartels accepted him. Zave had money, and it wouldn't take them long to figure that out. He'd made news with his parties and was known for enjoying women and indulging in fetishes. The cartel wouldn't ask questions about where all these women were going after he bought them.

They probably assumed he had a harem or that he was slicing them into little pieces and scattering them across his private island. Zave had the perfect cover for what he did, especially now that he was a recluse. Except Bess had said Bronwyn's death brought him *out* of his seclusion.

"If he was such a playboy," Devon said. "So full of himself and uncaring, what made him choose to become a hermit?"

Bess became more subdued. "Unfortunately, I can't answer that. I can tell you the event that sparked it," Bess said. With one hand under Devon's, the other stroked the top. But Devon didn't know if Bess was offering her comfort or taking it instead.

"What happened?"

"His parents died. They died and it was a shock to us all, none more so than to Zave, who believed himself invincible. He believed nothing bad could ever happen to him or around him. Then suddenly in a flash, they were gone. I don't know what went through his head. We weren't close. Not at all. Except he was alone and no matter how much of a cocky idiot he was, he is family. It didn't take us long to see that he wasn't going to face his first real trial with courage."

"That's awful," Devon said, thinking of how horrific his first experience of grief was.

"For months, Brodie was the only person he would speak to, maybe because Brodie lost his parents when he was young, so they could identify with each other. Zave was in his twenties, but he took it just as hard. The poor boy didn't have a childhood, but he'd been blessed with wealth and intelligence. His charmed life had seemed untouchable, and then just like that, he was alone without siblings, without parents. Maybe it just hit him how superficial everything in his life was. He stopped going to the office, and it was his father's trusted colleagues who kept the corporation going."

"It still exists?"

"Knight Corp? Yes, and it's about to get bigger," Bess said. "It's in the midst of merging with a company that Brodie just inherited and has no interest in, so he's signing all control over to his cousin. Zave still makes the corporate decisions at KC, he just does it on speakerphone from here and doesn't go to the office. He hasn't been in the Knight Corp building for a long time. He limits his interaction with his colleagues to just a few. He never leaves this island unless it's for Kindred business."

Anyone with knowledge of Knight Corp or the business world might recognize Zave while he was at these auctions. The risk he took with his reputation and his livelihood were great. In light of this, limiting his contact with the women they saved seemed smart. Except she had a feeling his reserve was more about his aversion to conversation than his concerns about being exposed.

Some of the blurred edges were becoming crisper. "The death of his parents," Devon murmured. "He shut himself up in this house and that's how he became what he is now?"

"Thad and I moved in here to give him support. I had to make sure he was eating and looking after himself, which of course, he wasn't. Every day was a battle. And Thad had to deal with plenty on his own while I was busy trying to support Zave," Bess said, so solemn that it was obvious she was still affected by that time. "But we pulled through as a family. Brodie did his best to get Zave to open up, and eventually he started coming down to eat with us every once in a while. Brodie and my brother, Art, stayed here as often as they could. Zave joined us more when Brodie was here. But he spent most of his time alone in his private part of the house, tinkering. Because those devices are not just his trade now, they keep him sane."

"He likes logic," Devon said.

"Yes," Bess agreed with a smile that didn't reach her eyes.

So, after losing his parents, he'd become a recluse. "You said Bronwyn's death changed him?"

Bess took a long, deep breath as if cleansing herself before moving on with the story. "Bronwyn was staying here with Thad. Thad had been on the mainland, working at the hospital, and hadn't seen her for a few days. I wasn't here, either. I'd been away from the house for about a week."

"They were alone in this house? Zave and Bronwyn?"

"Yes," Bess said. "At some point, for some reason, nobody knows why, she left here."

"On her own?"

"The boat was gone from the dock, so yes, and she made it back to the mainland. Zave didn't know she was gone. No one did. We still don't know exactly when she was taken or even when she left here."

Concern furrowed her brow. "But the technology that monitors sound and movement—"

"It wasn't long after we lost Bronwyn that Zave put those up everywhere, but it was too late. Art and Brodie did what they could to find her, and they did, I don't know how. But it was too late. They found her body in the desert, not far from one of the cartels' headquarters. She was there with half a dozen other women, and we still don't know why they were killed."

The story was so horrific that Devon's tears came again. "I'm sorry," she whispered, trying to brush away the tears.

"I don't mean to upset you," Bess said, using the back of her hand to wipe Devon's damp cheek. "I'm telling you this because you've said you'll join us. I haven't seen Zave take an interest in a woman in years, but he's punished himself for too long, Devon. If there's a chance we can pull him through this and make him see that he deserves to be happy… I know it's a chance that Thad, Brodie, and I, have to take."

So Devon was here not just because of what she knew, but because of how Zave had reacted to her after the auction. "He told me I was special," Devon admitted. "But I don't know if that means anything."

Bess tightened her grip on Devon's hand. "I'm not

asking you to fall in love with him. I know you can't make yourself feel something that's not there. All I'm asking is that if you do feel any kind of attraction or any glimmer of a connection, that you don't let yourself be discouraged by his indifference. It can be scathing; it's hurt us all. It still makes Zara uncomfortable at times. Just be patient with him, can you do that?"

The man was more complex than she could ever have imagined, and he'd been to hell and back. Now, he was subjecting himself to these horrible environments as some kind of penance, dealing with disgusting men and saving women to assuage his guilt.

Devon wasn't discouraged by the story; she could understand why he was reluctant to get close to Zara. If he blamed himself for what happened to Bronwyn, Thad's girl, he may see Zara in the same sort of light and may worry that he may one day be responsible for her downfall.

"I'll be patient," she said. This woman was so accepting. "He's been through some terrible things, but he's extremely lucky to have you and the others."

"He knows. He has grown a lot, he's more serious and responsible these days. He couldn't ever go back to the way he was. We're family. We do whatever it takes to get through these things together. And you're going to be a wonderful addition to our little group."

Bess pulled her into another hug, and Devon tried not to read too much into the idea that she was being welcomed into this family. Even if Bess didn't say it, Devon felt the expectation they'd put upon her to rescue a man far stronger than she was.

Dinner tonight would be revealing and once it was through, Thad would take Zara and Brodie back to the mainland, leaving her alone with Bess and Zave. Devon might come back to her room when they departed, or maybe she'd get a chance to get to know her host better.

TWELVE

EATING DINNER AT the Knight house was a revealing experience. Observing the way these people interacted with each other betrayed so much about their personalities. It was a wonder that they chose to spend as much time together as they did. Though if they hadn't been blood, she doubted that they would elect to be in each other's company because their personalities were so different.

Thad and Zara laughed with Bess. They told stories, shared memories, and projected nothing but openness. Brodie said little and was rarely addressed by the others as though they knew he had no interest in being a part of their chitchat. But he did contribute. Once in a while he'd interject, he and Zara would flirt. Devon would be fascinated to know how this couple had been brought together. But she didn't yet have the confidence to ask.

She, too, was invited to speak. Devon told stories about her life pre-abduction, and if it hadn't been for the ominous cloud sitting at the head of the table, it might have been a benign experience. While most of the table were speaking and Brodie was following along, Zave didn't say a word. It wasn't that he said little. He literally didn't say a single thing.

When it came to the end of the night and the plates were being gathered up, Devon offered to help transport them into the kitchen. As she left the dining room with her hoard of dishes, she noticed Brodie and Zave rise in unison and move toward the window. That was the first time she saw Zave's lips move in speech all night, although she couldn't hear what was being said.

Instead of joining the men or helping the women, Thad disappeared out another door. To do what, she didn't know. Perhaps to prepare their helicopter for flight or to pack whatever was being transported.

Shown through the passageway that led to the kitchen, Devon put the dishes down on a central island and was about to ask what other chores she could do when Zara pulled out a stool.

Slapping a hand on the seat, Zara smiled. "Sit down, Devon, we'll take care of this," Zara said and went to join Bess, who was rinsing dishes to stack them in the dishwasher.

Self-conscious at remaining still while they were working, she made another offer. "I should do something to help," Devon said.

"You need to regain your strength," Bess said.

"I'm sorry that Rave and I have to go," Zara followed up, changing the conversation before Devon could object. "It would've been nice to get to know you better. Though from what I hear, we'll be seeing a lot more of each other."

"Devon is joining us, isn't it exciting?"

Resting her forearms on the island, she was glad of the physical support. "At least for a while," Devon said, trying not to raise her caretaker's hopes too high.

"I think it's great," Zara said, bending to put another plate into the dishwasher. "It's about time the Kindred expanded their ranks."

Bess touched Zara's cheek before turning to retrieve the dishwasher detergent. "Since you came into our lives, young lady, we've done nothing but expand."

Zara had been smiling and relaxed all night, but while Bess' back was turned, Devon saw a tightness cross the beauty's shoulders as her eyes wandered sideways. "No amount of new members can replace what we lost," she murmured.

Bess stopped what she was doing and turned back. Rounding the open dishwasher door to take hold of Zara's arms, she was firm. "Don't hold on to the past," Bess said. You know that he'd be proud."

The kitchen door opened and Brodie came in. His semi-neutral expression pounced into high gear. "What the fuck did you say to her?" he demanded of her and Bess, marching over to take hold of Zara.

"Nothing," Zara said, forcing a smile. "No one said anything."

He grabbed the back of her neck in one strong hand and tugged her forward. "You want to stay? We'll stay."

"No, it's not that," Zara said. A man who'd change all his plans for his girl without questioning her or hesitating was a rarity. "We'll say our goodbyes and get on the road. We have business to take care of, beau."

It didn't take long for them to say their farewells. While the women held onto each other for a considerable time, no tears were shed. Then they were gone and life carried on.

Bess put the dishwasher on and turned to her. "Would you like a nightcap?" Bess asked. "We have a nice sherry, or there's port and—"

"No. I was a complete lightweight with alcohol before all of this."

Bess laughed. "Okay then, why don't you go through to the dining room and I'll bring some coffee through."

"I can—"

"No! Let me deal with it… I could use a minute to myself."

Devon couldn't tell if Bess meant it. Maybe what Zara had said reminded Bess of something she wanted to reflect on by herself. Whatever the reason, Devon wasn't going to question the woman who'd been so good to her when her request was so simple.

So she got up and followed the corridor back to the dining room. It was lucky she'd been in this room so many times, she was beginning to learn the route. Although it was the first time she'd been to the kitchen, she recognized the hallway one of the corridors intersected and so she found her way back.

Bess might need a minute, but if she brought coffee through, she might want to talk. If that turned out to be the case, Devon wanted to be there for her as Bess had been her shoulder of support earlier in the day.

When she walked into the dining room, she didn't expect to see Zave, standing facing the window that she'd been looking out when she first laid eyes on him. The window was closed now, but it was night, so there wouldn't be much to see out there.

His static silence and lack of reaction to her entry should've intimidated her. But it didn't. In fact, she was so overwhelmed by the many things that she wanted to ask him that she couldn't settle on a single sentence to begin on.

She wanted to talk more about what Bess had told her about his past. Wanted to express condolence for the loss of his parents, wanted to ask questions about what had happened before Bronwyn left this house.

Devon wanted to know about his company, about his inventions, about his process. She wanted to know why he felt it necessary to say nothing while in a room full of people who were making an effort to be social.

Why did he hold himself away from everyone? Segregate himself? Why did he lock himself away in a room and only come out when he had no other choice? Devon wanted to ask about his wild youth, if he held happy memories of that time or if he had regrets.

She wanted to know why he'd been skulking outside her bedroom door. Why he'd kissed her. Why he'd told her that he'd never do it again.

Except instead of speaking, she began to move. She walked past the table, across the room, to the window where he stood. Whether he sensed her presence or not, he didn't acknowledge her, and knowing she would never be able to logic him into admitting his deepest secrets, she had to take a different approach.

Bess had told her that it had been a long time since he'd shown any interest in a woman, and all she could assume was that he was punishing himself with self-exile. Standing at his back, she opened her arms and wrapped them around his torso. He tensed. But he didn't say a word.

Coiling her arms all the way around him, she pressed her chest into his back and rested her temple on his spine. Zave didn't seek emotional comfort from anyone. Didn't venture into intellectual debate. The man shied from any form of conversation.

But this, physical proximity, affection, they hadn't been a part of his world, maybe ever. Sure, Bess spoke of sex parties and women, but she'd never mentioned love or comfort, care, or fondness. Devon didn't want this man to exist alone because she knew what that was like, having existed that way herself for most of her life.

She had Rig if she was stuck, just as Zave had Bess to keep him fed. But having one person choose to simply be a comfort was a luxury that no amount of money could buy or replicate. It wasn't even something family could provide because this was choice, not obligation.

"What are you doing?" His low voice vibrated from his chest through her body.

"I hate seeing you in pain," she answered because honesty was the only answer. Maybe that was what she'd seen in him that drew her to him, the agony he exuded while trying to project to the world that he was untouchable.

"I deserve to be in pain," he said. "I should be in pain."

"Is that why you do it?" she murmured, sliding her arms further around him. "Is that why you won't let anyone in?"

"You don't understand, shy."

Closing her eyes, she could sense that he wasn't comfortable with her proximity, but she had never felt more content. The stress and trauma she'd carried since arriving here melted away, and her body slackened. Aches began to wane. Anxiety faded and with the scent of him permeating her, she languished in the shelter he provided her. No person had ever made her feel as safe as this.

"I do," she said. "I do understand."

She might not be in his head and she certainly didn't have any psychology degree, but so much of him made sense to her after her conversation with Bess. "There are things in my past—"

"I know," she said. Bess couldn't have told him what they'd discussed. Devon wasn't going to lie to this man; she wouldn't give him any excuse, ever, to push her away. There and then, she made that assured decision.

"How could you possibly—"

"Bess told me," she confessed.

That was when he pulled away. In the same instant, he spun around, and although her breath was stolen from her by surprise, somehow her arms remained around him. "She what?" he snapped.

His anger was boiled and she sensed a shame intermingled with it, but that made her pull herself closer to maintain their connection, to keep him here with her during the subsequent shared silence in the dimly lit room.

"She didn't tell me more than facts," Devon said.

It wasn't like Bess had spent hours going into every detail of Zave's emotional reaction to the various personal situations. She hadn't tried to deconstruct him, hadn't betrayed any confidences about moments of weakness when he may have let his cultivated exterior crack.

"Why would she do that?" he barked.

"I assume because I'm joining your team. I have to know some of the history."

"No," he said. "I said no."

He took ahold of her shoulders to jolt her body away from his, so he could withdraw from her hold. "Tonight was my initiation, that was what Bess told me," Devon said, watching him stalk toward the cleared dining table. "I think your attendance was taken as your acceptance."

"Well, it's not," he said, slowing down to curl his hands around the back of one of the chairs. "You can't be here, Devon. You have to go. I should've sent you with Brodie. He'd have kept you safe."

"I'm safe here."

"No, you're not," Zave replied in another burst of anger that made him whirl around to glare at her. "You're not safe here, Devon. No woman is."

"I don't believe that," she argued back, moving away from the window. "Everything about this place is wonderful and your family is incredible, and you…" Clasping her hands between her breasts, something warm rose within her. "It breaks my heart to think I could've left this place without ever meeting you."

It seemed like so long ago that she'd been locked in that room with the four-poster bed, demanding to meet the man who had bought her only to be told she would never see his face. But she'd seen it now, and it was one she didn't want to live without.

"You're grateful," he said, trying his best to push down any glimmer of emotion. "You were in a bad place and we pulled you out. You've latched onto—"

"Maybe," she said. "Maybe it is gratitude that you saved me, but don't you see I'm not the only one who's been locked in a cage? Zave, you can't live like this forever. It tears Bess apart. Thad worries for you. Even Brodie and Zara—"

"You don't know them."

She could sense how he was struggling to restrain the emotion he'd tried for so many years to rid himself of. "I know that after your parents died, Brodie was your lifeline, the only one you trusted. I see the way you talk to each other. You have trust deeper than most brothers would. Maybe I don't know him and Zara well, but they have each other and they're in love. Anyone can see that. He lost his parents, too, but he doesn't punish himself like you do."

"What do you think is going to happen here?" he snarled, lunging forward a step. "Think I'm going to suddenly agree with you, start smiling and laughing and going to the office every day? Is that what you want?"

"No," she said. "I want you to accept me. It's a first step."

"I can't do that. I can have Thad take you to Brodie's—"

She wasn't going to let him shut her down when progress was so close. "No. I only deal with you. That was our agreement."

"That was made before everyone decided you joining the team was a good idea. I don't even talk to Zara, and I've known her for months. What would make you think I'd talk to you?"

Because all throughout the meal, she'd felt him watching her. Devon tried to be covert about looking at him, but he wasn't nearly as subtle. He stared at her eating, watched her lift her water glass, examined the nuance of her smile, and scrutinized her hand that lay on the table.

"Because you noticed me," she said, moving in close again. "You told me you noticed me at the auction."

"You were naked," he said, and though he plastered his face with disgust and kept his tone cold, she shook her head.

"That didn't arouse you. There's no way you could be surrounded with pond scum like that, watching me be led around like an animal, and be sexually excited by it."

"Maybe I was."

"If that were true," she said, taking her hand to his cheek, and once again, he grew rigid. "Why did you tell me we'd never kiss again? If you wanted me, why wouldn't you be doing everything in your power to have me?" He tried to move his face from her hand, but she put the other on the chair he'd been leaning on, meaning if he wanted her to move, he'd have to touch her. "I know I'm not in your league, that's not why I'm trying to reach out."

Touching him wasn't meant to be a sexual advance. She didn't bat her eyelids or rub herself all over him. She was trying to remind him what a simple human connection was, what it felt like to have someone, to have skin touch his skin.

She kept going. "I want to be your friend, Zave. Not because of the Kindred, not because of the gifts, but because it hurts me to see you in pain."

Swatting her hand away from his face, he gave the other a shove, and marched away from her. "I did notice you," he said, turning his chin down and his head to the side while keeping his back to her. "I knew I was there to purchase you. I'd seen your picture. Knew all your stats. But when they led you through that door, something snapped. I was so angry to see the way they treated you that it took everything in my power not to leap onto that stage and rip every one of them apart with my bare hands.

"It can't be easy to see what they do."

"No," he spat the word loud and strong, making her jump. "No, that's not it. I've seen them treat women like shit. I've seen innocents thrown to the floor and kicked like dogs. I've seen those bastards spit in women's faces. I've seen the most horrific things, things that would make you weep. But you… when I saw him yank on that chain connected to your neck, I began to think of ways I could take him apart. I wanted to grab the chain off him, wrap it around his throat and squeeze the life out of him." He ran a hand through his hair in a gesture that was anxious and completely out of character. "And I'm not the killer in the family. That's not my purview."

So, she was different, but he didn't seem happy about that and didn't understand it.

"And that's why you're trying to push me away now?" she said. "Because you're worried that reaction means something?"

"It does," he said. "I don't know if it means something about you or about me. But it means something."

"That you might be attracted to me? Or maybe that you're getting past your need to be alone and could be ready to seek out something more with a woman, any woman? Could be I was just the one to cross your radar first."

His hands curled into fists at his sides. "I haven't been with a woman in a long time. I haven't looked at one and felt anything for longer than I can remember. Maybe it was sexual, or maybe my subconscious was trying to tell me something."

So all she'd done was cause more confusion in his life, and this was a man who'd admitted to craving order and logic. And here was Devon, a variable that he couldn't label.

"Bess said you carried me up to the room," Devon said. "You didn't always put this wall between us."

"It's easier to relax in the company of a woman who's

unconscious," he said. Some might think that statement sinister, but she was sure she heard an attempt to joke.

"I want you to kiss me," she said, after about a minute of silence.

"I can't," he breathed.

"I don't understand why, but I won't force you," she said, still aware of the enormous gulf between their social levels. She came from the ocean trenches while he'd always existed in orbit. "But that doesn't mean we can't be friends."

"You don't get it." Pivoting, that scowl was back on his face. "You have to go to Rave's."

"Why?" she demanded. Infuriated and hurt, she strode toward him. "Why are you so determined to toss me away like trash?"

"Because I want to kiss you!" he shouted, and the sheer volume stopped her in her tracks. "Because I've held you in my arms, shy. I've carried your lifeless body through the halls of my sanctuary. I've lain you down in my sheets and let your hair run through my fingers. I've tasted your lips, the softest, sweetest, most tempting lips I've ever been close to. Since that first moment my fingertips touched your body, I've been hounded by thoughts of sliding myself inside you to sate the desire that won't stop throbbing through my veins! The sound of your name echoes in my ears. My mind pulses when I think of your scent! And every morning, I wake up solid as fucking concrete thinking of your body, lying so close to mine!"

To say she was shocked was an understatement. "You... you want me?"

"For years I've fought to keep control, I promised myself I would never, ever indulge in unhealthy obsessions again. I spent too many years drowning in decadence and selfish depravity, thinking only of myself, of the next thrill. I was the most important thing in my world. I thought I was the most important thing in the universe.

"I treated everyone like crap. Stepped on people who wanted to help me. Laughed in their faces when they offered support! My parents died hating me, and I'm sure I hated them. I had never faced up to my responsibilities in my life.

All the money, the firm, the products, it all meant nothing. They were so disappointed in me. I disgusted myself, shy, I couldn't look at myself in the mirror. I still can't."

Gritting his teeth, he leaned down, getting into her face, and blocking the faint light in the room. "I am the monster! And you should be afraid of me. You're not safe here. You'll never be safe here, not because they out there will get you," he said, thrusting an arm toward the window. "But because I"—he smacked his palm on his chest—"am hanging on to my control by a motherfucking thread." Bringing his thumb and index finger up to her face, he held them an inch apart. "I'm this close, shy. This fucking close to…" He sealed his lips and a growl heated his throat. "I don't dare leave my fucking room while you're here, shy."

"Zave—"

"You want to know why I was standing outside your room that night? Because I couldn't stay the fuck away. Because I knew you were here, in my house, sleeping in one of my beds. And I couldn't stop myself from getting as close to you as I could. Next time, who knows? You could wake up under me."

A pulse of pressure went through her body, and while his words left her stunned, the first thing she became aware of was the tingling building in her core. Devon wasn't afraid of this outburst, of this man. She was in awe. She was enchanted. She was in heat.

Grabbing his face, she didn't ask his permission. Leaping from the floor, she forced him to catch her. When their mouths clashed, she coiled her legs around his hips and compelled his mouth to take her tongue. She'd never been a bold lover; she'd blushed when he used the word "sex." But he was so attracted to her that the man of infinite control couldn't hold it together around her.

He didn't seem to be objecting to her brazenness, the embrace of his arms got smaller and he didn't allow her tongue to be in control for long. He pushed her own back into her mouth, urging it down, flicking it up, moving it to the side for him to lick the roof of her mouth and her teeth. Zave kept her guessing about his next move. All she could do was react to his movements that were meant to excite and entice her.

That stimulation grew when he bent, and she clamped tight around him because she didn't know what he was going to do with her body until her back landed on the dining table and with his feet still on the floor, he remained bowed over her. Taking her hands from around his neck, he pinned them onto the table at the side of her head. Locking their fingers together, their mouths remained entranced by their mating.

The rest of her body felt neglected. It ached for his touch. She tried to arch her breasts into him, but his body, his strength kept her flat on her back. Taking her heels to the edge of the table, she opened her legs wide, doing her best to work from side to side, trying to feel if his frenzied state equaled hers.

But he was so much taller than her that all she could do was rub herself against the ridges of his abdomen, which in itself was enthralling. The suction of their mouths broke in time for him to kiss her jaw. She couldn't breathe right. The sound of her panting was violent to her ears; she'd never been so blinded by overwhelming desire before.

When he kissed a spot under the curve of her jaw, just where it met her neck, she yelped. Instinct forced her chin higher to let him lick her throat. Biting her lip as he got lower, she couldn't wait for him to reach her chest. She wanted to beg him to hurry and go faster, to take her here and now like this, in this place he'd been so sedate only an hour before.

Now he seemed enflamed and feverish, and this was how she wanted him, out of control, emotional, embracing the truth of what was inside instead of trying to deny it or being ashamed of it. She heard nothing but the rush of blood in her ears. Zave must have heard something because in one abrupt move, his lips disappeared, and although his grip on her hands didn't disappear, he pulled them down to her sides, allowing him to rise.

Noticing that he was focusing on something to the side, she twisted her head up and around, and that was when she saw the agog Bess just inside the door. "I'll be going to bed now," Bess said and backed out of the room, one careful step at a time.

step at a time.

THIRTEEN

ONCE THE DOOR was closed again, Devon looked at him and could feel him retreat from their intimacy. Twining her legs around his hips again, she tried to maintain her grip on his hands when they receded from hers. But she didn't succeed.

He took hold of her calves and freed himself from the circle of her legs to walk away from their passion.

"Zave," she said, without sitting up or moving. "If this is what you want, you can't hide from it forever. You can lock me up. You can send me away. You can banish me from your island. But I'm a part of this now. Whether I'm here in your house, staying with Brodie and Zara, or naked in your bed, I'm not going to disappear. It doesn't matter how many times you turn your back on me."

This time when he twisted to look at her, it was as if he'd realized how the physical act of striding off and turning his back to her was emotionally draining for her, more than that, it hurt her. But she wasn't going to let it discourage her, as she'd promised Bess and because she knew Zave was acting in learned behavior. He'd said it himself that he'd promised to never lose control again and it was that training that caused him to act this way with her, not because of his personal feelings as had just been demonstrated.

"Nothing good can come from this," he said. "Even if I let it happen. Six weeks from now…" He trailed off.

She lifted to lean on her elbows. "Six weeks from now, what?"

"I take you to my bed and then… what?" he asked, turning his head toward the window. "We enjoy each other's bodies, sate our desires, satisfy our fantasies and curiosities, and then what?"

She didn't understand the question. Because this was just chemicals, electricity between two people, the kind of instinct that made one lover seek another out in a crowded bar or in a busy workplace. This was attraction. So as for what came next when they hadn't even explored this, she didn't know what he meant.

"Given that we haven't slept together," she said, sitting up on the edge of the table. "And that we haven't had a full and open conversation." She'd learned more about him from Bess, and that was hardly the basis of a deep, emotional connection. "We would need trust and communication before we could start to think about if this was ever going to be—"

"Communication," he said, "has never been my strong suit."

She shrugged. "We'll adapt, if we need to, we'll figure it out. You are flawed, but I'm far from perfect… I can't bear to see you lock yourself up, Zave. I can't bear it. How many hours do you spend alone? You have so much to give and you choose to withhold yourself from the people who care about you.

"I have to tell you what I know. I have to tell you what I heard those men saying to each other. I have to tell you about some of the things I went through for you to understand the context of when and where I heard these things. But I just can't understand why you reject me, and that makes it difficult for me to open up."

"You shouldn't try to understand me," he said.

"But I want to. I want to know what you do with all those hours you spend alone in the parts of the house you won't let any other person see. I want to know how you can be so thoughtful and generous and still think of yourself as a monster. Your milkshake made me cry," she said, and his attention snapped to her as she slunk off the table. "That's right." She smiled. "I felt like an idiot. But I just couldn't figure out what I did to deserve it. Every time I tell you that I want something, you find a way to get it for me."

She stopped and rested her fingers on his abs, which again, made him flinch, but she didn't remove them. "Shy…"

Trying to peer into him, she couldn't see through the shutters behind his eyes. "Why is it different when I tell you that I want you?"

"It's the one thing I can't give you," he said. "Anything else in the world you want is yours. That one I'm just not capable of."

"I think you're capable of anything," she said, because she would believe in him, even when he struggled to believe in himself. "I'm not naïve. I'm not the most beautiful woman in the world or the most sophisticated. I don't have money or material possessions. I'm not cultured or worldly, and I'm sure not as smart as you. I don't have anything to give you except my promise that I'm not going anywhere."

While he scrutinized her features, she speculated on what could be going through his mind. Was he trying to think of a way to let her down gently? Was he trying not to laugh in her face? Whatever it was, he had enough practice at remaining deadpan and holding himself aloof, that she couldn't begin to reach any conclusions.

"I know you're not in my league," she said. "I'm so far beneath you that I'm not surprised you won't share your secrets with me. But I am loyal, and I'm sure you don't deserve what you do to yourself. So, please, at least, accept me as a friend."

Just when she expected him to walk away and leave her, she felt the tickle of his fingertips on her palm. When her focus shifted down, she saw him link his fingers between hers. It wasn't an advance but initiating physical contact of any kind was a major breakthrough for him, which was perhaps why their first kiss perplexed him so much. Maybe he hadn't expected himself to be capable of that.

The real shock came when he began to move toward the door, the one she'd never been through. The one he, Brodie, and Zara emerged from whenever they came into this room. Through that door was a rectangular corridor.

Zave took her to the end and into a stairwell with a spiral staircase. Up they went and into another corridor. The next door they stopped at used fingerprint access. But that wasn't all. It had a green keypad that required a number to be punched in, and it had a retinal scanner. The door also wasn't wooden like the others; it was metal, painted to blend in with the décor.

He took her inside to a narrow foyer, and a second door stood before them, with equal levels of protection to the first. Either he was paranoid or dealing with some sensitive things. Her heart was pounding; she didn't know where they were or what to expect. But when he flicked on a light, the first thing she was awed by was the size of the space they were in.

The large lab stretched out, it had a bank of computers to the right, and spread across the left and center were various work desks and drafting tables, each with their own angled light. Beyond this workspace was a glass wall. A section filled with components stood on one side, and on the other were power tools far too complex for her to understand.

Another glass wall stood on the other side of those sections, but the furthest space was so far away, she couldn't decipher much of what was beyond it except what looked like more equipment.

"This is where I spend my time," he said. "This is what I do."

She couldn't imagine what all of these things were for. On the work desks around them, there were various schematics, diagrams, sketches and drawings, some of which she couldn't begin to decipher.

"There's another level," he said, looking to a door at the far right of their position. It stood at the end of a dark, narrow hall beyond the computer banks, and she wouldn't have noticed it was there unless he'd fixated on it. "In fact there's two, but this room is where most of the work is done.

Below the lab floors, in the basement, I have a gym with a pool. That's sealed off from the rest of the house. This whole section of the house is."

"And that's the only access?" she asked, speaking of the door they'd come through.

"The only one I'll tell you about," he said, and when he let her go to move forward, she tried to figure out if that was a joke or if it was one of those, 'if I told you I'd have to kill you' scenarios.

"This is your lab. How many people have—"

"No one."

Going to a high draftsman stool at a drafting table, he sat down and pulled an angled light closer to the surface. His position faced the door, so she couldn't see what was going on over the highest edge of the tabletop.

Everything here appeared functional and she saw nothing designed for comfort. "This is where you sleep?" she asked.

"I sleep in the tower, which is above us."

A tower. His bedroom was in a tower. She wished she could see this building from the outside, to try and put together a picture of where it was she'd been living for weeks.

"Why did you bring me here?" Moving across the empty space, she stopped at the back of the table that was angled so high she could rest her chin on the crest. "It's wonderful, it's amazing. And I'm honored, but why?"

Picking up a pencil from a lip on the lower edge, he added something to the paper that she couldn't see properly because the lamp was so close that the glare of the light blanked the image. With a crease between his brows, he drew a couple of lines, then brushed a hand over the paper before he put the pencil back down.

Then he looked at her. "You're right that if you join the Kindred, we need trust. All of us need that."

"So this is your way of showing that you trust me?" she asked. But he hadn't done it for Zara, hadn't even done it for Thad or Brodie.

"This is my way of showing you that I don't consider you beneath me. But there can never be anything between us."

She didn't understand that, and he must have read her confusion. "Could you be with a man who spends all his days here?"

Devon could see there were narrow, horizontal windows on the farthest back wall, past the equipment room she couldn't make out well. The rest of the light came from florescent overheads. If this was where he spent all his time, he'd barely see the sun or smell the sea.

"Maybe."

He didn't believe her. "You would be with a man who would rather spend his time surrounded by electronic components, circuit boards, and wiring than be anywhere near you?"

"I don't believe that's true," she said. "I think you're trying to push me away. Just like you do with everybody else." And like he'd already tried to do with her. "Who says we have to have anything more than friendship?"

"Didn't you hear me downstairs? Have you forgotten what almost happened on that table? How many friends do you do that with?"

None. In fact, it had been a long time since she'd been with a man. After her last disastrous break-up, she'd begged off relationships and it had probably been more than a year before her abduction since she'd been intimate with anyone.

Men had just never made sense to her. Except the most complex of all, this man in front of her, somehow seemed straightforward. Yes, his motivations, his personality were complex, but he wasn't deceptive. His revelations downstairs, his outburst, they had opened her eyes. He wanted her. He was just afraid to let her in. Either because he thought he didn't deserve the love or because he thought he would let her down.

"So it's six weeks of sex, isn't that how long you said it would last?" she asked.

He had an answer for everything. "Kindred don't screw other Kindred."

That wasn't true. "What about Raven and Zara? They screw, anyone who sees them together would know that."

"That's complicated," he said. Something on his

drawing caught his eye, and he picked up his pencil to make another adjustment. "They're married."

She loved that little crease between his brows, the sign of his concentration. His intent focus moved with the swipe of his pencil. What he didn't understand was that although his drawings were technical, the sound of the graphite scraping across the textured surface of the pulp was arousing to her artist's ear.

The artist in her was mesmerized by the sound. Her eyes drifted shut, imagining every time she'd held that kind of pencil in her hand and the pleasure she got from creating, watching an image come to life with every new stroke of her hand.

He'd put pencil to paper, paused to make a measurement, and brushed a fingertip down a line. Every sound was one she recognized as something that fired her soul. Her nipples were strained to such tight peaks that they began to throb. He'd stirred her up downstairs, let her in to his private domain, and now he was teasing her with his scent and the sound of her greatest passion.

"You said I could have anything I wanted," she murmured.

Still in the haze of her high, Devon slunk around the table and although he was still working, Devon rubbed a hand over his leg to his inner thigh. That was when the sound of pencil on paper stopped. But she was already breathing his earlobe in between her lips.

"Anything but that," he said, picking her hand off his thigh to put it on the drafting table.

Devon kissed behind his ear and the side of his neck. She laid one arm across the back of his chair and rubbed her breasts against him. Not to stimulate him, but because it was her impulse to imprint herself on him, to try to mark him with her scent. Despite knowing it was pure fantasy, the notion he might belong to her was invigorating.

"You said *anything*." Maybe it was because her eyes were closed and she was still ensconced in her own illusion, but she told the absolute truth. "I want you to make me come."

The back of the stool twisted away from her reach, and she opened her eyes to find he'd discarded his pencil and turned the stool to face her so she was almost between his knees.

Devon expected rejection, she expected him to argue. Instead, he picked her hand off the drafting table, brought her knuckles to his lips, and kissed them once.

"I can work with that request, shy."

Now it was her turn to crease her brows.

As if he anticipated the torrent of questions he'd just provoked, he stood up and led her from the room, cutting off any chance she had to bombard him. He took her all the way back downstairs to her own bedroom and she was lost by the time they got there, partly because she was distracted by what his end game might be. Could he be taking her to her bedroom to make love to her?

No. When they got there, he stopped at her door, opened it, and urged her inside. "Go to sleep, shy," he said. "You've had enough excitement for one night."

Not giving her a chance to ask questions or make another statement, he closed the door, leaving her alone in her bedroom. He was right about one thing, she'd had plenty of excitement. Her day had started with the gift of a milkshake that made her cry and ended with a peek into his inner sanctum.

He wasn't going to make this easy. Zave had accused her of making him lose control, but he restrained himself more than he took credit for. Devon couldn't chase after him; even if she tried, she'd get lost. If by some miracle, she got to his lab, she wouldn't get through the door and pounding on it wouldn't help when she now knew there was a double entry system.

So, in a stupor, she went through the motions of getting ready for bed and climbed beneath the covers. At first, sleep seemed elusive and then she realized, the sooner she gave into slumber, the sooner she'd be able to wake and discover what progress tomorrow would bring.

FOURTEEN

A COUPLE OF days passed, and she didn't see Zave at all. Bess fed her and let Devon help with the household chores in short bursts, giving the women time to bond. After lunch on that day, Thad had come to see her. He'd popped in and out over the last two days, but his visits had been social not medical.

On this occasion, he performed a full check-up. He took all her vitals, asked all his standard doctor questions, quizzed her about her diet, weighed her, calculated her body fat, and noted everything down on a clipboard.

Every time he examined her, he wrote things down. Given what Bess had said about his aversion to updating patient notes, Devon doubted he kept a file on her. It was just habit that made him write these things down, and it would make them easier to remember while he went through the motions. That piece of paper was probably tossed in the trash as soon as he walked out.

Afterwards, Devon had moved into the dining room to sketch through the window using the easel Bess had brought her on the previous morning. Zave might not be physically present, but he was still showering her with gifts at every opportunity.

Instead of focusing on the vast view of the ocean, she explored the rocks, the grass, and the path with the tip of her pencil on the paper. The scene she created was the same as the one she'd seen him in for the first time. Devon couldn't fool herself. That was exactly why she was here doing this now, in hope that maybe he would run by.

Somehow, he'd known she was there the first time, so she figured he would know the second time too. Curiosity played in her thoughts. Would he acknowledge her if he sensed her here? Would he turn and wave? Didn't seem like his style. It was more likely that he'd turn and glare, then he would wait until the next time they saw each other and he would chastise her for stalking him.

Bess was sitting at the dining table folding linen napkins and had been there for some time, though the women hadn't spoken for a while. "You can go outside, you know," she said.

"I've thought about it," Devon said, although she'd never gotten as far as trying the front door to see if it was unlocked. "I wouldn't want to get lost out there."

Bess put a folded napkin in her neat stack and reached for another. "You can't get lost," she said. "Zave monitors everything from his lab. He'd be able to track your movement on the island. He monitors the weather from up there, too, taking readings from all the gadgets he has scattered around the place. He'd send a search party for you as soon as the temperature dropped a degree."

Bess' amusement was a consistent attribute of her gregarious personality. Devon wouldn't think to mock such careful behavior on Zave's part. Some might see it as overbearing if he did such a thing; she'd just be awed that he was paying such close attention. Adding some details to her sketch, she put some lines on the rocks and enhanced the shade. It began to lift off the page with life.

When the door clicked, she expected Thad to be coming in. Except movement in her peripheral vision betrayed that it was Zave's door that had opened, not the one from the hallway.

"It's time," he said.

While Devon wasn't sure what he meant, Bess did because she gathered up her linens and scurried from the room without saying anything else.

"Time for what?" Devon asked, putting her pencil in the tray at the bottom of her easel.

He stayed by the door. "We were waiting until your strength was back," Zave said. "We didn't want to rush you. But Thad has given me the go-ahead."

"Go-ahead for what?"

While watching him move across the room in a few long strides, a whisper of hopeful excitement simmered. Maybe he was talking about crossing that boundary he'd said he wasn't capable of broaching. Maybe he would come to her, sweep her off her feet, and return them to the tower he'd spoken of before.

Except it wasn't her direction he came in; he went to the side of the table and sat down. "You said you'd only deal with me," he said.

Anxiety overtook her excitement, hope became dread. "You want to talk about them," she said.

Living in this beautiful house was like living in an opulent bubble. All of her needs were catered to and there was nothing to fear here. Their literal island protected them from the dangers and evils of the world. That they'd ask her to confront those evils was inevitable, and she couldn't argue for more time or say she wasn't ready because they'd been patient. More patient than other groups would be in their position.

Using the time it took her to close the window, she gave herself an internal pep talk, repeating that she'd be able to say the words without letting emotion incapacitate her. Zave was a professional and she was a source. Whatever was going on between them personally had no place here in this conversation, it had to be sidelined.

"We've already established that you were unaware of being taken and of the journey," he said as she took a seat opposite him.

The width of the table may as well have been the width of an Olympic pool. In the gulf between them, she felt no warmth, but that may have been caused by her own discomfort rather than his attitude.

She sensed patience from him and he paced his words. For a man who'd shunned society for so long, it couldn't be easy to cast off his brusque exterior, but she could tell that he was trying. So, while he wasn't completely successful in putting her at ease, she appreciated that he made the effort.

"I don't remember any of that," she said, recalling how dark it had been when she'd come out of the gallery, and how she'd mishandled the keys, almost dropping them when she locked the back door in the service alley.

Considering how she'd still been stuffing one of her sketchbooks into her painter's satchel as she receded from the structure, she didn't remember hearing anyone, didn't remember feeling a needle or having anything planted on her face. Maybe she'd been aware of it at the time and had blocked out the trauma. Or it could be that whatever they did to her played havoc with her memory.

"We don't know how they select their women," he said. "What is the first thing you were aware of?"

The smell. Her eyes closed as her hands opened on the smooth wood beneath them. It was putrid, like nothing she'd ever inhaled before. Dirty. Unhealthy. Rank. Devon knew now it was the smell of bodies, encased in iron, existing in their own filth. Unwashed. Unkempt. Baking in the heat of a sun they couldn't see.

Learning to be quiet had saved her from the beatings. But she wondered how many of those imprisoned were lost to the scorching heat of the day or the frigid cold of the night.

"It was dark," she said, still with her eyes closed. "The whole time. It was dark. And I… my mouth was dry, they had… Something made my jaw hurt. There was grubby cloth wedged between my molars, pressed against my tongue. It kept my mouth open all the time, and it took a while to learn how to breathe like that. Sometimes I woke up choking."

"Did you see anyone else?" he asked.

Shaking her head, she couldn't believe she'd thought she could separate emotion while recounting the experience. Tears were already seeping from her ducts. "Other prisoners?

No. I heard them, all the time." Covering her ears, she pressed her palms into them until they formed a seal. "The screaming. The crying. Some sounded so young. All they wanted was to be set free. Like me, they just wanted to go home."

"Did you beg?" he asked when her hands slid away from her ears.

"At first. At first, I did. I didn't call out because in those first few hours, maybe it was a few days, there was nothing but shouting. A dozen women cried out for liberation."

This was significant enough to intrigue him. "They must have brought you in in a batch," he said. "Some of the gangs bring in one or two women at a time, it makes it easier to deal with integrating them. Others, like the ones who took you, ship women like animals. They pack their vans and trucks full before they slip across the border."

He could explain some of the things she hadn't known. "How do they do that?" she asked, opening her eyes to see he was unaffected. "How do they take women from one country to another without—"

"It's easier than you'd think. Some of the cartels do it by plane. Airspace is impossible to monitor at all times, especially when they fly beneath radar. Those who go by road, or rather off-road, have their own private points to cross. They travel specific routes a dozen times before switching to another, then another, making it difficult for authorities to track where they are or where they'll be. So you didn't call out?"

"No. I might have if I hadn't heard so many others, but I knew I'd be drowned out and all of the pleas were ignored. My hands were locked together at my lower spine," she said, and of their own accord, her arms moved behind her into the position she'd existed in for months. "Then they were locked by a fixed bolt or something, attached to a single point on the wall. There was no light. There was never any light."

"You're doing good," he murmured, soothing her bubbling emotions.

His confidence prompted her. "Later on, I figured out how small the box was. I stretched as far as I could and could touch the three walls surrounding me with my foot. There was no space to lie down, not that I'd have been able to because of the way my hands were bound."

"But they came to you?" he asked, getting her back on track with the narrative.

"Yes. The men, they came to me not long after I woke up. They threw water on me, maybe to wash me or wake me up, I don't know, but the door opened and I was hit with a wall of water. One of them pulled the gag down to stuff some food in my mouth, I don't know what it was. I wasn't paying attention, but I'd said it wasn't a taste I recognized. That was the first time I asked what was going on. I asked for help, for mercy, to be released. He demanded that I eat. Demanded that I stopped talking. But I wasn't thinking straight and I kept babbling until he hit me."

Zave's shoulder moved, but she didn't read too much into the reflex because she was thinking about that first hit and how quickly it was followed by a second and a third.

"He hit you?"

"He just kept saying that I was theirs now, I belonged to them, that my life was gone, and I'd been erased. He told me to be quiet. Told me to be grateful. He hit me so many times, and I couldn't do anything to protect myself. I couldn't lift my hands. I must have passed out because when I woke up again, he was gone. There was less shouting. The place was so quiet, it was eerie. Sometimes I heard crying probably coming from one of the cells flanking mine. But I didn't open my mouth. For one thing, my face was swollen, and I'm not sure I'd have been able to speak. The gag was gone, but the blindfold hadn't moved. I was too numb to cry. Shock stopped me from losing it. Maybe. My injuries distracted me. But from then on I gave up on asking too many questions."

"You survived."

But at what cost? The lives of others? Her own quick thinking didn't save her life, the Kindred did. "Coming to terms with where I was, it was difficult. I didn't want to give up. I didn't want to be there. My life became nothing but that cell, those men, and whatever they gave me. They'd take me out of my cell maybe twice a day, long enough to use the toilet.

They were tired of cleaning up the mess, that was what they said to each other. They'd learned, they'd obviously been doing this a while, because it hadn't been policy to let the women use the bathroom when they started their operation. Buckets in the corner of the room would mean they had to give the women freedom to move. It also gave the women a weapon, something they could assault their captors with."

"They spoke of these things?"

She nodded. "They would laugh about the women they'd murdered for drenching them in urine. They'd laugh about the way they punished them. About how they'd pay her back in kind for days. Every man on site would soak her bound body every time he needed to relieve himself."

Stopping, she could feel her voice beginning to waver. Devon didn't want to drown in emotion when they'd only just started talking. She had to show strength, to remind herself that she was free, and that sharing this experience would help those still imprisoned.

"Take your time," he said, displaying more patience.

Sealing her lips, Devon swallowed to provide respite to her dry tongue. "I know it wasn't brave of me, but stories like that terrified me, and they had dozens of them."

"They told you these stories?"

"No," she said, once again spreading her hands on the table, keeping her fingers wide apart, maybe just because she could experience this kind of freedom to do what she wanted to with her own limbs and digits. "No, they told each other, they boasted. They didn't address us as fellow human beings. We were poked and prodded, pushed and shoved. We were rarely given explicit instructions, which was part of the reason I figured something was going on before the auction, because the procedure that night was different."

"We'll get to that. Let's take it a step at a time," he said. "So they spoke to each other? Told each other these stories?"

"Yes," she said. "They would jeer and laugh, reminisce about certain girls. They would talk about different things they'd done to them. It didn't seem to be policy for them to touch a girl, to rape her, unless that girl was never going to make it to auction. Except they didn't call it that, though, they just said, 'make it to the end' like it was a game, like there was a finish line, a goal to be achieved."

"There is for them," he said. "The goal is to sell the girl and steal a new one to take her place."

These men thought that what they did was a game. Devon knew they didn't take it seriously, not as anything more than a way to make money. "Will it ever end?"

"We know where you were located," he said. "But storming the place will blow our cover and we'll be blacklisted. We can't afford to take a risk like that to eliminate just one cartel."

To take down one, she thought, and a memory of something she'd overheard surfaced. "What if you could take out several?"

"What do you mean?" he asked, straightening up.

"A few times, they were talking about a meet. Something the head guys do several times a year. Something to do with turf and clients and clarifying territory. They meet."

"Who?" he asked.

"I don't know their specific names, not all of them," she said. "I can give you a list of the five or six they mentioned."

"Five or six?"

When he was this dry, he was difficult for her to get a handle on and she began to worry. "That might not be all of them," she said, sorry that she may have disappointed him. "There could be others, they never specified how many different groups were allowed to be part of the meeting. Only that each boss was allowed one body man and no more."

"They're paranoid," he said.

"Anyone who shows up with more than that is fair game. They were talking about it because there was some kind of war going on at the top as to who their gran jefe was going to take with him this time. Those who were vying for power want to be seen at his side. It makes them seem valuable and important. No one could decide who that could be and Yago, their boss, he hadn't fingered anyone yet."

"This meet was soon?"

Considering this, her attention drifted. "They didn't specify a date, although they said that it would happen between their next two market days… that would mean auction, right? That would mean after the day I was sold and before their next auction?"

"That would be a rational assumption," he said.

Glad that she had recalled something which might be of use, she shared more. "They said whoever went to the meet with Yago would probably be in charge of the next gig, which made it tough for them to make decisions about the women they should gather."

"Auctions happen several times a year. Each cartel has their own schedule. Some are pretty reliable and others are erratic. But this is useful. We know which group held you. We can talk to Carlos and find out when they plan to hold their next auction."

If they weren't a gang that the Kindred usually dealt with, this could be a good opportunity for them to start rescuing women from there as well. "How will you do it?" she asked. "You can't be honest about why you want to know."

"It won't be difficult," he said. "These men are desperate for money. When they hear someone like me is interested, they'll start talking about special orders."

Squirming, disgust flavored her throat. "You can do that?" she asked. "Order a woman?"

"Most men with my means, who are into this lifestyle, do."

"What kind of things do they ask for?"

He shrugged and linked his fingers. "Something as simple as hair or eye color sometimes. Some like them young, virginal. Others like their women to be feisty, to be fighters, women that they can break. Some like those who fight back because the harder a woman fights, the more violent he can be."

Her ragged breath didn't relieve her aching lungs. "How can there be men out there who enjoy other's terror?"

"You're not supposed to understand. The fact that you don't and that it repulses you proves you're a decent person, shy, one who doesn't deserve to be caught up in this."

"Are you going to make another attempt to push me away?" she asked. "Is that your subtle way of telling me again that I don't belong here?"

"You don't belong here," he said. Before she could voice any protest, he held up a hand to silence her. "After I lost my parents and faced who I'd become, I treated this place like my prison. I chose to limit my access to the world because all I ever did when I was out there was damage."

"That's not true," she said, thinking of the products that had made the world better and the people he'd touched with his generosity. Even if they were shallow sorts who were taking advantage of him, they'd still learned something from their association with the great Xavier Knight.

"My basic needs were met, but I wouldn't allow myself to indulge, and I promised I would spend the rest of my days here to protect the world from my detrimental effect. I worked to create items that could make up for some of my disgusting behavior."

Devon had found a way in just by fulfilling her promise. "You're too hard on yourself."

"What happened with Bronwyn made me hate myself more," he said. "After we discovered her fate, I shut myself up here again because my beliefs had been reinforced. While what I make might be good and fun, or interesting and useful, my impact on people, individual people that I had one on one interactions with was negative. I made people's lives worse. I know that Thad blamed me for what happened, he blamed himself, too, and he might have slid into a despair similar to mine had it not been for the Kindred. Brodie, Swift, and Art, they got Thad through and roped me into doing what we do now when I would have preferred to close the doors and block everybody out."

"Why didn't you?" she asked. "Why didn't you tell them to go to hell?"

"Thad needed me. He didn't fly then, his funds weren't up to much, and his social scope is limited. He's outgoing and happy, he gets along with people far easier than I do. Except a sense of humor doesn't wash with these guys south of the border. He didn't have my rep as a guy with plenty of money and a penchant for partying. By then it had been years, half a decade since I'd lost my parents, but I convinced that scum that I'd come out of retirement and found myself a new hobby."

"Slave auctions," she said. "And because you felt responsible for what happened to Bronwyn, you couldn't say no when Thad asked for your help."

"Right. So here we are, four years later. We buy the women, we fix them, and send them on their way. But Thad's itching to hurt these guys hard. The more I see, the more I want to take them apart. This information, it's useful. If we can hit these guys during the meet, we'd be anonymous, they wouldn't be expecting me to be around, like they are at the auctions. If we can find out when, then Swift can find out where, and we'll be able to set the place up before they get there."

"Set it up how?" she asked. "What is it that you plan to do?"

"I don't know. I'll talk to Rave and Swift, we'll come up with a plan. But this helps. You've helped. I want you to know that we're going to take these guys down for you and Bronwyn and every other woman that they hurt."

"That doesn't explain why you think I don't belong here," she said.

Resting against the back of his chair, he curled his fingers around the edge of the table. "Because this is supposed to be my prison. The auctions are my penance, my hard labor, if you like. When I'm not there, I'm here. Being here is supposed to be punishment."

Sometimes he frustrated her. "You're locking yourself up for a thousand years because your parents died hating you, according to what you believe," she said.

"Because I didn't deserve what they gave me. My father built Knight Corp. Without him, it wouldn't exist. I wouldn't have the money and the house and the ability that I do now to go to these auctions. I'd have squandered it all. I'd have lost everything."

"Zave—"

"The drugs, the women, it was juvenile indulgence,

and I'm embarrassed by it. I hurt people. Good people. I used women, stole them from good friends who cared about them. I wasn't a nice person, shy. I didn't deserve to come out of that period of my life intact, with a successful company, an expensive home, and a nest egg larger than most people could make in ten lifetimes. My father set me up, proved he cared about me, even when I was ridiculing him. My mother adored me. When I was a kid, she was so proud, and had high hopes for what I'd become when my intelligence began to shine through. By the end, she couldn't look at me."

"So you think that by having me here…" she said, trying to figure him out. "I'm some sort of extravagance you shouldn't have in a prison meant for punishment?"

"It's a prison like no other, I'll give you that. It would be laughable to suggest that my life here isn't privileged. I have my work. Access to everything that I need. I have privacy. I have facilities for exercise, grounds that you wouldn't find at any penitentiary."

It was a metaphorical prison, she understood that. Exiling himself not only protected the world as he claimed it needed to be, but it protected him from experiencing further grief. As long as there were no people in his life, he couldn't lose or disappoint them.

"Bess is no jailor," she said. "And Thad worships you, you have to see that. I think this has gone on long enough. Maybe I had to go through that horrific thing to bring me here to you. Let's face it, we'd never have met otherwise." If he was always here and she was in New York, there was no way their paths would have crossed.

Pain was the emotion she read on his face, which was usually so free of sentiment. "Please don't tell me you went through that because of me." Panic made her hold her breath. "Shy, I thought that saving you was maybe the reason for everything else. But don't tell me that you were in that place because of me."

"I didn't mean that," she said and tried to reach for his hand, but the table was too wide, he would have to offer it, to lean forward and meet her halfway if she had any hope of touching him. It was little surprise that he didn't. "Do you know what I dream about? I dream about you holding me. I dream about you looking into my eyes and telling me that you don't want me to leave, that you want me to be by your side. I dream that you'll stop trying to chase me away. I dream about you touching me, about you kissing me, about you giving in to what you've told me you want. It's torture, Xavier, to know you're in this house, wanting me, and you won't let me in. Sometimes I wake up aching for you, wishing I could just speak to you. My whole body is alive when you're around, every nerve is so sensitive to the dream I've had of your hands on my skin."

His steady eyes landed on hers. "I think now is the time to give you your gift," he said.

Devon waited for it, because she hadn't seen him carrying anything. He got up and left the room only to come back a moment later carrying a long narrow box. Jewelry? No, it was wider than it would need to be to contain a necklace, longer than a bracelet, and what use did she have for jewels here?

He seated himself again and with a single finger, pushed the box to the center of the table. She didn't know what it was, but his gifts had always hit the mark before. She picked it up, and after narrowing her eyes on him, she glanced down at the box and then tried to see if he gave anything away. Except he didn't. He never did.

Pulling off the lid, she put it down and unwrapped the tissue paper that was cradling the item inside. The long, narrow cylinder of plastic was smooth, its coating soft, and although the gift shocked her, she smiled.

"Where did you get this?" she asked. "It's a vibrator."

"I made it," he said.

That in itself was impressive. They were on an island in the middle of nowhere, and he could toss something like this together. "No man has ever…" Her blush made her self-conscious when she ran her fingers over the device. Putting it back into the tissue paper, Devon found herself unable to look at him. "I don't know what to say. Why did you…?"

"You said you wanted me to make you come," he said, and while he could say the words without flinching, her face must have burned brighter.

"That's not what I meant," she whispered. "I appreciate this, but…" Drawing her finger around the rim of the box, she did what she could not to look him in the eye. "I thought you might be in the room, that you might participate."

"It's my craftsmanship," he said. "You can reach climax with a tool I've provided."

"Not the tool I was thinking of," she said, flashing a timid smile at the table.

"You're altering your request."

"Not altering," she said. "Defining it, being more explicit."

But he didn't sound offended, he was enticed, intrigued by her adjustment. "You're issuing a challenge."

Surprised by her own daring, she looked him in the eye. "Will you rise to it?" she asked.

Bess came in and got a few paces toward the table before she stopped to observe the charged atmosphere. "I'm interrupting again."

"No," Zave said, not shifting his gaze.

With Bess in the room, Devon became more self-conscious and folded the tissue paper over the object to secure the lid again. "We were just talking," Devon said, which was a ridiculous thing to say because they were sitting at opposite sides of the table, what else would they be doing?

"Shy has a challenge for me," he said, titillating her with his plotting.

"A challenge?" Bess asked. "You like those."

Zave got up. "You did well today, shy," he said. "Now I have work to do."

Kindred work or work rising to this challenge he claimed that she'd extended. Sliding the box toward her chest, she covered it with her forearms. Bess came over wearing a grin. "Another gift?" she asked, and Devon nodded hoping that the flames in her cheeks would prevent the woman from asking too many questions. "You keep tying him up, dearie. You're doing a fine job so far."

Bess went to the sideboard to begin arranging space for the napkin she must have finished folding. Devon found herself fixated on the door Zave had exited. This gift wasn't what she'd intended, but she knew that she would indulge because if nothing else, he'd made it for her and it would be rude not to utilize it.

Except that was only half the truth. She wanted pleasure at his hands, and this was the closest she would get. This was a gift she could keep forever, one she would always treasure.

FIFTEEN

TEMPTATION DWARFED FEAR on the first night with her new gift. Although she'd been alone in the dark, she'd been self-conscious when she first turned on the toy and listened to the sound she knew he'd heard after creating it.

Getting used to the buzz, she'd run it across her fingers, up the inside of her sensitive wrist, and while telling herself it was an accident, she let it graze across one nipple and then another. It hadn't taken long for the item to find its way between her thighs. Soon, the endorphins of pleasure had erased all traces of embarrassment.

Devon had used it again on the second night, and when she woke up in the dark, disorientated after a nightmare, she'd retrieved a glass of water, washed her face, and returned to bed. When slumber didn't come to meet her, she sought distraction with the intimate toy.

It was late on the third night when she reached for the drawer in the nightstand to take out the toy she'd secreted there. As far as she knew, Bess had never gone through her things. But Devon always nestled it in the back corner beneath every other item she kept there, just in case.

The thrill of sharing the secret of her toy's existence with Zave intensified her pleasure when she used it. It was only him she thought of when she played with it. Devon had just twisted the base and parted her thighs when she heard the tapping on the door.

Turning it off, Devon grabbed for the sheet when the door began to open before she'd uttered a word. The pounding in her heart dried her throat, and she was afraid to breathe because she had no idea who would be coming to her this late or why.

Her eyes had adjusted to the lack of light while she'd been lying here contemplating whether or not to indulge herself on another consecutive night. So it didn't take long to recognize her benefactor.

"Zave?" she breathed, and the heat of awkwardness made her squeeze her legs together, which only reminded her that his gift was still beneath her thighs.

"Do you want to be alone?" he asked.

God, that was a loaded question. It was easy to want him. It was easy to feel comfortable with him when her senses were seeped in a haze of arousal as they'd been during each of their kisses and physical encounters. But when he was a powerful figure standing in her doorway, while she sat naked in the middle of one of his beds covered only by a thin sheet, she couldn't help but be intimidated.

"That depends," she said because the last thing she wanted to do was reject him when she'd been so blatant about her desire for him.

That he was even present proved they were making progress. She'd often wondered if he still loitered outside her room at night and had been tempted to check on several occasions. But she liked the illusion that he was there and didn't want it to be shattered if she peeked out to find the hall empty.

"I have something for you," he said.

Another gift? "Then come in."

Although her heart hadn't slowed and if he had come down here to slide into her bed, Devon wasn't sure her skills would impress him after the extremes he was used to with more experienced women. Despite the apparent interval of celibacy between then and now, it would seem a shame for him to break that streak and be disappointed.

Yet her own selfish interest made her almost pant when he slipped into her room and closed the door. Here he was, the Lord of the Manor, in her room, in the middle of the night, without any other occupant of the house knowing he was here.

Their clandestine affair had moved up a level and after what his last gift had been, she could infer from this late arrival that she was going to get another sensual surprise.

"Have you enjoyed my last gift?" he asked.

The bass in his tone was laced with an innuendo that constricted her throat. Her insecure nature made her want to deny the truth, because she'd never shared her self-gratification habits with anyone. Yet having him here, like a living, breathing fantasy, she was compelled to loosen. Reminding herself that he was taking great strides and showing immense trust, which he hadn't given to anyone else, just by coming here, Devon bolstered her courage.

Either he'd taken time to psyche himself up or had just been unable to stay away from her. Had he been so drawn to her that he couldn't resist her pull? Could she be that much of a temptation? Allowing herself to believe that she was, Devon wanted to tempt him more and prompted herself to be bold in this dark night, to pretend this was a dream, a fantasy come to life, that it wasn't real and she could be anything she wanted to be without fear of ridicule.

This was simply her mind giving her a tangible taste of her deepest, darkest desire.

"Yes," she admitted and liked the shot of adrenaline that leaped from her heart to her clit.

"Good," he breathed. "I have more for you. I'm going to meet your challenge, shy."

Rising onto her knees, Devon held the sheet in her cleavage. "You are?"

"You told me to be present and participate."

Inching down the bed, anticipation threatened to make her drool. "Yes."

"Tell me what you think about," he said. "When you're playing with that toy."

"You," she said. "I think about you, how your hands have touched the thing that gives me pleasure. How it would feel to have you touch me with the same kind of dedicated, skilled care."

Standing at the end of the bed, he loomed in the shadow over her private space. Devon could only make out the occasional glint of his eye. "What else?"

"I think about your mouth, how it feels to kiss you, what it felt like when you picked me up and I wrapped my legs around you. The strength in your arms and the security of your grip. The way you laid me down and never stopped kissing me."

"Is that enough?" he asked. "Does that make you come?" He was enough, and the images and scenarios she'd built in her mind had brought her to release every time she'd used the toy. "Lie down."

The expectancy that came with the uncertainty of what he planned to do made her comply. Devon lay on her back with the sheet over her body and then she lifted one knee to let her leg peek out from beneath the white cotton spread across the bed. Revealing her bare limb to him, her hip, and her abdomen, too, she kept the most intimate corner of her body concealed.

"What now?" she whispered, eager to know what he'd request next.

"Where is it?" he asked. Lifting her butt, she groped for the toy she'd been lying on. When she found it, she showed it to him. "Hold it in both hands." Again, she did as she was told. He moved half a step toward the window. "Close your eyes."

His commands were sure, whispered in a masculine grumble. Tightening her hold on the solid shaft he'd gifted her, Devon didn't know what to expect. Then something touched her ankle and without a single sound, a vibration moved through her.

When her lips opened, she breathed in. "More gifts?" she asked and the vibration stopped.

"Yes. Only if you want it. I want you to know something."

"What?" she asked, opening her eyes.

"There have to be ground rules."

"Like what?"

"Number one, we do nothing that you're uncomfortable with. If you don't want to do something or you're unsure, say no. We don't need a safe word, we don't need code. A simple 'no' is all I need to hear to make me stop."

Some of the illusion was lost in this pragmatic declaration. But the implication that this would be more than a one-off excited her. Reality was more gratifying than any dream. "Number two?" she asked.

"You do nothing without permission," he said. "Which means your eyes shouldn't be open."

The sincerity of his words made her smile and she closed her eyes, because it was just as important for him to be as comfortable as her. "Sorry."

"That doesn't mean I won't let you, it just means you have to ask."

"I understand, lord," she said. "What's the next rule?"

"Number three, your pleasure is the only thing that matters when we play."

That didn't seem fair to him, that she should be the focal point of all the fun while he deprived himself. "But—"

"No buts," he said. "See number two. You don't question me. You may ask permission to do something, but my word is final except in cases of number one."

Her smile returned. She was getting a glimmer of the business man in him. "Number four?" she purred, feeling her body loosen as she wriggled between the cool sheets.

"This is temporary. I'm doing this because it's your wish, and I find myself compelled to fulfill those. One day soon, we'll have to stop."

But he gave her no specific end date, and maybe if she kept telling him that this was her wish, he would keep fulfilling it because he still hadn't explained exactly what it was they were going to do. "If I object?"

"Then we go no further."

Okay, so she wasn't going to voice any opposition to his rules. "Anything else?"

"Number five, anything that happens between us, these toys, these games, what we say to each other, it stays private at all times, in all circles."

If she'd been making up rules herself, that would've been one of her top ones, so Devon was pleased that he thought in the same way. "I haven't told anyone and I won't."

Sharing this secret with each other, it made her feel special in his life in a more concrete way than just some fragment of a feeling that they might be connected; now they actually shared something physical.

"I'm not shy about sex," he said. "But I know you can be."

Was that his way of implying the last rule was to protect her modesty? Devon chose to share the primary reason for her discomfort. "Because when you're around it seems to be all I think about."

"Don't ever worry about disappointing me, you can say no at any time and it won't change my opinion of you."

"And if I agree to absolutely everything you say? Would that make you think less of me?"

The length of time it took him to answer made her stop moving. She feared a negative response and didn't want him to think of her as a slut when he was so eager to avoid memories of his indulgent past that had been filled with easy women.

"Nothing could sully my opinion of you, shy. All I care about is making you happy."

He'd come down here with a plan, and she was desperate to know what it was. "I trust you to do that," she said.

"Do you accept?" he asked.

"Yes," she murmured like there could ever have been a question mark over her obedience.

The vibration touched her ankle again and ran down the front of her foot to the tip of her toe, making it point toward him. "If I asked you to put this inside of you, would you do it?"

She didn't know what it was, only that it felt nice buzzing against her. It was a warm, arousing sensation. With her eyes closed and her body relaxed, she bent her knee higher, away from the toy, but it wasn't a refusal. Letting her leg fall to the side, she gave a physical sign of obedience.

"Yes," she breathed.

With her eyes closed, she could slip back into the fantasy. Devon imagined what it would be like if he would pull the sheet aside, lean over the end of the bed, and be the one to do the honors. Instead something bounced on the bed beneath her elbow.

"Pick it up," he said. "Leave the first one where it is."

Putting the vibrator in her cleavage, Devon kept her eyes closed and fumbled for the item he'd tossed to the bed. She found it and picked it up. It wasn't long, it was fat and short, and it had a short, silicone tail at the base.

"That's right," he said. "Explore it." She hadn't realized she'd been touching it with all of her fingers, stroking them over it, learning the size, the length, the width, the texture. "It's not too big." She wondered if he was easing her in with the modest size of this bauble. "I made it just for you. How does it feel?"

"Nice," she said. "Smooth. Warm."

"That's just a taster," he said.

As her fingers ran over the plastic, it began to vibrate, and she gasped. "I don't know how I—"

"You didn't," he said. "I did. You wanted me to participate."

Those had been her conditions, that he was to be present and participate. He'd found another way to manipulate what she'd meant to meet both of their requirements. He was here and he was in complete control.

"Let it touch your body," he said. "Over the sheet… on your breast."

While it still vibrated, she lowered it to her nipple, rolling it over the already sensitive peak. This experience was more intense than when she was alone, thinking of him. Pressing it down with her fingertips, an invisible elastic tightened between her nipple and her clit. It thrummed in time with the rhythm of this toy.

"The other," he commanded. Rolling it down,

through her cleavage, past the other vibrator, she treated her other breast to the same treatment. "Slide it down your body, under the sheet."

One gradual step at a time, he was easing her into each new request, giving her the chance to refuse. Tempted to open her eyes, she wanted to see how he was reacting to this performance. But she'd agreed to the rules, so she kept them shut.

Taking her hand under the sheet, she whimpered when it touched her responsive flesh. Tracing it down her sternum to her navel, her belly began to pulse when the vibrating egg dipped inside. "Keep going, shy," he whispered.

Anticipation made her hold her breath as it descended on her stomach, went over her pubis and then the vibration stopped just a whisper from her clit. Her disappointed moan probably came off as petulant.

"Put it in your pussy," he said.

It was already dipping into her juices. She was slick, ready to accept it and wouldn't need any further foreplay. If only she could tempt him to take the final step and join their bodies. But she would have to be patient, her whole body was raw, and if he did that, she'd be lurching into climax before he was buried in her passage.

Forgetting for a second that he was standing over her, Devon brought up her other knee beneath the sheet. Allowing her inner thighs to stretch, she opened herself to slip the toy he'd built for her into her most intimate crevice.

The sensation of it sliding inside was odd. After pushing it past the tight muscles of her entrance, she wriggled to get used to its bulk. Each movement sent a strong surge of pleasure to her mind, making her hips rise to meet the vacant spot where his should be.

Maybe because it had been so long, or because she was unaccustomed to this, but it felt larger than she would have assumed.

"Close them," he said. Flattening her legs to bring them together, the action made the occupier feel even bigger, and she whimpered. "How does it feel?"

There were no words for how it felt to have this thing

he'd crafted nestling inside her in a place none of them could see. No one but them would ever know it was there. Devon didn't respond and the vibration started. After a gasp of surprise, her hips began to move. Instead of up and down, they writhed around, trying to experience every whisper of joy that he was bringing to her.

The space inside her was heated and enlivened with throbbing arousal. "Zave," she whispered and began to massage her own breasts.

The vibration grew. "Only with permission," he said. "Put your hands above your head."

Devon did as he said, but it was almost too much to hear his voice and at the same time feel the stirring sensation build to critical mass in her core. The power of vibration increased in time with her gasped breaths and desperate exhales.

"God," she breathed. "God!"

"How does it feel?"

Each word though husky was louder than the last. "It feels so good. So good," she said.

"What are you thinking about now?"

His voice delivered a dose of agitated endorphins to her. "About you," she said. "About how you're doing this to me. How you're here in this room watching me." When he ratcheted it higher, she yelped.

"Is that what you want, shy? More?"

"Yes. God, Zave…"

"Touch your breasts," he said. "Feel them, squeeze them. Think about my hands on them, how it would feel to have me touch you."

"Yes," she cried out. "Yes! I need you to touch me!"

"No," he said. "You imagine it. Think about what I'm doing to you and the pleasure building in your pussy. That's my gift in there, making you feel so good. My hands are making it work to get you off. Forget the world, think about that one spot in your body, under my control. The way you feel now, it's a reaction to what I'm doing to you. I make you feel good, shy. I want to make you feel good."

"You do," she said. "Oh, lord, you do!"

Her hips were rocking, rising and falling, pressing down deep into the lush mattress and then lifting to squeeze her thighs together. The vibration amplified to beyond what she could handle. Her hands ran over her body and down her abdomen, to push between her thighs. Her feet left the bed when she bent her knees up to open her legs wide.

Clasping herself, her fingers played over her clit. "Oh, I need you," she called. "Please!"

The vibration dropped away and she cried out in dismay. Devon was so close to the verge of orgasm, and yet he'd just snatched it away. "I'm going to make you come," he grumbled.

"Yes!" she begged. "Yes! Please!"

"Just like you wanted, I'm right here, I'm in control. I'm going to make you come, shy."

"Yes!"

"Our secret, shy?"

"Yes!" she screamed out again, ready to promise him anything.

Rubbing her fingers between her own folds, she began to tease her opening. "Only with my permission," he said. "Hands above your head."

And although it pained her to do so when she was close to release, Devon complied. Her reward was a return to maximum vibration and the cascade of hormones took her to a point of no return. "Zave! Oh, God, yes! Please!"

"You want it?" he asked, playing with the rhythm. Tormenting her with an ebb and flow of speed, enticing her to what would be a powerful end. "Tell me what you want."

"I want you," she said. "I want this! I need you!"

Overcome and out of control of her senses, Devon couldn't be here, writhing on this bed, with every inch of her alive and aroused without feeling more than gratitude toward him. Turning to crawl to the end of the bed, she clambered up. Barely looking at him, she managed to wrap her arms and legs around him to plant her mouth on his in time with the pinnacle of orgasm.

He didn't object to her kiss, he welcomed it, and twined his strong tongue around hers. Devon couldn't breathe, and didn't want to, as she poured all of her desire into this kiss. Throwing her head back, she gasped and called out his name when an aftershock turned into another full-blown climax.

"You're going to need practice."

The depth of his voice almost scared her because it was so close. Somewhere between laying on the bed and launching herself onto him, she'd developed an amnesia that was just starting to clear. The chemicals of arousal had made her bold and forgetful.

This wasn't a dream. It was reality.

She'd literally mounted the man standing at the foot of her bed. Still heaving in breaths, Devon panted them out, and although her eyes were open, her vision was blurred by the hormones pulsing through her. Every vein was stretched by the torrent of blood rushing through its journey.

"Practice?" she asked.

"This is against the rules," he said, his hands nowhere near her skin.

"Against the rules?" Repeating what he said was easier than trying to come with new sentences of her own.

"On the bed, shy. You're supposed to stay on the bed."

Because this was about her pleasure. He developed these toys, not only for her enjoyment, but to negate the need for him to touch her. Reluctant as she was, she climbed off him, over the footboard, and sat down in the middle of the bed.

"Practice," she said again. "If I need practice, then you stick around, right?"

"Not tonight," he said, recognizing her ploy to try and keep him near. "I want you to give them to me. Both of them."

She knew exactly where the egg was, the vibrator she wasn't so sure of. But before she could think about removing the now-still egg from inside, she became aware of her nudity. Sitting cross-legged, with him just a few feet away, she had no modesty.

He'd seen her naked before, but this was different,

this was by choice, and they were alone after sharing an intimacy.

"Take it out," he said. Leaning back, she lifted her knees and found the silicone cord that allowed her to follow his instruction. When she noticed how intent his focus was on what she was doing, she wanted to kiss him again. "Find the other one."

Rolling onto her front, she fumbled around on the mattress, under the pillows, only to find that the vibrator had fallen onto the floor. Hanging off the edge of the bed to reach it, Devon probably gave him a better view of her ass than he'd expected. But the man had just watched her screaming for him, climaxing around the gift he'd given her while he controlled her experience.

One toy was wet and one was dry, and she was going to offer to wash them, but he took both from her after she sat up and before she could open her mouth. Something about holding her hand over his, with her juices smudged between them, gratified her all over again.

That was evidence of what he'd done to her, and she prayed it would entice him to want to do it again and maybe to get closer next time, so she could leave her juices on another part of him.

"Lord," she said, curling her fingers. "Thank you."

"Satisfied?"

"For now," she whispered. Incremental progress may be all she could ever hope for, and she wouldn't push too hard too fast. If she took each concession and was encouraged by each victory, eventually they would reach the summit of her true desire.

"Get some sleep, shy."

"Yes, lord."

Sinking back into the sheets, she slid her hands up beneath the pillows and closed her eyes. Wearing a broad smile, she dreamed of the next ecstasy he'd deliver her to.

SIXTEEN

"I NEED TO talk to Zara." Those were the first words Devon heard when she walked into the dining room the following morning.

Though they weren't directed at her, they did make her stop because she hadn't expected Zave to be in this room, sitting at the head of the table. Yet, there he was, talking to Thad who was seated at his left eating brunch.

The table was covered with food, and Bess stood at the foot of the table folding laundry from one basket into another.

"That will give Zar the shock of her life," Thad said in reaction to what Zave had said, and the doctor raised his brows at her in what she guessed was a *good morning*.

Thad carried on eating. Zave was taking notes in a pad to the left of his plate that was clear now but showed signs it had been used. Moving forward, she sank into the chair at his right and rested her palm over his knuckles and curled her fingers, sharing with him a more physical good morning.

In another surprise, Zave twisted his hand in a quarter turn to squeeze her fingers, just for a brief second, but it was more than she could've hoped for.

"It needs to be done," Zave said, having not missed

a second of his writing.

"What's the problem?" Thad asked.

Devon selected the juice pitcher and filled up her glass as she listened to the men converse. "Some of the language is a bit hazy," Zave muttered.

"Ambiguity has never been your friend," Thad responded. "You think you'll be able to hold a conversation with Zara? I guess she'll hold it for you."

Zave kept writing, while Thad ate. "She's been the liaison for this merger, and she's done a fine job," Zave said. "It's not her fault that the talking heads at the top of the chain want a slice of the pie for themselves."

"But you have to shut them down," Thad said. "Make sure they know who's in charge."

"Thad can do it," Bess said. "He can call Zara, if you're uncomfortable doing it."

"No," Zave said. "Brodie entrusted this to me."

"And much as he hates it," Thad said, watching his cousin write. "He'll put his discomfort aside because he has some weird bond with Brodie. And given what we expect Brodie to do for the Kindred, he takes the greatest risk. So it's sort of right that the rest of us should pick up the slack when he asks us to."

"When he so rarely asks for anything," Bess said. "Brodie has zero business experience, while Zave has plenty. Kindred members use their skills for the good of the group, those are the rules."

Brodie took the biggest risk, she wondered what that meant and what skill he used to benefit the Kindred. "Brodie has a company?" Devon asked, picking out a bagel.

"Inherited it," Thad said. "The McCormack family firm, after his brother died. Brodie never took anything to do with it, it was always his father and brother's domain. But there's no one else left in that line, so while he remains the majority shareholder, he's signing all decision-making over to Zave and allowing the companies to be merged. Which is easy, because Zave is the sole shareholder of Knight Corp, so he can pretty much do what he wants. And everyone who knows him knows, as long as he's in control, Zave is happy."

She hadn't expected Zave to be looking at her when she drew her eyes around to him, but he was. While his gaze tested her, she smiled. Yes, she knew all about how he liked to be in control, and she'd learned a lot about herself last night in allowing him to have it over her.

Placing her hand on his again, he turned his hand to hold her fingers like before. This time, he didn't let go even after he went back to his writing. Devon hadn't put anything on her bagel, but she'd happily eat it dry if it meant holding his hand in this public place, so that was what she started to do.

Thad was preoccupied by the physical connection. "Is it really the time to be thinking about business?" he asked. "Or other distractions? Did you forget about the message you got this morning?"

"I didn't forget," Zave mumbled, writing something else. "I'm getting these things in order now, so we can move when we have to. We have plenty of time for prep, this is a standard mission, one we've done before. It could take weeks for them to confirm."

"I'll have to talk to my boss," Thad said.

"Wait? A mission?" she asked.

Thad didn't answer, neither did Zave, and Bess stopped folding. "Once they get the next call, it'll be just you and me for a couple of days," Bess said.

But Zave never left the island, he'd told her that himself except to fulfill one specific need. "There's going to be an auction?" she asked, panic was the only discernable emotion in her voice. "But what about—"

"It's a different group," Zave said. "We haven't missed our chance, this doesn't affect the information you gave me. Swift is figuring it out. The men who had you only hold one or two auctions a year."

Okay, so that was something of a relief. The special "meet" that she'd heard them talk about was happening before the next auction of the group who'd held her. That didn't stop another gang selling their merchandise, they worked to a different schedule.

"We haven't heard from these guys for a while. It will

be interesting to see what they have," Thad said.

"I'm more interested in their setup than their stock," Zave said. "But I'm sure we'll bring something home."

A woman, one who would occupy the room that Devon had woken up in. It was odd that even though she'd been intimate with this man and their relationship was nothing but ambiguity, she didn't experience jealousy.

It didn't occur to her to be insecure about him seeing other vulnerable, exposed women. No jealousy, despite the fact that he would select one, spend money for her, and bring her back to his private abode.

All Devon felt was concern, terrible worry, that he was going to such a dangerous place to do such a righteous thing. At any second, he could be discovered, and there would be no mercy. He may have done this before, he may know he could hold his own if questioned or accused by the criminals who ran these human trafficking operations, but she felt sick.

Devon was a novice, she'd never watched Zave go to war before, and she didn't like how helpless it made her feel to know all she'd be able to do was sit here and wait as each second ticked by until he returned.

"I have work to do," Zave said. "I'll meet you downstairs in an hour." Thad nodded, his mouth full of food.

When Zave stood up, she didn't let go of his hand. "Lord," she said but wasn't quite sure what question she wanted to ask or what reassurance she needed.

He drew a knuckle from one of her ears to the other, following the line of her jaw. "I haven't forgotten about you," he said. "I'll come to you."

And while the others might not understand what that meant, she did. Although she was reluctant, she let him go because she was going to cause more of a scene than she already had if she didn't. He stalked away to his door and disappeared.

"Lord?" Thad asked. "You guys are into some kinky shit."

Bess clucked. "Oh, you be quiet. Couples the world over have pet names for each other. I think it's lovely. He calls her 'shy.'"

Devon knew that but couldn't remember if he'd done it in front of Bess or if maybe he used her pet name in private when she wasn't around. "Is there anything I can do?" Devon asked.

"Not at this end of the deal," Thad answered. "Zave's right, we have time. Carlos calls ahead to see how many buyers he can round up and if they have any specific tastes they want fulfilled." Just as Zave had explained. "And it gives their customers a chance to make plans. When it's time, we get a message no more than thirty-six hours before. They like to keep the details as vague as possible until the last minute, just in case any uninvited parties try to drop in." See: law enforcement. She understood his implication.

What had happened to her seemed like a distant memory and one she thought was secure in her past. This made her realize just how present the situation was for all of them and specifically how dangerous it was for Zave.

"They can just call you at any time?" she asked.

"Sometimes it's a week after the initial call, sometimes it's a month, sometimes it's as many as three."

"Then what?"

"We go, find the girl who looks most in need, most vulnerable, usually she's the last one of the night, the one the real sick fucks pay big bucks for. We bring her back here and… you know what happens next."

Zave would have to sit there while girl after girl was put on the block. "Have you ever thought about bringing back more than one?"

"Sure. But it gets unwieldy. We only have so much space in the chopper. Plus, if they wake up and learn there's a dozen more here just like them, they might think we're another factory. Who's likely to spill the beans? Who's likely to keep our secret? When we're dealing with a large group, it gets difficult to read them and keep a lid on things."

"We always wish we could do more," Bess said.

Thad was more pragmatic. "We are only a small band of people, and I hold down a full-time job. Zave always keeps his distance, so it's down to Mom to figure out our guests. If we were to bring back too many girls, I'd never be able to ensure all of their medical needs were met, not single-handedly."

He didn't sound guilty, but the rush of his words betrayed that he'd thought about what she was asking, probably more than once. Maybe he did feel guilty that they couldn't help more people. Yet everything he said made sense. Devon was sorry she'd brought it up and made him uncomfortable.

"You can help me," Bess said. "I thought we might take a tour outside today."

"Outside?" Devon asked. "I think I might like that." She smiled. "I think I'm ready. I've seen so many slivers of the sea through these narrow windows… I've been thinking about swimming."

"Swim?" Thad asked, glancing at his mother. "In the ocean?"

Devon didn't share their concern. "Why not?"

"It will be freezing for one thing and the currents for another."

"The rocks offer some protection. If I stay in their shelter, near shore, I should be okay."

Bess wasn't any more enthusiastic than Thad. "There are two swimming pools in the building," Bess said. "Heated ones. One is in the gym in the basement and the other is in Zave's suite. I'm sure he'd let you use either."

A test perhaps. If he did then Bess would have confirmation on the relationship. Except she probably got that from the earlier hand-holding. "It's not the same as being outside," Devon said. "I've always loved swimming in the open."

"What would you wear?" Thad asked, clearing his plate. "You don't have a bathing suit."

That was true and a point she hadn't considered, but she wouldn't let it stop her. "There's no one around," she said. "You guys have told me that we're alone for miles."

Again, Thad looked to his mother and while Bess was smiling, there was a distinct rosy hue in Thad's cheeks. "You mean… you'd go skinny-dipping?"

Devon smiled and wondered if she was so cute when

she blushed. "You're a doctor, what do you care? You see a thousand naked women every day. Bess has all the same parts that I do."

"And Zave?" Bess asked, drawing out his name in a drawl laced with innuendo.

Devon could only laugh. "The first time he saw me, I was naked. I don't think he'd bat an eye."

"If he learns you're planning to prance around naked outside, I think he would have plenty to say," Bess said.

"Do you think I should ask his permission?" Devon asked, considering how far their numbered rules reached and if she should be doing as he commanded outside the bedroom or not.

Bess was folding again. "I think it would be an interesting conversation if you did."

"What did he mean he would come to you?" Thad asked, giving Devon an opportunity to blush.

"Nothing," she said. "Nothing important." Although she'd already eaten half her bagel, she started to spread cream cheese on the other half to busy herself while the other two exchanged their furtive squints. "Going outside would give me a chance to draw more of the water. It would be great to have oils and—" she stopped herself.

"What's wrong?" Bess asked.

"Nothing, it's just, I should learn to watch my mouth." Rolling her eyes upwards, she knew Zave couldn't hear but knew he would find out what she'd said. "I have a habit of making wishes and finding they come true pretty quick."

Bess laughed and even Thad joined in. "Yeah, he's not subtle," Bess said.

"Always trying to compensate for something," Thad said.

Compensate for what? Devon wondered, taking a bite of her bagel. Was spoiling her supposed to make up for what had happened to Bronwyn in the same way what he did at the auctions was supposed to make up for it? Devon liked being in his thoughts, liked that he cared about her needs, but she didn't want him fulfilling them out of obligation.

"It would be nice to get a wide view," Devon said, moving the conversation on. "I can't get that in any of the rooms I have access to. I'm limited in—"

"Not too limited," Thad said.

Devon clarified. "I can get up and down several of the hallways, but as far as rooms go, I have this one, the kitchen, my bedroom…"

"You have access to more than that," Bess said and came closer. "I'm sorry, I didn't think to say. I supposed you would be naturally inquisitive… like Zara, she's always opening doors and sticking her head in just to see what she can find."

"What are you talking about?" Devon asked.

Thad answered, "Last I looked at the grid, your fingerprint had been authorized for most of the rooms in the house."

"My fingerprint?" she asked, having never thought to try any of the restricted rooms, in part because she was worried her attempt would be flagged on some system somewhere. It might upset the Kindred to know she was snooping where she shouldn't be. "You fingerprinted me when I arrived?"

He scoffed. "Nothing so crude," Thad said. "We got it digitally."

"My fingerprint exists digitally?" she asked. "I've never been arrested. I've never—"

"No, but you had an iPhone," he said and stood up. "You should snoop around, most of those rooms only see Bess here when she goes in to clean them. Zave won't be upset. You won't get in anywhere he doesn't want you to be… If he's getting his shit in order, I better do the same."

Thad left and Devon turned to Bess. "I suppose you have some more exploring to do," Bess said, returning to her laundry. "Eat up, girl and get to it."

There were some rooms that Devon was more curious about than others. Zave's private lab, where she'd been only once, was the place she was most interested in. Except if there was any room that would have remained restricted, it would be that one.

She wasn't sure she'd even be able to find it again. But if she did, that was one room she didn't mind being caught trying to get into because its occupant was the one she craved time with, whether he was happy with her or not.

Besides, she had to ask his permission to skinny-dip, and as Bess had said, that could lead to an interesting conversation.

SEVENTEEN

THE ANXIETY OF that morning lessened over the days that came after it. For almost eight weeks, Devon's life bloomed on its new path, becoming something altogether too wonderful. She'd gone from abject depravity, living with almost nothing, to existing in the lap of luxury with a man who had the power to give her anything in the world her heart desired. And he frequently did.

Sitting at the end of her bed, Devon's hands covered Zave's that were curled over the footboard. "I don't know how I'll feel in this house without you," she said.

He was crouched on the other side of the footboard, with his forearms resting along it. Devon slid her fingers between his and squeezed before brushing her palms up his bare forearms and back down again.

"You survive in this house without me every day," he said.

She still slept in her own room, and it was certainly more hers now than it had been when she first slept here. Filled with the possessions Zave provided her, he made sure her every craving was fulfilled. Either the Knight Corp CEO made items for her personally, or he got Thad to bring them back during his frequent commutes.

Having access to most of the rooms and all of the island, there was plenty for Devon to explore. Following Zave's example, Devon had tried the running thing but found that she preferred to walk so she could absorb the beauty of her surroundings.

Zave would lap her on his runs, but she'd come to enjoy their brief encounters. As he passed, he would touch her, sometimes on the arm or hand, other times he tugged her hair. Emboldened by their nights together, she often gave his ass a smack as he ran by.

For a time, she'd try to keep up with him, but she loved staring into the wild landscape too much. Her walks were interrupted by her need to stop and sketch when inspiration struck, and Zave had, of course, provided her an artist's satchel for all her supplies after he saw her struggling to carry everything in her arms.

Devon could sit for hours on the rocks or on the beach. Bess and Thad had been sure that Zave would veto the idea of her skinny-dipping in the ocean, and they'd been right. But she'd since discovered that the island was much larger than she'd assumed it would be, and it held some wonderful secrets.

Four miles long by almost two wide, Devon hadn't begun to cover all of the land. One of her greatest discoveries was of an enclosed lagoon, hidden by overhanging rocks and trees. Although the water was cold, it was sheltered from the wind and gave her an escape when she wanted to get out of the house.

But it was their after-hours fun that added the true thrill to her life. Zave came to her almost every night these days. On the few occasions he didn't, she tossed and turned, tormenting herself with notions of where he was and why he wasn't with her.

Zave brought all sorts of gadgets to tease every inch of her body. All of them were activated and controlled by him using remotes that she never saw. Each toy contorted her pleasure, and Zave had made bringing her to climax without ever laying a hand on her body into an art form.

Her lord didn't knock anymore and she was used to

being exposed for him, she enjoyed it, anticipated it. Their rules hadn't changed, and while she loved what his toys did for her, she wished he'd spend the night. She wished he would let himself take from her instead of doing nothing but give.

"Can I ask you something?" she asked, leaning forward enough that her breasts touched the footboard.

Except he anticipated that and lowered his forearms to ensure that part of her body never made contact with him.

"You may," he said.

She was getting used to asking permission during their illicit encounters in the dark, and it was becoming habit whenever he was near. "Do you ever...?" He'd made it obvious that he didn't want to touch her, and he didn't allow her to throw herself on him and kiss him as she had done on their first night. But he didn't shy away or flinch anymore when she touched him with her hands. So Devon let a fingertip move to his temple. "Do you ever think about me?" she asked. "When you leave here? When you're alone?"

"I think about you all the time," he said. "Some of your toys take time to figure out."

"Not that." Sensing that he was being deliberately obtuse, she smiled. "When you're alone, you know? How many times have you seen me come now? It's been two months since you first came into my bedroom. You came in here and watched me... I just want to know how you do it, how you keep your hands off."

"It's not easy, if that's what you're asking," he said, taking her hand from his temple to enclose it in both of his.

"Sometimes I feel like an experiment," she said. "Like you're observing me to keep note of the results."

"It's nothing like that," he said, his voice full of offense. "You told me you wanted me in the room with you. If you want me to leave—"

"No," she said, that would be a punishment, a torture more than she'd be able to endure. Twining her fingers between his, she wouldn't let go. "I just... what I feel..." With the hand he hadn't captured, Devon brushed her palm over his cheek. The solid wood of the footboard acted as a barrier between them, just the way he liked it. "I feel so selfish. You get nothing from this."

"I get more than you think," he said. "It's not conventional."

She laughed and bowed lower to let her cheek rest on her arm. "A billionaire living in exile on his own private island who rescues the girl from the evil sex slave merchants, I wouldn't have expected conventional."

Devon had enjoyed his toys, their games, and the words he used, as well as the questions he asked her in the night. During the days, she helped Bess and did her chores then went about her exercise and her sketching. All the while Devon thought about the man and why their relationship was the way it was. It didn't take long for her to reach an honest conclusion: Zave was still punishing himself. He wasn't ready to let himself be happy with her, with anyone.

Bess had expressed admiration for how much more engaged he was in company business and how he spent more time with the executives at Knight Corp to ensure the CI merger was supervised by him. No project had been so closely monitored by a Knight since before his father had died.

Bess complimented Devon on how she'd drawn him out in a way they could never have done without her. Although Devon didn't think she was responsible for his awakening. He had to have been on the verge of it before he came to the auction where she'd been sold to him.

Devon and Zave kept their after-hours activities to themselves, but it was obvious to Bess and Thad that something was going on between them. They were never overt in their affection, and Zave did his best to hold her at arms' length. But there was no doubting that something was thriving between them.

Devon imagined it was only a matter of time before he made it real and joined her in her sheets. "You never touch me," she said. "Yet no guy has ever satisfied me so thoroughly. I guess I just want to know if you get any satisfaction from me when you're… alone…" There was her word again and he must have heard the smile in her voice.

"Like in the shower?"

"Yes," she answered. "That's exactly what I mean."

Picking up their joined hands, she rubbed the back of his against her cheek. "I try not to," he said. "But, yeah, I might have slipped a couple of times."

She guessed that he was being modest in underestimating what went on when she wasn't around. Despite not being present during these slips, it boosted her confidence to know that she was in his thoughts when he was being intimate with himself.

"You should get some sleep," he said.

Devon whined because the saddest part of her day was when he slipped out of her room at night. "You're going to leave me with that thought? Haven't we got time for another round?"

"That would be your third tonight," he said.

Lowering her own tone, she murmured her words on his knuckles. "We've done three before."

"And I would stay for a four, five, and six, but you know I have to fly before sunrise."

The call had come. The auction was on. His reminder made her let him go, and it cooled her desire. Folding her forearms on the footboard, she laid her head on them, because she was back to her original point of how she would feel about being in this house without him.

"What will I do? How will I sleep?" she asked. "I always sleep after our visits, when you command me to close my eyes. I won't without your instruction, I never do."

He picked her hair from her face and tucked it over her shoulder, managing to touch only her hair and avoid all contact with her skin. "I command you to sleep well now. I command you to stay here, to sleep well, and not to worry for a second."

An impossible request. But he was trying to reassure her. "How can I not worry?" she whispered. "I know where you're going and what those people are capable of. If they found out—"

"They never will," he said. "How could they? I'm looking at the last girl we saved. They could never know that you are still here. Even if they did, they'd never assume that you were happy here... you are, happy here, aren't you?"

"Happier than I've ever been," she said.

The gang would assume that she was being subjected to his deviant pleasures when in truth it was her own gratification that was his sole priority.

"This is a different group anyway."

The message had come through earlier that night. He and Thad had scrambled to make plans. But Zave had stolen this time to be with her, this was an intermission from planning and resting. He shouldn't be here. He didn't have time and this wasn't part of his tried and tested routine. Usually they got the word and followed a strict procedure. But this was the first time they'd gotten this call since she'd come into his life, and he'd come to her room because he'd known she needed him to.

"I'll worry every minute," she said. "And what if I need something? What if I need you?"

She'd never be so selfish as to ask him to stay. What he did out there was important, it was his job, his mission. But Devon wanted to make it clear to him how much he meant to her without putting too much pressure on him or their relationship.

"Write me a list," he said. "Anything you need. I promise I'll get it to you as soon as I get back."

"I have a feeling there will be only one thing on that list," she said, opening her arms to stretch them out to rest them on his shoulders.

Despite the hours that he spent in the gym making his body hard and fit, it couldn't be comfortable for him to remain crouched for so long. Though inviting him into the bed would be met with opposition. This was as close as he allowed them to get. The thick plank of the footboard reassured him that there was no way for their bodies, or rather their hips, to come into contact with each other.

"What will that be?" he asked.

"You."

Bending her elbows, Devon tried to hold him, to pull herself closer, but he resisted. "Shy," he warned.

Whenever he left her to go to his room, she was disappointed. This time was different, he was going to his room now, sure, but in a few hours, he'd be leaving the island, and she'd never been here without him. "Please," she whispered. "You can't leave without…"

There was no wiggle room in his certainty that he wanted to stay out of her bed, and he was losing patience with her constant requests. "Without what?" he said. "Every night you ask me to spend the night, and every time I say the same thing."

No. She didn't need to be reminded of that. "I won't ask you to sleep here when I know you need your rest."

"So what are you asking?"

Something much simpler. "For a kiss," she said. "And a promise."

"Of what?"

"That you'll come back to me. That you won't leave me here without you for a minute longer than you have to."

"You've been encouraging me to spend less time locked up alone," he said. "Isn't leaving the island a positive step?"

Yes, it might be in another situation, if he wasn't going away to put his life on the line to save other people. If he went down there and got into trouble, said the wrong word to the wrong person, or got caught in someone else's crossfire, she might never know what had gone on.

"Will you promise me that you'll do whatever it takes to be away from me for as little time as possible?"

"I can promise that if something happens to us out there, you'll be bequeathed all of your toys."

"But I'll have lost my lord." Without her puppet master, they would remain inert and would never mean the same without him pushing their buttons to stimulate hers. "Zave," she murmured, pulling herself higher to hang over the end of the bed, getting as close to him as she could.

"Yes, shy?"

"Promise me," she exhaled the words so quietly but was dazed by her proximity to his lips, and he wasn't withdrawing.

In fact, it was him who closed the hair's breadth of space between them. The press of his kiss was so thorough that she tasted her promise, and she let herself be swept into it with the movement of his tongue as it comforted hers. He soothed her worries and assured her there would be a tomorrow and a time for more games and intimacy. That this wasn't finished. That this wouldn't be the last kiss.

Except it didn't last long enough. Before she could get too excited or try to build the pace, he pulled back. "This was never meant to happen," he said, and when he stroked the hair that was loose over her face, she caught a ragged breath.

He so rarely allowed himself to touch her. If his kiss was a gift, then his touch was a blessing. "What wasn't?" she asked.

"I was supposed to live the rest of my life in celibate isolation," he said.

"Isolation works for me."

Having spent her life chasing her next paycheck to pay bills, she'd never been able to submerge herself in her inner passion for art so thoroughly. Not only did Zave provide all the supplies she needed, but he had some wonderful pieces in his own collection that she'd discovered while investigating the rooms and halls of this house. Each new space was a treat, and she never got bored of learning the new corners she came across.

"But not the other part," he asked.

The celibacy. "If it was a choice and not a punishment, I'd support it," she said. "But you don't abstain because you want to. You do it because you believe you don't deserve pleasure and happiness."

"I had those things in abundance in my youth. Enough to last me a lifetime."

Zave wasn't the only one who struggled to hold onto his patience at times. "Maybe you had an abundance of sex and drugs and fun, but you weren't happy then. You underestimate how much of my happiness will come from yours."

"Will come? Future tense? I don't make you happy?"

"I'm happy every minute I spend with you. But I'd like to be able to lie in your arms, to wake up and see your face. I can't feel relaxed and secure here until I know that this is real, as real for you as it is for me."

"It's real," he said. "I wanted to refuse to let it be and tried to deny to myself that it was… I should've put a stop to this long ago. But it's real, shy. I don't need to stick my dick in you to know that."

"Maybe it's something I need," she said, trying to nuzzle his lips. "You do make me happy, Xavier. But until you can share your bed with me, you can never share your heart. I guess your dick is like a symbol of completing our relationship. Until you can give it up, I'll never be able to look you in the eye and tell you how I feel."

"I've been avoiding this conversation," he said. "Those bastards brought us together and because they're tearing us apart, they're forcing us to confront what this is."

Devon wasn't comfortable giving the cartels credit for anything positive. But his point was valid. "We don't need to work it all out. I just need you to swear you won't stay away."

He tasted her, and when the tip of his tongue ran the width of her lip, she almost fell right off the end of the bed. "I swear. I won't be gone a minute longer than is necessary. I will come back to you, shy. You're my sun, the light that I revolve around now. A star that exudes energy and life, scorching me with your fever, sustaining me with your radiance. You give me an anchoring orbit to a sure and certain path I never want to waver from now that I've found it."

He was romantic. She had no idea that he could charm her like this. "Zave," she exhaled.

"Leaving you is a new kind of cruel punishment, worse than any I've endured before. I won't survive away from you for long. I won't stop thinking about you."

"Lord," she murmured. "My heart won't beat until it's near to yours again. Hurry home to me."

"That you can count on."

He had to go and do his job and she had to let him, but she'd worry every minute they were apart. She'd think of him, wonder where he was, crave his safety. Already she anticipated the joy she'd experience when he came home safe.

But the time between now and then would be torture for her, as well as him.

EIGHTEEN

"I'LL LET YOU fold his laundry, if it will make you feel better," Bess said, having just brought a hamper into the kitchen from one of the back rooms. Putting it on the opposite side of the island where Devon sat, she opened it.

Devon smiled and rolled her eyes away from the woman, whose offer hadn't been serious. After tapping her pencil on her lip, she carried on writing.

"You've been scribbling in that since the minute he left," Bess said. "What's so important for you to get down on paper?" If she'd been close enough, she would've given Devon a nudge because her lips curled in a saucy smirk. "Or are you writing raunchy love letters?"

"Not love letters," Devon said, considering how Zave would react if she did write to him that way. "I'm trying to get it all down."

Examining the words she'd already scrawled on the paper she was working on, she reflected on how she understood the definition of each word but couldn't think about the meaning they took on when she put them in the order that spelled out her ordeal.

"Get what down? Your experience?"

"I don't want to miss anything," Devon said. "And I

feel… I don't know, Zave and I have had so many conversations about it now that I just… I want to get it down in a linear way."

Bess laughed, which startled Devon, given what they were talking about. "I knew you were having an effect on him. I didn't realize it was working the other way. Since when have you been so logical?"

Devon had never been accused of being logical before. Yet it made her smile. "I guess I know if it makes sense to him, it makes more sense to me. It makes it easier for him to share with the others and, I don't know, maybe Swift can pull out some details that I'm not seeing. So many people came and went… I didn't see faces, so I gave nicknames to the voices I recognized. But one could easily have been another and when you're malnourished and dehydrated, sometimes my thoughts were muddled."

The dishwasher beeped to indicate that it had completed its cycle. "That's understandable," Bess said.

The women had eaten dinner late. Once the men were gone, Bess admitted a secret, that she enjoyed walking the grounds at night. It was something Zave and Thad discouraged her from doing because they were always worried she'd hurt herself in the dark or that the temperature would be too low.

While walking arm-in-arm, Bess told stories about her brother, Art, who had founded the Kindred as a lone man before he took on Brodie. It started with him and a hodge-podge of friends who weren't particularly loyal, they just helped each other out.

After Brodie's parents died, Art had taken on the teenager. Art straightened out for a while, but Brodie had needed a focus and Art had missed the adventure. So they started taking on projects together. Somewhere along the way, in the Far East she believed, they'd met Swift, an American with no ties, a high IQ and an axe to grind.

Art had mentored Brodie and molded him into a capable marksman. Swift had natural talent in his own field and had honed his skills in the underground. Art gave him stability, offered light and a helping hand. The three men had come to rely on each other as family.

At various points throughout their walks, Devon had freaked herself out after hearing strange noises or experiencing unexpected, strange feelings. Bess had reminded her that they were alone. Bess admitted to feeling uneasy at times, but as long as she stayed near the shore or kept the house in sight, she couldn't be scared here. Devon had come to enjoy her strolls with the woman.

They walked while their meal slow cooked and ate together in the kitchen rather than at the large dining table that reminded them of their missing men.

Leaving her paper, Devon went to the dishwasher to begin unloading it. It seemed only fair for her to do this job while Bess dealt with the linens that she was folding to be ironed. Devon had noticed the number of chores Bess did and had considered how unfair it was that she be treated like a housekeeper. Except since the men had gone, the intensity of her cleaning and the amount of tasks she took on grew. Devon deduced keeping busy was Bess' way of coping while the boys were far away doing something dangerous.

"That's sensible," Bess said. "Putting everything down on paper in black and white. It will help you process your trauma too."

"It means there's something permanent that can stay here, in case something happens to me."

Bess stopped folding. "And just what do you think will happen to you?"

"I don't know," Devon said, putting away the plates. She'd gotten to know her way around this kitchen while prepping and cooking with Bess every night. "Anything can happen at any time. I was snatched off the street once, there's no telling when it might happen again."

"You don't really think that," Bess said, propping a fist on her hip. "Do you think that my Kindred boys would let anything happen to you? Besides, you're here. You're not planning on going anywhere, are you?"

Devon didn't know what she was planning. She could stay here, but even Bess went back to the mainland sometimes. Thad spent more time there than he did here. "I can't stay here forever."

"Why not?"

"I don't know if that's what Zave wants."

"It's exactly what he wants, and you can't let him think that you're uncertain about being with him or he'll use it as an excuse to push you away."

"I'm too worried about him to think about that," Devon said.

When she did take the time to think about their relationship, she kept coming to the conclusion that she was running out of rabbits to pull from her hat. She'd used every magic trick she knew to tempt him into being with her wholly and completely. Nothing had worked.

"Worrying is part of the job," Bess said.

"I can't…" Devon trailed off when she registered a noise, and Bess perked up at the same moment. "What is that?"

Bess' smile was brief, and she dumped everything she'd been doing to rush toward the door. "They're back."

The noise she recognized as it got louder was the sound of a helicopter returning. Devon stayed in the kitchen listening to it come nearer until she was sure it was going to land right on top of her. She didn't know what to do. Bess had rushed out with purpose, but she knew the procedure, Devon didn't.

Zave and Thad wouldn't be alone, and Devon didn't know if she could face a strange woman being brought here because it would mean witnessing what she'd endured on her own arrival, which was a memory she didn't have.

Torn between a desire to be helpful and her concern that she might get in the way, she didn't know what to do. These people had done this so many times, they had to be a well-oiled machine.

The rotors slowed and the sound died off. The silence became unbearable, and when she couldn't stand it anymore, she followed Bess' route out of the room but didn't know which entrance the women were brought in. It didn't take long for her to find out.

She was standing on the bottom stair, against the

newel post in the foyer, considering whether or not she should try to locate the room she'd awoken in. That was the one place she hadn't tried to go and knew that part of the house had been remodeled for the purposes of the women they brought here to save. Whenever she recognized the décor change while on her expeditions, she turned and walked the other way instead of confronting it.

The front door opened and Bess came in fussing over an unconscious woman in a wheelchair who was being pushed by Zave, while Thad did something with a band around the woman's arm. They carried on across the foyer to a set of double doors on the left in the shadow of the arch under the mezzanine opposite where her bedroom was located.

Zave glanced at her once, but she said nothing, sure that she must look like a rabbit in the headlights, observing a scene that she'd once been party to. Although if what she'd heard was true, she hadn't been wheeled in a chair, she'd been carried by the lord.

Something was said within the trio while the doors stood opened. When they closed again, Devon wasn't sure if she was alone until Zave appeared from the shadows, striding toward her. He didn't greet her with words, and she couldn't find any that would fit the moment.

The fixed growl on his face made her clasp her hands beneath her chin, as she tried to figure out if he was angry at her, traumatized by what he'd seen, or if something else was at play. Zave didn't slow down, he just crouched to sweep her off her feet. Wrapping her legs around him, their mouths clashed in a full-tongue, no-hesitation kiss.

She was gripping his shoulders and gasping for breath when he finally broke the seal of their mouths, and that was when she discovered they'd ascended the stairs and were now moving along a corridor that that she didn't recognize.

Dazed by his show of passion, she tried to recall where he'd been. "Shouldn't we help?" she asked.

So intent on her mouth and his path, Zave showed no compassion. "They've got it," he replied.

"She was in a chair, and there's stairs—"

"There's an elevator," he said. "You never had reason

to be in it."

Because Devon had been unconscious when she arrived here and been in his arms. Stroking his face, she ran her fingers into his hair and teased his mouth with hers. "I missed you," she said. "I was so worried."

"I told you not to worry, didn't I?"

They stopped at a door at the end of the corridor, he got them through it with his fingerprint, and took her up the spiral staircase she recognized. Going through another door, they were traversing the corridor that brought them to his lab.

He was taking her into his lair. Except, instead of stopping in the lab, Zave swung a right to head for the door in darkness. Taking her up another set of curved stairs, they reached a grand room in a circular space with windows too high to see out of.

The bed to the left had a high wooden headboard, and although the frame was ornate, the sheets on the bed were plain white. There was only one pillow and only one blanket. He'd been right when he said he considered this a prison. He gave himself no luxury, the room was all but bare.

Devon only noticed these things after he settled her down, placing her head on the single pillow. She expected a game and while she wasn't quite prepared for it, his kiss had warmed her up. Except instead of retrieving the toys from wherever he kept them, Zave went to the end of the bed to slip her shoes off her feet.

Picking one up, he pressed her instep to his cheek and kissed the tip of her toe before laying her leg back down on the bed. He was never affectionate, never let himself touch her, and he'd never brought her to his bed before.

After sitting on the edge of the mattress, he unbuckled her jeans. Devon lifted her hips to let him pull the clothes off her lower body. Thinking she was helping, she pulled the string at her clavicle to unfasten the first knot on her top, but he grabbed her hand.

"Let me," he said, more fixated on the clothes he was removing than the skin he was exposing. When she was naked, she expected the game to begin. Instead, he stayed on the edge of the bed, perched beside her hip. "Being down there. After this…" He shook his head once and focused on her navel. "It was almost too much, shy."

After this. After them. Now he wasn't just there to save anonymous women. Every one of the women in that place was synonymous with her.

Sitting up, she rested a hand at his throat. "Thank you," she murmured, leaning forward to kiss him. "For going back there, for doing it again, for saving another innocent life. Thank you for saving mine."

Reaching for her temple, his fingers got lost in her hair. When he angled her head, she closed her eyes, expecting his kiss. But she didn't get one. "I've been saving something special," he said. "Would you like to try it out?"

"In your bed?" she asked, her mind drifted and her lips curled with delight. "I'd do anything for you in your bed, lord."

"You'll like this one," he said. "I promise. Now, lay down and close those eyes and let me take care of you."

His lips brushed hers before his body receded and she sank down, stretching her arms out and opening her legs, reveling in the luxury of this bed that was more basic than hers, but its significance was undeniable.

This was his most private space and he'd just invited her in. If he wanted her to leave, he'd have to demand it. Even then, she wasn't sure she'd go without a fight. But for this minute, they needed a distraction. Their craving for each other would deliver them to oblivion.

Devon would let him pamper her, and she'd give him the control that helped to ground him. But tomorrow, she was going to have to let him see that he wasn't the only one progressing in this relationship. She wanted to give him more and she'd find a way to do it.

***

COMING DOWN THE stairs in the nude, Devon yawned, and scratched her fingers through her chaotic locks. Sloping up the hallway, she entered his workspace, assuming she'd find him here since she'd woken up alone. Sure enough, there he was hunched over his drafting table, scribbling something at a frantic pace.

He was so busy concentrating that she considered leaving him alone to work, but she was feeling selfish so kept on going. Drawing a fingertip along the top of his desk, Devon let the digit carry on down the perimeter as she moved around it.

Stopping next to him, she touched his shoulder. Although he glanced at her, Zave kept on working for a few seconds before the pencil fell from his fingers and he turned his stool toward her to examine her exposed flesh.

Her nipples reacted, her face heated, and urgency made her core begin to pulse. "What's this look?" he asked.

She grinned. Putting both hands on his shoulders, she climbed astride his lap. The rules were different now, it was daytime, she was in his private space, and she'd just woken up in his bed. Testing the boundaries seemed appropriate.

"I don't have anything to wear up here," she said. "All of my clothes are in my room downstairs." That was only part of the reason. She could've raided his drawers. Although, snooping may have upset him. She could have put on her dirty clothes but would have been uncomfortable in them. "What are you working on?"

"Hmm?" was his response, which took her attention away from the page she'd glanced at. She saw that he was enraptured by the sight of her breasts.

His concentration made her hope. "Does this do something for you?" she asked, presenting her body.

His hands skimmed onto her hips and she thought just maybe she'd broken through, so she leaned in to close her mouth over his. Kissing him made her confident and wild and bold, things she'd never been anywhere else.

How many other nude women got to interrupt their boyfriends while they were working? To climb on top of them to sink their tongues into their mouths in an attempt to entice them into crossing the carnal line?

"Easy, shy," he said, rubbing her arms as he pushed her away.

Devon was tired of moaning at him about her desire.

"Why can't I have you?" she asked, letting her mouth dance near his. "You create wonderful toys for me that get me off, but I've never pleasured you."

"You pleasure me every day. This is a pleasure. One I shouldn't be taking advantage of." He'd resorted to stroking her shoulders and her neck, avoiding anything further south.

Frustrated, Devon wanted him to relax with her. "It's not the same as what you give me. You pamper me. Spoil me with climax on top of climax. Each day there's a new, incredible gadget and I love every one of them, but I want a part of you."

"There's a part of me in every piece I craft for you."

"Not the part of you I want inside me," she said, kissing him again. "I want to make you feel good, like you make me feel." An idea made her reach for the hem of his tee shirt, but he snatched her wrist and held it up, suspicion prevailing in his gaze. "I promise not to touch your penis. I just want to try something."

His dubious expression was as vehement as the grip of his hand. He wasn't going to give in yet. "It will make me feel good," she said, having learned how to push some of his buttons. "It will make me happy. There's nothing more important to you, right?"

This was enough to make him release her hand, and he allowed her to pull his tee shirt up, over his toned arms, and off over his head. She dropped it to the floor. Drawing her index fingers from his collarbone to his navel, it pained her that he held himself stiff because she was testing the limits of their latest development.

Skimming her hands the width of his shoulders to meet at his spine, Devon let them carry on up into his hair until her elbows rested on each side of his neck. Squeezing herself close, she pressed her torso into his, crushing the cushions of her breasts into the hard planes of his chest.

It felt so good to be touching so much of his hot form, more than she ever had before. With her lips on his, she released a single, long breath into his mouth. The sheer gratification of this progress was almost as good as any orgasm she'd ever had.

"You feel good," she whispered and let her forearms fall against the width of his shoulders behind his neck.

She hung around him, sagging deeper against him. Laying her head on her own arm, she kissed his neck and began to rock her hips, getting closer and closer to the monolith she wished he'd let her sink onto.

Rubbing her cheek on his, Devon whispered into his ear, "You can take off your pants if you want to."

Seizing her hips, he shunted them further down his thighs toward his knees to prevent her center from making contact with his. "I do that and there's a chance…"

"What?" she asked when he didn't finish the strained sentence. "A chance that you might accidently penetrate me? If it was up to me, it would be no accident."

He groaned. "Shy, we've talked about this," he said. Picking her up off his lap, he put her on her feet and then bent to snag his tee shirt from the floor. "You know the rules. Our numbers. Do you want me to make you recite them?"

But their limits were being pushed. "Are we never going to have sex?" she asked.

"I can't."

"You can," she said, eyeing the unmistakable mountain jutting up from inside his sweats. "That looks to me exactly like you can… We can have Thad test me for diseases if you think—"

"Don't be stupid," he said, leaving his stool to push it in. "You're in perfect health."

"Then, what?"

Irritation made him drive a hand through his hair and then ball it into a fist. "I give you pleasure," he spat out. "Every night, every time you ask, I'm there. Anything you want, you get. You get more of me than any other person ever has."

"I don't want to be selfish," she said. "But I want to know what it feels like to have you inside of me. Not one of your toys or something you cooked up in your lab. You, me, flesh, together. Old-fashioned style. You laid me down up there, played with me, and left. You won't even sleep with me."

"Because if I do…"

"What?" she asked, but when she took a step toward him, he retreated one. "Do you think this boundary stops you from caring about me? Is that what you're scared of? You don't want to care about me?"

All of his actions suggested to her that he already did. "No."

"Then, what? Explain to me why you won't touch me with your own hands. How can we be together when you've never touched my breasts or kissed me anywhere beneath my neck? You've never felt what it's like to tease me with your fingers, to sink your dick into me—"

"You think I'm not aware of that?" he asked, his brows leaping up. "Do you think I've failed to notice every opportunity I've ever had to take advantage of you? I get it almost every night. You think I don't think about that all the time?"

Did he? "I wonder," she said. "If you wanted me as much as I want you, you wouldn't be able to help yourself. Look at me swanning around naked, trying to get your attention, trying to find out how to turn you on, how to make you want me, or was I right? Is this just some kind of warped experiment?"

"I'd never use you!" Startled by his own outburst, he took a calming breath. "Shy, I do want you."

"Then have me," she said, opening her arms. Slow in, quick out, her breathing mimicked the rhythm she wanted their bodies to share. "What's stopping you? We're alone. I'm naked. I've already distracted you. There won't be a better time."

Once again, his eyes traveled over her and when he began to inch backwards, she knew she'd lost him. "I'm going for a run."

"A run," she sighed. "I guess that's my cue to get out of here."

"You should get something to eat. Bess will be looking for—"

"Whatever," she said, walking away from him to go back to the bedroom to gather up her things.

He may be able to switch off and cope with his feelings by running along the battered island shore, but she couldn't. Zave thought she made him lose control, and for a minute she'd thought it too. Nothing could be further from the truth.

Devon had done everything in her power to make him want her, to make him wild, but she'd failed. He'd never touch her like she wanted him to. Either she had to get used to living her life with a boyfriend she'd never sleep with, or she had to realize she just wasn't enough.

NINETEEN

AFTER EATING LUNCH alone, Devon was writing at the dining table. She'd tried to complete her latest piece earlier in the day, but her creative juices had been parched by what had happened that morning in Zave's lab.

Thad and Bess came in, one after the other. "She's beautiful," Thad said, continuing the conversation he must have been having with his mother before they entered. "White blonde hair, porcelain skin, and the most striking blue eyes you've ever seen. We paid more for her than we've paid for any other girl."

Both had moved into the room but had yet to acknowledge her. "It's so horrible," Bess said.

"I'll say," Thad agreed on his way to the large wooden cabinet in the corner that was designed to fit in with the antique furniture throughout the house but was actually a fully-stocked, double-wide fridge and chilled wine rack. He pulled out a bottle of water and gulped down most of its contents.

They hadn't spoken to her but were talking freely, so Devon interjected. "How is her health?" she asked.

Thad didn't hesitate to answer. "Tough to tell," he said. "We've got to let her sleep it off. She's thin and weak, but they always are. I've done what I can without being invasive."

"I'll take something up for her to eat," Bess said. "She's dehydrated, she might need one of your IV things."

"If she lets me do it," he said. "The last girl we brought in here was tricky."

Devon gave him a smile as he dropped into a chair further up the table. "How different was her setup to mine?"

"Don't know," he said. "We don't see behind the scenes."

"Do you go to the auctions?"

Thad picked at the label on his bottle. "Sometimes. If Zave's allowed a body man, I go in under that role. Most of the time, I provide backup from outside and that's when our tech comes in handy. If we think it might get sticky, we'd call in Brodie or Swift, but we would need to know ahead of time for that. There was no need this time, it was standard stuff."

Most of the population went about their lives without ever thinking about the disgusting underbelly that existed around them. Crime was rife in streets across the world. Men and women were subjected to horrific treatment that profited others.

After doing the job for so long, she could understand why Thad was apathetic to it. Devon was still adjusting.

"Back to your writing?" Bess asked, nodding at the page on the table in front of Devon as she folded her arms on the back of one of the dining chairs.

"Yes," Devon said. With a new guest in the house, Bess had been busy, and Devon hadn't seen another person since leaving Zave's suite.

Zave would be doing his best to avoid not only the new rescuee, but the previous one as well: her. "I can talk to her," Devon said. "If you think it will help."

Bess and Thad exchanged one of their looks. Devon used to think it was a mother/son thing that allowed them to communicate without speaking. Bess had raised Thad on her own. They'd always been close according to what Bess had said, and she doted on her child.

That bond was a contributing factor. But Devon

began to recognize it as a Kindred trait, as well. Maybe facing so many life and death situations together allowed them to share thoughts based upon their similar experiences.

"It could go either way," Thad said. "It's either the best idea in the world or the worst."

"I think it would help our new friend," Bess said. "I'm not so sure it would help you, Devon, dearie."

Devon was surprised Bess was still concerned. "Me? I've had weeks to come to terms with what happened to me. I've been the woman in that bed, terrified. I can relate to what she's going through. Maybe it will help us breakthrough."

"But you're not Kindred," Thad said. "You haven't been briefed on the rules."

"Then brief me," she said, not in the mood to be marginalized. "Anyway, I know how it works, I've been on the other side of your silence. I shouldn't tell her where she is or who any of us are. I should use everyone's code names. I shouldn't give out any details or answer too many questions. I have to reassure her without being specific. I think I can manage all that. Especially since there's still so much I don't know."

Thad inhaled. "Finch," he said, linking his hands around his bottle when he put it on the table.

"What?"

"Zara came up with it. If you're going to do Kindred business, you need a Kindred name."

"The first thing they usually ask is for a name," Bess said.

Being a part of this process gave her the focus she'd lacked today. "You use your real name," Devon said.

"But who would know me?" Bess asked. "I don't give out a last name, I'm like every other busybody on the street. There are people out there who know your brother."

The Kindred had experience that Devon had to trust. "People who could hurt him. You take the alias and use it, or you go nowhere near this girl," Thad said. "It protects you and the people you care about."

Thad didn't equivocate and Bess broke the tension. "Everyone I care about is capable of looking after themselves," Bess said. "I still don't think going in there will do you any favors. You're still regaining your strength."

Bess liked to mother everyone and Devon often felt like the sheltered daughter being clucked over, but she refrained from rolling her eyes and exhaling a teenage-type scoff. "I've had months to regain my strength," Devon said. "You've looked after me, fed me. Thad's given me constant check-ups. If he wasn't happy with my progress, he'd never have let Zave question me."

"Maybe we should talk to Zave," Bess said.

"I think he's confident in her strength," Thad said. "He wouldn't be screwing her otherwise."

Bess' mouth fell open before she gasped to chastise her son. "They're not screwing."

The woman could be completely in the dark, or she was protecting Devon's honor. But what she said wasn't untrue. "As long as I have the clearance of my doctor, I think it's safe," Devon said, and all eyes fell on Thad.

He wasn't convinced but conceded. "We'll let Mom go in first. She can try to feed her and get a measure on how our guest feels about visitors. If and when she's ready, Finch can go inside."

Getting a Kindred name was as exciting as it was peculiar. Devon had never needed an alias and had avoided everything in Rigor's world that might require her to need one. Here she was in the most expensive building she'd ever slept in, being given a secret name and told not to reveal her true self.

Bess could be right and this could set Devon's recovery back. But everyone else in the Kindred worked hard for others, putting their own needs aside.

Devon could do that. She could use the skills she had for the benefit of the group. That was the Kindred way. Right now she was the only one with the experience that could allow her to identify with this woman. It could speed the rescuee's recovery and the turnaround of the mission.

Setting to work, she wanted to finish writing her narrative before she walked back into that bedroom and began the next chapter that would involve her helping others through their trauma.

***

THE FIRST ODDITY that brought Devon up short was the flash of acceptance under her fingerprint when she pressed it to the door Thad had guided her to. The same door Devon had been imprisoned behind when she first came to this island.

Thad was going to stay outside for moral support. It couldn't be anything else, because even if he suspected that she planned to let the woman go, there was nowhere they could flee. Devon had proof that this was an island, and although she knew where the helicopters were, she wouldn't know where to begin in getting it off the ground.

Besides, it wasn't her intention to disrupt the process. She wanted to make it as easy as possible for all parties to be involved, not be a hindrance.

When she went inside, the girl was sitting up, hugging her knees, leaning against the headboard wearing the same kind of white nightgown that Devon had woken up in. Closing the door, she smiled. It hadn't been as hard to come here as she thought it might be. Maybe having the focus of helping this terrified person aided her in forgetting her own trauma.

Thad was right. The woman was beautiful. Devon could see that she was stunning even from across the room and in her distressed state. Although, when she lifted her forehead from her knees to look and see who had come in, her eyes were bloodshot and swollen. Still, Devon recognized how flawless her features were.

"I'm not here to hurt you," Devon said. She hadn't considered how she would begin, nothing she could say would be reassuring. "You're safe here. No one will hurt you."

Even if this woman didn't believe her, Devon had to say the words. "Who are you people?" the woman sobbed. "Please let me go home.

Feeling more confident in her ability to give this woman what she needed, Devon stayed calm. "We will. We just want to make you well first."

"Why did you bring me here?"

"The place you were," Devon said, moving to the end of the bed. "How did they treat you?"

"Horribly," she barked out.

The cartel Devon had been with had a rule about not violating the women they planned to sell. But there were no guarantees that this woman had benefited from the same treatment.

They knew nothing about this blonde. Devon had asked, thinking that having some facts about the woman she wanted to help might prepare her. Except she was told that this woman was a stranger.

When Zave and Thad had come to rescue her for Rig, they'd known everything about her, because her brother had directed them to her and filled in all the blanks.

Being that this was a standard mission, they'd traveled to purchase the prize of the night without knowing a single thing about who she was. Devon had come here to help this poor soul, but she was getting an insight into why the Kindred worked the way they did too.

She hadn't always understood why they brought the women here and held them while Thad nursed them back to health. Devon assumed that the women could get that care at home, except not all of them would have health insurance or be able to answer the questions posed to them by healthcare professionals. They might not be believed. They might face opposition. The Kindred could be returning them to a situation that was worse than, or similar, to the one they'd come from.

The Kindred needed time to learn whether or not the women were being returned to a safe place and to make sure they didn't have any friends or family who might come after the people who'd purchased them, no matter how well they'd been treated. They needed to gain the trust of the women to make sure they were looked upon favorably and understood.

Rushing the women home and dumping them off might hurt the women and it might hurt the Kindred. "What's your name?" Devon asked. The woman just blinked. "You have no reason to trust me or my friends, and I know that you're scared. A few months ago, I was sitting where you are now."

The woman's shoulders went back. "You were?"

"Yes. The people here rescued me, the way you've been rescued. And when I sat in that bed, I challenged them. I didn't trust them, but they helped me. I got sick and their doctor made me better. Bess fed me. They gave me back my strength."

Bess had already been in. The girl hadn't eaten or drunk a thing. A water bottle stood on the bedside, still untouched. With all the crying and emotional exertion, Devon wondered if Bess had been right about the need for intravenous fluids.

"But they didn't let you go," the woman said and sobbed again, though her hands fell down to her sides, and Devon registered the victim's sunken eyes and lack of tears despite her obvious upset. "You're still their prisoner and you've been here for months!"

"No," Devon said, having not thought about how her continued presence would appear. "I'm here by choice."

"They probably want you to think that. How many of them are you forced to have sex with, huh? Do they share you? Do they pass you around? The other girls said—"

"It's not like that here."

Devon shook her head and propped a hand on the footpost nearest the door. Wherever this girl had been, she'd had contact with other women. At least she hadn't been completely isolated. Although that did mean she would've witnessed everything that happened to the other women, good and bad.

"What is it like?" the woman whispered, probably dreading the answer.

"Bess and I are the only women here. We're not expected to have sex with anyone. These people have done this with other women, and all of them have gone home."

Watching her relax some more, Devon hoped she was making progress. "Then why did you stay?"

"I stayed because I wanted to help," Devon said in truth. "Because my experience gave me knowledge that can make a difference to other women trapped in places like we were."

Her head thumped back against the headboard. "You stayed to help me?"

"Not just you. What I went through changed me, it made me want to fight back, and you can do that, too, or you can go home to your family. You make your own choices. You just have to let us help you first."

Her eyes closed and her head rolled to the side, making Devon worry about the way she seemed to sag. "Jennifer," she slurred. "That's my name."

She slumped and her mouth opened. Devon rushed to open the door. "Wren!" she called out. Without hesitation, he leaped forward when she gestured for him to come in.

"What happened?" he asked, going over to help the woman onto her back.

"I don't know. We were talking and then she just… passed out."

He tossed the pillows away and turned to listen for breathing. "She's alive," he said, counting her pulse.

That was a relief, but Devon clung to the footpost and watched with wide eyes as he went through a series of checks. "Will she be okay?"

Devon got no response, Thad was in doctor mode. "Fuck it," he said and stormed out of the room, leaving the door open.

Devon didn't know what to do, but it wasn't like the woman was going to run away while she was unconscious. Still, she stayed, just in case there were any changes in Jennifer's condition.

Thad came back in with a full med-kit and an IV stand which had to have been close by because he hadn't been gone that long. There were other doors on this floor that led to rooms she hadn't explored, so Devon guessed one of them held supplies.

He put a needle in Jennifer's arm, hung a bag, took blood, and all Devon could do was stand and watch, being useless. "She won't drink anything," Thad said. "If we don't increase her fluids, she won't be with us for long."

"You're doing the right thing."

Jennifer's face was gaunt, it had gone a disturbing shade of gray and Devon shivered wondering if she'd looked as ill when she lay in the bed delirious with her fever. "You don't have to be here, I've got this," he said, concern for his patient written all over his face. "Go back downstairs."

Devon didn't know if she should push to stay or follow his orders. He wasn't happy, probably because he'd forced treatment on a woman without asking her if she wanted it.

Devon had been part of his journey onto that slippery slope, she'd refused treatment, and he'd been instructed to force it on her. She'd become so sick that he had no choice. Now she was thankful for what he'd done, but his discomfort over that decision had to linger and must create havoc when he tried to make ethical decisions.

"I can stay," she said.

"No!" he snapped, and she'd never heard him snap. "Just go, Devon, please."

Not only had he lost his temper, but he'd used her real name, which wouldn't matter because Jennifer was unconscious. But it did break a Kindred rule that had been drummed into her.

"Jennifer," Devon said as she retreated. "Her name is Jennifer."

He glanced up, and although there was an apology in his eyes, he didn't voice it, and she didn't request one. Devon slipped out and went down the corridor thinking about what lay behind Thad's usually outgoing and optimistic exterior. He'd lost the woman he loved to monsters like the ones who'd taken her and Jennifer.

Yet he went back to those despicable places to help other women. Every time he did, he had to be reminded that he hadn't gotten there in time to save Bronwyn. Women like her and Jennifer had been saved, but Bronwyn had been lost because there had been no Kindred there to save her then.

As far as she knew, Thad wasn't seeing anyone, although she'd never asked. Zave was used to tormenting himself and now he had her for support, whether he chose to embrace that or not. Thad came back and was expected to give each woman full medical service while Zave could close the door and never address any of them, never face the truth of what he had in his house.

Thad had to confront it. He saw every injury these women had. It would be human nature to compare those wounds with what Bronwyn may have endured.

Zave could shut himself away. Bess could busy herself with housework. But Thad had to fly himself back to the mainland and hold down a job where he was surrounded by people who had no idea what he did in his spare time.

He had to see patients with trivial problems who acted as if their worlds were falling apart. He probably lost patients, too, ones he could be close to or care about. He would watch them wither and die, then deal with more without taking time to process. Other Kindred members could be selfish and ignore the world. Thad was still a full-fledged member of society.

So although she'd always sensed that he wasn't her biggest fan, especially after witnessing the way he acted with Zara when she'd been here, Devon couldn't give him a hard time or dislike the man. Because he held it together and was stronger than anyone else she'd known. If he wanted to snap and send her away, she'd take it and wouldn't pout, berate him, or go complaining to the others.

Thad had to uphold a façade more convincing than those who didn't have lives beyond the Kindred, and he couldn't enjoy letting it slip. Devon would support him in her own way, and make sure no one ever knew about any of his moments of weakness that she witnessed.

TWENTY

JENNIFER WAS EATING for the first time. She'd been with them for three days now, and after Thad's treatment, she'd been more receptive to conversation with Devon. Going in with Bess, Devon had encouraged Jennifer to eat, and it reassured their guest to see them interacting. Although Thad had thought it would be intimidating, it turned out to be effective.

Devon did feel self-conscious about sitting around the dining table with Bess, Thad, and Zave when Jennifer was upstairs eating alone in the other wing. But at least she was eating. Baby steps were more likely to be successful in the long term than trying to rush the woman into a hasty recovery.

"Her vitals are getting stronger," Thad said. "So if she keeps eating a little every day and doesn't stop drinking, I don't think she'll have any major problems. There's some bruising on her back, and I'm worried about some of the cuts between them. I think we got to them in time, I'll keep cleaning and dressing them. There's no sign of infection in her blood."

Bess was smiling, and Devon understood that her optimism came from a kind place. But just as she'd felt when she'd been in that room, Devon's thoughts often returned to the other women, the ones the Kindred hadn't bought. They'd be enduring torture, not sanctuary.

"I'm going into the city tomorrow," Zave said.

The statement was so shocking that everyone stopped eating. "What for?" Bess asked.

"A meeting." Zave's tone was so clipped that it was obvious he was more uncomfortable with this conversation than he was about the trip he planned.

"You're going into Knight Corp?" Thad asked as though this was the most unbelievable thing he'd ever heard. It was like he'd just been told aliens had landed outside and they were asking to come in for coffee and donuts.

"I have to," Zave said. "I'm getting bored with the fucking around. Zara can only do so much from her side of the country. It's about time I knocked some heads together."

Devon could read the surprise in Thad's open expression, and she understood that reaction. Bess' grin and her whoop of delight made less sense. "This is fantastic!" Bess declared and leaped out of her chair to come over and hug Devon.

Devon laughed, just because the reaction was so bizarre and extreme.

"Mom, don't make a big deal of it," Thad said, understanding in the way she did that Zave wouldn't want a spectacle.

But when Bess rushed over to hug Zave's head, Devon had to laugh again. "It's wonderful!" Bess said.

"You're scaring him. Let him go," Thad said. "You're going to give yourself a heart attack."

Bess scoffed. "There's a doctor present and a chopper right outside," Bess said, talking to Thad while still clasping Zave. She bent to kiss her nephew's forehead. "I'm proud of you, son." She kissed him again before coming over to pull Devon out of her chair. "Aren't you proud of him?"

"Very," Devon said, although she hadn't been waiting quite as long as Bess had for this kind of progress.

Zave drew in on himself. "It's one meeting," he said, tempering Bess' expectations. "Going in should provide enough shock value to get them listening."

"Yes, one meeting," Bess said, nodding but squeezing Devon closer. "One step at a time. One step at a time. One meeting."

Thad had relaxed enough to let his own amusement show, but that didn't slow down his eating once he started again. "You weren't this happy when I got my MD."

"I was," Bess said. "You know how good it is that he's making this effort, and we have to encourage him."

Thad swallowed and forked up some more food. "I think Von's been encouraging him enough for all of us," he murmured from the corner of his mouth with a grin almost as wide as his mother's.

Zave straightened his cutlery and was doing all he could not to look at the faces that were so entertained by his simple statement. "Do you want to come?" he murmured.

Bess let her go and all the smiles vanished. Devon didn't know what was significant about the question until she saw both Bess and Thad were looking at her. "He's not asking us, we go back all the time," Thad said.

The question was for her. "Me?" Devon asked, stepping away from Bess to move in his direction. "You're asking me to go to Knight Corp with you?"

"Not to the meeting, I can handle that. But you've been cooped up here for months. You must want to get away. You can go shopping, eat a meal in a restaurant, you can be free."

"Free?" She didn't like the implication of the reserve Thad was sharing with his mother through a solemn expression.

"Come and help me with dessert," Bess said, holding a hand across the table for her son.

Like any dutiful child, Thad rose and joined his mother enroute to the door that would lead them the back way to the kitchen. When it was back in its frame, Devon licked her lips.

The others had made such a solemn exit that dread cooled her for a moment before anger began to simmer. "Why phrase it like a question?" she asked, getting his attention.

"What?"

"If you're evicting me, why not just say I've outstayed my welcome? Just tell me that you want me to leave." Exhaling, she rubbed a hand over her brow and reversed a step. "God, I'm an idiot."

Shoving his chair back to stand up, the legs scraped on the hardwood floor. "What the fuck does that mean?"

"She is beautiful," Devon said and spun to make for the door to the hallway.

But she didn't get to it. Zave came up behind her and grabbed her arm to whirl her around. "Don't you fucking dare imply—"

"Imply what?" She jerked her arm away from him. "I don't know what kind of sick game you're playing, Xavier Knight, but you're not the man I thought you were."

"No?" he asked. "Because you think that now we have a new woman in the house, I'm moving on, like I make a fucking habit of this."

"Do you?" she asked. "'Cause that's the way it looks to me."

His anger out-scorched hers. "I'm doing what's best for you. All I ever do is try to meet your needs."

Exhaustion made her beg. "Then why do we keep fighting?"

Since the morning in the lab, he hadn't come to her. Maybe inviting her into his bed had been a step more than he could handle, because he'd locked himself up tight since them. Now he was standing in front of her, telling her he would take her back to the mainland and grant her freedom.

"We fight because this has gone as far as it can go… as far as our comfort zones will allow."

And those were the words she'd dreaded hearing him say. "Because I'm too horny for you, because I'm the slut who wants to sleep with you."

He calmed. "I didn't say that. I don't think you're a slut, I just can't."

"And I'm tired of hearing that. So you're right, this has gone as far as it can go and it's not just about sex. You wouldn't let me stay here even if I promised you I'd never ask again, would you?"

"Is that what you want?" he asked. "To stay here?"

"Not to be a member of your harem. How will you seduce Jennifer if I'm standing in the way?"

"Don't fucking do that," he said, sneering at her. "You're cheapening what the Kindred do. I have never touched any of the women we've rescued."

"Is that why you're reluctant to touch me?" she asked. "You've made up this arbitrary rule that you'll never put your hands on a woman you've purchased? I might not have cost the most, but you do technically own me. You haven't gotten your money's worth out of me yet. But I guess since you're pushing me away, I've given you all I can."

Instead of reacting to her anger with his, he cooled. "I asked you to come because I trust you."

"Trust me to what? To walk away or to stay?"

"To make your own decision," he said with a bite in his words. "We brought you here without your permission, and we've never given you a chance to leave. I'm giving you that chance. It's up to you to decide to come back… or not."

Sighing, Devon was tired of him deferring the pressure to her. "Up to me. I can't go shopping and lunching and run away from you. I don't have a cent to my name, I haven't seen my purse since—"

"Money is irrelevant. You'll have everything you need to start a new life if that's what you want to do."

Was he testing her to see how serious she was about him and their relationship, or had she been naïve and manipulated all along? Taking one step back, she opened a hand on her hip. "We've spent our whole relationship focused on what I want and what's best for me. It's time we talk about you. All I hear is what you're not allowed to do, what you're not capable of. Just for once, Xavier Knight, tell me what you want."

"No," he said, without pausing to inhale. "Anything I say will influence how you feel."

Her frustration burst. "That's the point!" Opening her hands at face level, she wanted to wring his neck. "That's the point, Zave. In a healthy relationship, we should influence each other. You should compromise for me as much as I compromise for you. What we have now is one-sided. You focus everything on me. I get what I want. You pleasure me until I orgasm. I sleep safe. You spend your whole life looking after me, and you won't let me do one single goddamn thing for you."

He sneered. "So a blowjob will even everything out? Is that it? What shall we say? Once a year? Twice? Every month? Is there some equation I can balance—"

"Don't be snide."

Turning his back on her, he marched off. "Isn't this what women want? For fuck sake, you get all the attention you want! I dedicate myself to you and it's not enough!"

Despite his volume and obvious anger, she wouldn't be deterred from her position. "This is not about sex," she said. "We're talking about what you need."

Spinning, he gestured down with his flat hands. "I need you here not giving me shit. That's fucking it."

But she wouldn't be another avenue of punishment for him to subject himself to. "You build up walls, surround yourself with rules you won't let anyone break either. You still won't tell me what you need to make your life better. I tell you that I need a pencil, you bring me one. I tell you I want an orgasm, you deliver it. I demand food, you bring me a feast. You won't even let me bless you when you sneeze. Can't you see how it makes me feel to be constantly pampered while you shut yourself off? I don't know you any better than any other person on the planet, but I've given all of myself to you. I am the idiot who's fall—" Sealing her dry lips, her eyes dropped when she cut herself off.

"Idiot who's what?" he asked.

But she couldn't answer, finishing that sentence was wrong for too many reasons. "If you want to go to the city, then we'll go. You want me to melt your credit card setting myself up with a new life, I'll do it. I agreed to follow your commands, this is just the continuation of our theme."

She hadn't managed to force herself to look up, so she felt him coming over before she saw him move into her space. "Shy," he started and lifted his hand toward her face.

Usually she jumped at any chance of physical contact,

but this time, she backed away. "I'll be ready, Bess can tell me when, I won't make you wait. I should tell you that I've never ridden in a helicopter before," she said.

He swallowed, which worked his jaw. "Actually, you have. You're one of the few women who don't get air sick."

And there was another reminder of how their association had started. A blank space in her life that he knew everything about, while she remained in the dark on everything about him.

"That's good to know. Thank you." Frost began to build on the wall that stood between them. "I'll see you tomorrow."

The message in those words was that she didn't want him in her room tonight, and she didn't. If she was going to lose this, if this was her last night here, then she had to face the fact that what she thought was the beginning of her future was actually the last chapter of her past.

***

BESS HAD KNOWN something was wrong when Devon cried over the milkshake she'd been surprised with before departure. Devon didn't know why she'd cried and Bess didn't ask.

The tears threatened again as she sat next to Zave in the helicopter with the island receding behind them. They were alone, but they hadn't spoken a word. She didn't expect much conversation while he was focused on flying. He was capable and sure and she didn't feel unsafe for one second, even though she was hanging in a metal bubble over a vast, choppy sea.

The bustling activity on land looked odd. For the first time in months, she saw cars and people. Even though the sound was indecipherable beyond the noise of the rotors, she could imagine what it was like to be on the streets down there. Devon didn't relish the idea of being one of those ants again, scurrying around in a meaningless life.

Instead of descending, they ascended, and for a moment, she thought about speaking. That was until she saw the words Knight Corp emblazoned on a black glass and steel structure jutting up from the landscape, taller than everything around it.

That was where they were headed. They landed right on the roof on a central helipad. Devon didn't move until Zave had powered everything down and turned off the rotors. Bess had told her that Thad often landed here. There was a second landing site at the edge of the building, so he could park here for as long as he wanted to.

Devon didn't know if the Knight Corp staff was expecting him. It would depend if the meeting had been planned for him or if he was crashing a scheduled meeting, and she didn't know the answer to that, either. His company was none of her business, so she kept her nose out.

Struggling with the buckle on her seat restraint because her fingers were shaking, Devon convinced herself it was due to anxiety about the journey. But if she was honest, she'd admit to herself that she wasn't looking forward to reintegrating herself into society. She hadn't been ready to surrender her existence on Zave's island.

Yet throwing her in at the deep end may be the only way to ensure that she'd take the plunge. The Kindred couldn't support her forever. She was nervous about what sinister elements might be loitering on the busy streets, but not as nervous as she was about the idea of never seeing Xavier Knight again.

He leaned over to loosen her harness. She couldn't look at him because the metaphor was too much to bear. He was freeing her from her shackles, from the sanctuary of the island and from the tethers of their relationship. Letting her loose from his chopper was a symbol of liberating her from captivity and from her obligation to him.

Maybe it was because her mind was in a dozen places, but she couldn't figure out how to open the door either and had to wait for him to come around to help her out. When they were on the concrete roof, she began to seek an exit.

Rig would be her first call. He'd called a couple of times while she'd been on the island, but he'd been so confident in her safety wherever she was, that he didn't ask too many questions. Her brother wasn't bothered enough to seek an explanation about why she wasn't coming home.

Things had gone back to the way they always were. Her big brother only checked in when he had to, and she only got in touch when she needed something from him.

"Hold up," Zave said, capturing her wrist to pull her back when she set her sights on a black doorway.

"What?" she asked and wasn't going to deny him the right to speak to her.

"Here."

He looked delicious in his suit but so different to the man she was used to seeing on the island. She'd seen him in a button-down shirt and slacks before, but this was different. His shirt was brilliant white, his tailored jacket pressed, even his hair had been tamed into a corporate style.

Pulling a wallet from his inside pocket, he opened it to pull out a wad of bills and a black plastic card.

She resisted when he tried to hand the whole bunch over to her. "What is that?" she asked.

"You'll need it."

Money she recognized; the other thing didn't look like any standard credit card. For one thing, it had no logos on it, no colors. There were embossed numbers, but the whole thing was solid black. "What is the card?" she asked.

"The card will get you anywhere in the world," he said. "There's no limit on it. You could buy yourself a fleet of cars and a fucking mansion if you wanted to. But, as I'm sure you understand, card transactions are traceable. So it's up to you. You can choose not to use it and stick to the cash if you want to disappear. There's only a couple of thousand there, but—"

"A couple of thousand?" she asked. Her anger had lingered since yesterday. "You already paid for me once, why are you doing it again?"

"Stop this," he said.

She tried to leave him, but he grabbed hold of her again. For a man who wouldn't touch her below the neck a week ago, they'd taken great leaps forward.

If he wanted rid of her then he couldn't keep pulling

her back. "What do you want from me?" she asked.

"This trip is about choice," he said. "Money gives you choice. You want to take it and spend fifty bucks, you do that. But, right now, you don't have two quarters to rub together. This gives you enough for a call if that's all you want to use it for. I don't know how long this meeting will take, and I'm sorry that I can't spend the day with you."

Was he? She wanted to believe that. "Zave—"

"I have a security man down the stairs who will stay with you until you tell him to fuck off, okay?"

Arranging to have her tailed was quite a compliment. "Security?"

"You didn't think I'd turn you loose to wander the streets by yourself unprotected, did you? That won't happen while you're my girl."

Confused didn't begin to explain her state of mind. She took a breath. "Your girl? But I thought…"

"I know you did," he said. "Everything we said yesterday is true, and this is your chance to leave and be free. I'm telling you, I won't make it difficult if you do choose to go. I won't come after you or punish you."

"But?" she asked, sensing that there was one.

"But I am expecting you to be back here at eight p.m. You have the rest of the day to make your decision."

He was expecting her back. Devon couldn't believe it. She thought he was cutting her loose, letting her down not so gently. Turned out, her assumption was wrong. "Eight p.m.?" she asked.

"There's a board room a couple of floors below us, I'll show you on the way down. Your fingerprint will work everywhere here, so don't worry about getting lost or locked in. If you're back in that boardroom at eight p.m., I'll know you're choosing to belong to me and to our life together on the island. But if that's not what you want, if you want to go home to your brother, or you want to disappear"—he held the money and the card out to her again—"I'm giving you the means to do it."

"You said the card was traceable."

"That doesn't mean we'll come after you," he said.

"Knowing where you are and what you're doing will just make it easier for us to look out for you." So she would always be on Kindred radar. That was reassuring, not distressing or discomforting. "You'll have all day to think about it. Either way, eight p.m. tonight, we'll both know."

A day to herself in a busy metropolis where she'd have to make a decision about the rest of her life. Devon recognized what he was doing, separating their obligation from freewill and conscious choice. She could be with him if she wanted to be, but he would never accept that while she was locked up at his house.

Eight p.m. tonight, he'd find out exactly what it was that she wanted: him… or not.

TWENTY-ONE

BREAKING A HUNDRED in the coffee shop guaranteed her a glare. Every time she turned around, she noticed the security guard Zave had put on her. At first, it was unsettling, like she was being stalked. Then she saw the guy put his body between her and a dude who was running down the sidewalk. He might not have been coming for her, but her bodyguard prevented her from having to think about it. If that guy had come rushing at her, she probably would've panicked. As it was, the act made her smile.

Payphones weren't easy to find, and she didn't want to stand at a busy booth to talk to her brother. By chance, Devon noticed disposable phones in a convenience store and picked one up so she could talk to her brother and walk at the same time. The initial call was short because Rig was busy. After they hung up, she stopped to peruse some windows.

Her thoughts went to Bess, and she wished her newest friend had a phone that she could call. Devon had never heard a phone ring in Zave's manor, though the place was so big that no one would hear a phone ring.

The card Zave had given her intrigued her enough that she wanted to try it out. Devon didn't like carrying a bunch of loose cash, so she bought a purse, half expecting the card not to work. But it did. Picking up a few essentials, she went for another coffee and thought about her relationship with Zave. Being with him was a big commitment, he would need constant coaching because if she didn't ensure someone was looking out for his needs, he'd neglect them.

This relationship wasn't going to be easy and laid back; it was going to be intense and need ceaseless nurturing. He'd given her a chance to walk away because he knew he was no picnic. Devon had always been insecure about her worth, but Zave gave her his everything and spoiled her in a way she wasn't sure she deserved.

He'd noticed her. That first day he'd seen her at the auction. He'd noticed her, he'd told her as much, and she became special to him. Devon had never thought she'd live her life in seclusion with a recluse. Some things would have to change, but she'd steer him because she could only do this if they were equals.

Rig had called her back before she left the second coffee shop and she spoke to him for a while but didn't admit what had happened between her and Zave. In her defense, her brother didn't ask. He just wanted to know what she'd been doing and wanted to update her on his own life. Rig always had a woman on the go, sometimes he had several, but he would always choose to tell Devon about his romantic liaisons rather than his criminal ones.

After hanging up, she felt much lighter. She'd had time to consider what she wanted from Zave and knew that her brother was safe. One thing Devon had learned over the last few months was to be grateful for life's small mercies. In this single moment, she had no reason to be afraid. She had food, liquid, money, and plans for a future that she could only pray Zave would accept.

She would have to talk to Zave before they got onto that chopper, and there was still a chance that he would leave her behind. Choosing hope, she decided to take this opportunity to gather what she thought she'd need on the island because if he did take her with him, she could be there for a while without any chance to stock up on what she needed.

The security guard stayed with her and she began to return to Knight Corp in the dark, and her anxiety did grow. That was when she asked the guard to walk with her, and she got the chance to have a conversation with a person who knew nothing about what had happened to her.

Pedestrian lights slowed her down, and when she entered the lobby of Knight Corp, the elevator was so busy it stopped on almost every floor. It didn't help that she got off a floor before her stop by mistake and was delayed by looking for the stairs.

But eventually, she got to the right place and walked across the conference lobby. The blinds were closed over the room Zave had told her to meet him in and she hesitated for a second, but there was no assistant around.

The bodyguard, Petri, was still at the stairwell door and must have been told to give her a wide berth in Knight Corp, so he offered no help. He'd returned to his passive, blank self, like he had been before she'd engaged him in conversation.

Although she wasn't wearing a watch, she knew she was late and didn't want to delay anymore. Taking a risk, she put her shopping bags on the floor to the side and opened the conference room door to step inside.

"I remain unconvinced," her man said.

Zave was seated at the head of the table with his back to her. There were four people on each side of the table and a few assistants on the perimeter of the room. Everyone was focused on him until he twisted his chair a fraction, just enough to spot her, and they all followed his line of concentration. Turning back around, he glanced at the wall clock then returned his focus to her.

"It's eight oh three," he said.

Subduing her smile, Devon loitered in the doorway. "Your elevator is slow."

"We'll do something about that," he said. "Somebody call maintenance."

It wasn't only the young assistants who shared confused and uncertain expressions, those at the table did too. Eventually one of the young women near the window stood up and that was when Devon moved forward.

"He's kidding," she said, although they could be forgiven for not inferring that. His delivery was more than dry, he looked pissed off and she guessed after a day surrounded with people, he was struggling to keep his cool. "Should I wait outside?"

"Hell, no. Come in and close the door. Where's your security?"

"Standing out here," she said. "I've been good. I promise. I'm sure he'll give you a full report."

Walking to his side, Devon didn't know what to expect when she got there. Graphs and figures lit up a projection screen at the far end of the room. Contracts and paperwork were spread out on the table, interspersed by coffee mugs and plastic water cups.

If she had to guess, Devon would say that they hadn't stray far from this room all day. "Maybe you can help us out," Zave said.

Getting worried that he might pick up one of these contracts and hand it over to her like she was supposed to understand any of the gobbledygook scrawled on it, Devon tensed. "Help you with what?" she asked.

With zero business experience and less than that at a multinational level, there was no way she was going to be able to follow whatever he said next. And there wasn't any glimmer of possibility that she would be able to do something that these other practiced folks wouldn't.

"We're split down the middle," he said. Devon rested an arm on the back of his chair, strands of his hair tickled her forearm, giving her some confidence. "Here we have Knight Corp." Zave gestured at the four people seated to his left. "They believe it's important to baton down the hatches. They want to downsize CI's presence on the East Coast, to liquidate as many of the fixed assets are as irrelevant to KC and absorb those which can be utilized. Anything that doesn't fit with the current Knight Corp image should be rebranded or sold."

So he wasn't going to throw a bunch of jargon at her and make her look like an idiot. Good, she could cope with explanations like these. "Okay," she said, signaling her understanding.

"On the other side of the fence," he said, this time indicating the four on the right. "We have CI who believe it's important to speculate in hopes of accumulating. They think Knight Corp should use this as an opportunity to diversify, expand the existing brand, and invest in the present CI structure to build on the reputation that they have."

"Except the reputation is floundering," said a woman on the left side of the table. "That's the real concern here. They've had no one at the helm for too long, and all the breakdowns indicate that Grant McCormack wasn't particularly focused toward the end."

"That may be," Zave said, switching his attention to the CI side in expectation of a retort.

They weren't reluctant to come up with one. "CI is well-respected across the world. We're a serious company who builds life-altering products. Knight Corp is known for frivolous ventures. A company that caters to the rich. CI saves lives, we facilitate medical advancements through scientific research and technology."

"At the end of the day, we all do the same thing," said the KC woman. "We invent new products and bring them to market."

"CI sells to expert industrial clients," CI retorted. "You sell to department stores and online retailers."

"Commercial clients," the KC woman corrected the CI man. "We're a global brand, recognized by almost every person in the Western World, and we cater to those in the upper income brackets, yes, but we have a vast range that appeals to the young hipsters too. If you walk into any coffee shop, university, or corporate board room, I guarantee you'll find a Knight product. No one has ever heard of CI."

"Yes, because we're busy saving lives in unison with the scientific community," the CI man said.

Zave opened his arms. "And so you see the problem I've been dealing with all day," he said, tilting his chin up without actually looking at her. "Both sides make valid points and are territorial, and it all means shit to me."

"You built Knight Corp from the ground up," said

the blonde on the KC side. "You're the reason we're here. The reason it exists. You have to understand that we're trying to protect—"

"My father built this company," Zave interjected. "Yeah, I made you all rich, myself too, but the hard work was my father's. Things are going to change, or this bullshit will bring both companies down. You'll find me more engaged, Anita. Lives are involved, the lives of our employees and customers, and they don't give a fuck about this kind of pissing contest."

Devon ferreted that piece of information away to share with Bess later if she should return to the island. "So you had no intention of listening to us?" the stuck-up CI man asked.

"On the contrary," Zave said. "You can't count on my loyalty being with KC. My uncle was a good man. He sacrificed his life for Cormack Industries. The man sold me his house, gave me stability. And it was the loss of my cousin's life that brought us all to this room."

Stuck-up CI man had the decency to lose some of his bluster. "We are sorry for your loss. All of us at CI share your pain."

Zave didn't respond to the condolence. "Both companies are family to me. I want what's best for them both. I'm acting not only for my interest, but for my cousin's too. So making the right choice is vital to me."

All of the faces at the table considered each other. It made sense that the KC lot were trying to protect what they'd built, and they weren't used to Zave coming in to pull rank. Devon understood that he'd continued to pull the strings from the island through the previous years, dealing with a few select members of management. She wondered if that included these four and if there was a professional relationship between him and these people.

CI was at a disadvantage, this wasn't their home turf. They would know nothing of Zave save for what they'd read on the Internet. The man who'd inherited their company, Brodie, was nowhere in sight to defend their interests.

"How would you like us to proceed, sir?" the blonde

on the KC side, who Zave had referred to as Anita, said. Devon didn't miss how the woman ignored her.

Zave took an arm off the table and stretched it around her to pull her closer to the side of his seat. With his arm coiled around her thighs, there was no mistaking his message to the others that she was important to him, that they were intimate.

Devon liked having that assurance and being next to a man who was proud of her. "What do you think, shy?" he asked.

If she addressed the room as a whole, she'd be too intimidated to talk. So she chose to pretend it was just this one man, the one she trusted, asking the question and expecting an answer, without the audience being a factor.

"I think there's always a middle ground," she said. "You do have to protect KC and you can't change what it means. That will affect your customer's opinion, and they might not like being associated with a stuffy medical company." Stuck-up CI man opened his mouth to object. "But the work that CI does is important, they can't be ignored. They're doing what they've always done, they're just under new management. There must be a way to share resources and save both sides money. But you shouldn't do it at the expense of one company or the other."

"I agree," Zave said, and she was so shocked that she gaped at the top of his head. "We need to streamline everything. This isn't the time to expand. We can't get our legs under us enough to have one productive meeting. We've been here for hours and come to no conclusions. Instead of presenting to me the facts about two different companies, I want to hear about integration, how we can help each other. I want a full investigation into how we can pool resources. I know a couple of consultants and I'll review all the paperwork myself, as well."

"Who will head it up?" Anita asked, edging nearer in anticipation, maybe seeking the job herself. "Which side?"

"I will," Zave said. Bess was going to be catatonic when she heard about this. "I want every department in every division in both companies to submit a full report of assets fixed and variable, labor costs, stock, everything they have that belongs or contributes to what we do. We're going to look for duplication, look for sites that can be merged. For now, both companies keep doing what they're doing until we figure this out."

"But I—"

Stuck-up CI man got no further chance to object because Zave stood up. Keeping his arm around her, it moved up her body to rest around her shoulders. "Leave us," he demanded in a return to the severe, impatient man she knew.

He didn't flinch during the time it took them all to realize they'd been dismissed. Everyone pounced to their feet and gathered up their papers to then shuffle out of the room in single file. The final assistant closed the door behind her.

There were still things on the table around where he'd been sitting, but he didn't pay any attention to them. Zave turned himself to face her and took both of her cheeks in his hands to marry his gaze to hers.

"You came back," he said.

Swaying forward, she was encouraged by his proximity. "Watching you be all CEO is sexy," she said but had yet to find something about him that wasn't.

"You're sex starved," he said, quick to dismiss her attraction to him as implausible. "I've neglected you these past few days."

Devon was spurred to flirt. "Maybe I've been taking care of myself," she said. It wasn't like she'd never pleasured herself before Zave came along. She just hadn't done it with an audience or had any tools to do the job for her. But if she tried, she was sure her fingers would remember how to work her into a manual release.

His brow arched. "Have you?"

She wanted to say yes, just to see how he'd react. Her smile probably betrayed the consideration of her tease because his smile became dubious. Devon couldn't lie to him. "No, I haven't been feeling sexy since what happened in the lab."

"We should talk about that," he said, perching her on the table and seating himself in his chair again.

Taken aback, she hadn't expected them to get serious

so fast. "You want to talk about it now? Here? It will take us a couple of hours to get home, and you must be tired."

"Home?" he asked. "So you didn't buy yourself a mansion, or come back here to let me down easy?"

Sinking down onto the floor between the table and his knees, she laid her hands on the front of his thighs. "Some things will have to change," she said. "But if you're question is do I want to be with you? I don't have to think long about my answer. You're difficult and pig-headed, and you frustrate the hell out of me, but I do love you, Zave, I do."

When he stroked her cheek, she turned her face into the caress, savoring the rare physical connection. "That's a big word. One I didn't expect."

"You keep forgetting," she said, sliding his hand down the front of her throat to press it against her upper chest. "This isn't all about me. You treat me like a princess, give me more than I deserve, and you're asking me to be sure. To return to the island with you by choice."

"Yes," he said. "That is what I'm asking."

"I choose to do that, but I don't want you to be under any illusions. I'm willing…" Pausing, to moisten her throat, Devon didn't want to say the words that would come next. But in the interest of honesty, she had to. "I'm willing to stay here and watch you go home alone if what I ask is too much for you. You were honest about why you brought me here, and now I have to be honest about my terms for coming back."

"Sex," he said, and she blushed probably in the same way she had on that first night he'd kissed her. Because when her head fell, he picked it back up. "I love it when you do that." Devon was sure there was a faint curve at one side of his lips. "I've watched you writhe naked in front of me, sweating and screaming. I've pitched you into orgasm more times than I can count. But whenever I say that word—"

"Don't," she laughed, moving to her knees to press her fingers to his lips. "We're having a serious conversation. You shouldn't make me laugh."

"Okay," he said, blanking his expression with impressive speed. "What are your terms?"

"We have to be equal," she said. "That means honesty and sharing and compromise, Zave. You can't run around after me anymore, handing me everything I want."

"Doing that makes me happy," he said, kissing her fingertips and then returning her hand to his thigh.

"Okay, so you can. But you have to let me do the same for you."

Devon didn't have the money to buy him expensive gifts or have the logistical infrastructure in place to do it either. Bess had explained that supply runs came by boat and by chopper and how different stores and companies had running orders to provide air drops at intervals through the year. In time, she would figure out how to use those methods and slip her own requirements into orders. But for now it wasn't possible.

She gave him a minute to think about her request and eventually he spoke, "I haven't been in an equal relationship," he said. "I don't mean financially, I mean…"

"Emotionally? You've always kept yourself shut off or hidden behind shallow behaviors. You've never opened yourself up to anyone."

"No," he admitted.

Devon tried to tempt his honesty by giving hers. "It won't happen overnight. I just need to know you're trying. I can't come back with you and feel like I'm a burden to you, always taking and never giving you anything. You have to let me give you something back."

"Okay."

But he didn't seem to get it, he appeared too serious, like he was trying to figure this out from a practical perspective. Like if he could put the right components together in the right order and fastened them with the right cogs and screws, everything would work out.

"We have to be equal in everything," she said. "And we can start with emotional, if you can trust me, everything else should follow."

Maybe she wasn't being clear, because he wasn't following her meaning. He narrowed one eye. "I don't know what you want me to do."

"Try it," she said, and he blinked at her.

"What?"

"Tell me something. Anything. Share a secret." Rising as high as she could on her knees, she put both hands over his heart. "Tell me one thing that no one else knows. Just one thing."

Adopting the look of a lost child, he rolled his jaw. The silence stretched for so long that she kept having to remind herself not to break it because if she started talking, the conversation would move on and she would never get the proof she needed, that he was willing to make an effort for her.

"I…"

It pained her to see him struggle, but hope made her lean closer. "Yes?"

After another lingering silence, he found something to admit. "I came here to make you proud," he said.

"Here?"

"You've been encouraging me to take more of an active role in the business. I've been psyching myself up for it for a while. I thought if I could come here, you'd see me as something more than just a broken man who lives behind two triple locked doors."

Devon had no idea that she was so embedded in his psyche or that he had any sort of insecurity that might make him consider, even for half a beat, that he wasn't good enough for her. Making demands was a risk that she'd known might get her tossed from his life. But already it was rewarding her, because she'd just learned something that he would never have offered without her coercion.

"Lord," she murmured and climbed onto his lap to kiss him.

Being close to him always felt good, but he kept his hands on the arm of his chair, a sign of another roadblock they'd have to address.

"One area down, what's next?" he asked.

Her logical love did like to tackle everything in its turn. "Practical," she said. Coiling an arm around his neck, Devon kissed his jaw.

"If we have a practical problem, I can fix it," he said, more comfortable with his expertise in this area. "Do you need me to build you something?"

Nothing so grand. "I have to be able to talk to you. Inviting me into the lab was a big deal for you, I know that. When you disappear for hours and days, sometimes I want to tell you something or ask a question. Emotional barriers are one thing, physical barriers are another."

"I can disable the security on the lab doors."

He'd missed the point. She didn't want him to be uncomfortable in his own haven. "I'm not asking you to give up your privacy. That's your space, I can respect that. I know you don't want Bess and Thad swanning in any time they feel like it. But there will come a point, if we're going to be together, that we have to share a living space, share a bathroom."

Blank, he was always most comfortable when he was stoic. "There are more than a dozen bathrooms in the manor," he said. "We won't ever have to share one."

Smiling, Devon chose to take his statement as a joke. "You know what I mean," she said, pressing her hand into his chest.

"You've seen my bedroom," he said. "It's not fit for a woman like you. You deserve—"

"You," Devon said, cutting him off. "You're what I deserve and I don't care where we are, I care that you want me around. Don't forget, I grew up in the 'hood. Most of my apartments have been roach-infested studios. Just 'cause your bedroom is sparse compared to the rest of the house, it's top of the line compared to most of the places I've ever lived in."

"Is that what you want? To share my bedroom? Is that what will make you come back?"

Devon was being honest about her expectations, but she hoped he wasn't just pandering to her needs and again sacrificing his own. "Everything else we can work on," she soothed. "We'll get there in time. We're not going to adjust to each other overnight. There's only one deal breaker."

Getting onto her feet, she pulled him up with her. "What's that?" he asked.

She could tell from the way the shadows in his eyes began to blaze that he knew exactly what she was going to say. "Sex," she whispered, forcing the word past her lips. "I want to be yours, to belong to you, and I can't until you claim me. I know you made a decision not to let yourself indulge and that I'm asking you to break that vow you made with yourself. But you didn't come looking for me, or this; it happened on its own. I'm a new factor in your life that has to be integrated into your decision making. Now that we've found this, maybe you might consider… readjusting your priorities."

"You're trying to logic me into it."

She liked that he could read her motivations, even if she had just been caught in the act of trying to use his trait against him.

"I'll come back with you," she said. "But tonight we go all the way. No more excuses. No more punishments. You have to give me what I want."

It was true that she was horny and tired of waiting for him. She'd been patient and wouldn't dream of cajoling him into this if she didn't think it was what he wanted. This wasn't a matter of him not being ready, he was. It was a matter of him believing he didn't deserve the happiness he might get from indulging himself in her body. Zave had to forgive himself, and she could help him to do that.

"To be with you or to lose you," he said. "To have your body submit to mine or to watch you walk away for good."

Yes, those were his options, and Devon didn't like how long it took him to pick one. If he chose to cast her out, she would be devastated, but she would rather know that he was never going to need her in the way she needed him if that was the case.

His next words weren't an answer. "What did you buy today?" he asked. "Anything fun?"

"Lots of things," she said. "I left everything outside here. I bought you a present too."

"What?" he asked.

She put a finger to his lips to indicate he should stay put while she darted out to retrieve one of her bags. Bringing it back in, Devon put it on the table to open it up. Handing over his gift, she waited for him to read the label.

"Pleasure gel. Do you think we're going to need this?"

"It's symbolic," she said, her shoulders sagged, but she understood that he wasn't offended, he was joking. "I'm giving it to you to show that I will do whatever it takes to make your body as happy as you've made mine. If"— she fidgeted with his cufflink—"you choose to take me home with you."

He put the bottle back in the bag, and her heart began to beat faster in anticipation of his rejection. Before he could give her an answer, the conference room door opened and a tall, black man, probably in his late fifties, entered.

"There's half a damn lingerie store out here," the man declared, and her face burned again.

"Is there?" Zave asked.

She felt his gaze move over her before he touched his knuckle to her cheek, but she was too embarrassed to look up.

"I heard that a girl came by for you. Are you going to introduce us?"

Zave didn't hesitate. "Devon this is Cedric Moore. Cedric, this is Devon.

"I had to come and see the girl who could move mountains," Cedric said.

Zave put his arm around her shoulders and directed her to him so they could shake hands. "It's nice to meet you," she said. "But I didn't move anything."

"You got him here," Cedric said. "We've been trying to do that his whole life."

"Cedric was one of my dad's best friends," Zave explained. "He's the guy who's kept the place going."

Cedric's teasing smile put her at ease. "Now I can retire. If you're back to take over, I'm off the hook."

"Let's not get ahead of ourselves," Zave said. "It's one meeting."

Devon had heard him say the same thing to Bess and he seemed adamant about it, but she wasn't sure if he believed it.

"And we have this beauty to thank," Cedric said. "You moved a mountain; this is an achievement. He's a stubborn sonofabitch."

The compliment startled her. "I don't think…"

"You're the only new thing in his life," Cedric said. "Just how new are you? Do you plan to stick around?"

"We were just figuring that out," Devon said.

"Figure it out fast," Cedric said, and his smile dropped when he looked at Zave again. "We're planning that merger mixer event in a couple of weeks. It will settle the troops to see you there. The Liberty Hotel. Just your standard dancing, drinking, networking shit."

"Maybe," Zave said, firm and sure. "I'm not back for good, Ced, I told you that."

"Once you get the taste, you won't be able to stay away," Cedric said, giving Zave's arm a pat. "Should I put you down for a plus one?"

Devon didn't mind being scrutinized by the man who was so important to Knight Corp. But she did mind the terror that had stirred her guts in the duration between the question and Zave's answer.

"Cedric, you can consider Devon a permanent fixture. From now on, where I go, she goes."

That was an answer not only to Cedric's question, but to hers as well, and when their eyes met, the fire of Zave's certainty stoked her relief. Devon reminded herself that they were in company, so she couldn't shriek or leap on him as she might do if they were alone.

"You're sure?" she asked, and he nodded once.

That meant one important thing to her: she was getting laid tonight.

TWENTY-TWO

"I FEEL NAUGHTY," she said, turning her body into his when he shut the bedroom door. The lights were still off when he closed his arms around her, making no move to put them on. Devon nestled into him. "I'm so glad we didn't run into Bess."

"Are you worried that she'll disapprove?"

"Disapprove?" Shoving at his jacket, Devon got it off his shoulders, then moved on to loosening his tie. "That woman's been encouraging me to find ways into your pants for weeks."

"You don't need encouragement," he said after she flung away his tie and grabbed his waistband to pull him across the room.

"No, I don't."

Devon was giddy, an over-excited schoolgirl who'd just drunk her first beer at prom. Usually her first time with a guy was a nerve-wracking experience. She would be anxious and fidgety until he touched her, and that's when she'd go stiff.

Zave had helped her out of the chopper when they landed back on the island. He'd rejected her kiss outside and collected up her shopping to move it inside. Devon was going to rely on his level-headed nature a lot over the course of their relationship because she tended to be more impulsive than he'd proved himself to be.

No lights were on in the rest of the house, signaling that Bess had gone to bed. She often retired to her room early when she was alone here. At that minute, it was somewhere between eleven and midnight, so Devon assumed that Bess was asleep.

"I went to a free clinic this afternoon," she said. "I got a couple of months' worth of birth control pills. It's the most they would give me."

His mouth slanted. "So sure of yourself, shy?"

But she was already pulling his shirt down his arms, though it snagged on his wrists. She'd never been with a man who wore cufflinks before, and her exuberance slowed as she tried to figure them out. "They wouldn't have hurt me even if you said no."

Loosening one link, and she figured out the other too. They were so heavy, and they gleamed in the shards of moonlight that broke through the lofty windows. She wasn't sure what to do with such expensive items, so she held them up in her open palm to ask him.

More interested in her eyes than her gesture, Zave took them from her and tossed them to the floor behind him. "I don't have any condoms up here," he said. "Thad will have them stocked in the med supply store, sometimes the girls ask for them before they leave. I can go check if—"

"I didn't say I wanted you to use a condom." Sliding the leather strap of his belt from its buckle, she inched backward. "I can't think of anything worse than there being another barrier between our bodies."

"There's math involved," he said, and his eyes went up a fraction then relaxed. "You're not ovulating."

Tickled, she stroked his obliques. "I don't know why, but it's hot that you know that." He must have been paying attention during their nights to when she requested external toys only and picked up on the timetable of her cycle. "Would it have mattered if I was?"

Without the slightest hesitation, he answered, "No."

For a man who was averse in so many other ways, this was a compliment. "That's a risk."

His eyes got wider yet smoldered at the same time. "You're a risk to my sanity, shy. I've been holding on to it by a thread for years. You might be the girl to make it snap."

A zap of electricity shot up her spine, awakening every nerve on its route. Anticipating that she'd lose grip of her own control, she admired the definition of his torso with her eyes before she let her hands explore.

"I've harassed you about this," she whispered. "About making love with me. But I haven't pressured you into doing something you don't want to, have I?"

Usually it was the male pressuring the female for sex. But the concept was the same in reverse. As sure as she was that he wanted this, she needed to hear him say it.

"Shy… I'm surprised I held out this long."

Pulling her top off, he began to walk her backwards, and she was flat on her back when he crouched to take off her shoes and skirt and everything else that was in his way. The bed cradled her while he got her naked, which he had practice at. Although his belt was loose, he wasn't nude yet.

Her anticipation was forgotten when he rose to lie on the bed at her side. With an elbow on the mattress by her ear, his torso rested on hers and that salacious contact of heated, sensitized skin was enough to empty her lungs in a satisfied moan.

This was what she wanted. "Zave," she said, stroking a hand from his pec, up his throat, to his cheek, and around to the back of his head to guide his mouth onto hers.

He'd resisted her like she was some kind of temptress, a siren sent to drag him from his path of redemption. But if that was who she was, he was the unattainable man to her. A god who stood high above her, observing her meager self, with the power to devour her at any given moment.

And devour her, he did. The speed and urgency of their mouths became a competition, not for dominance, but in a race to quench the thirst that had been building since they'd first stood together outside her bedroom. His mouth was confident in where it was, but his hands still weren't on her body.

Devon didn't want to lose the momentum of their kiss, so she skimmed a hand down his arm to seek out his hand that was hanging somewhere in mid-air above her body. Bringing it down, she clasped each of his fingers around her breast and that was when he broke their kiss.

His hand knew what it was doing, it kneaded the flesh in a gentle caress that grew bolder as it recalled the sensations her body was nurturing. Zave watched his hand stroke her, and the concentration on his face was so compelling that her legs opened in expectation of receiving him. Except his hips were parallel beside hers, not on top. Lifting a leg over his, Devon crooked her knee over the back of his thigh and felt the material of his slack still blocking their progress.

"How does that feel?" she asked. His eyes flashed to hers like he'd forgotten she was there. The question was usually his, it was one he asked while he pleasured her from afar.

"Better than the fantasy," he said, scrutinizing his caress. "I've imagined this body under my hands."

"And this is better?"

"Yes, and this is just the start."

His wet lips met hers just once, then he slid down the bed to enclose his mouth over her breast. Devon understood his reference to fantasy because this was one she'd had herself. The man who had been dedicated to pleasuring her for weeks was breaking his own rules and enjoying her form, just as she wanted him to.

The saliva of his tongue proved that he had dreamed about this because it was sure about where it wanted to go next and took its time to savor every second it had to taste her, as though she could be snatched away at any second.

The weight of his palm on her abdomen made her wriggle. On instinct, he followed her unspoken desire and let his hand descend until his long middle finger pressed to her clit and circled, stimulating her piqued awareness.

"Wait," she panted because she was quickly losing sight of the night's aim. "Wait, lord." Taking his shoulders as she rolled to her side, she forced him to do the same.

Their warmed bodies were pressed together, and he steadied her balance with his forearms flanking her spine. "Changed your mind?" he asked.

"No," she said, so blinded by raging hormones that she couldn't tell if he was concerned or amused.

"Do you need some help? I can get the toys if this isn't—"

He worried it wasn't enough, when it was actually more than she could handle. "No," she said again and panicked when his embrace loosened.

Pushing him onto his back, she imagined he expected her to retreat. Instead, she moved to her knees and down the bed to pull his pants off. "If you're not sure…" he said, grabbing her wrist to stop her getting far.

Leaning over, her breasts grazed his chest as she kissed him. "I'm the aggressor here, remember?" she whispered.

Well that was a joke, he was bigger, stronger, and much more confident, but she hadn't interrupted their seduction because she was unsure, she did it because once again he'd been pampering her. As the balance of their relationship stood, she had masses of orgasm credit and he was in severe debt.

She abandoned his mouth to move back to her previous task of stripping him. At some point, he'd toed off his shoes, so it was easy for her to work the clothes off his lower body, and he sat up to help. Once he was as naked as she was, Devon pressured his shoulder until he laid back down.

It wasn't in her nature to stare, but she was mesmerized by the thick column of his engorged shaft, so hard and long, and ready for her. Insistent in its jutting pride, it had been neglected for so long, yet now stood willing and able to cater to her.

"Come here," he said, opening his arms for her.

But she was still ogling him. Tracing a single fingertip from hilt to head, satisfaction spurred her on when his dick twitched in response to her attention. Without his permission, she pulled one of his legs toward her to make space for her to climb between his limbs. Bending forward to kiss his abs, she wanted to give him what he deserved.

"Shy," he said.

"I owe you," she whispered with her lips against his bulging base.

"Nothing," he said. "You owe me nothing."

But it wasn't about debt, Devon cared about this man so much. Her heart was heavy that he'd deprived himself of pleasure for such a long time. Wrapping her fingers around him, she held him still to run her tongue around his crown and up over the smooth head she'd have inside her soon. Carrying on down the full length of him, she cradled his balls and kissed them as she caressed.

Zave didn't let her stay down there for long. He sat up again and took hold of her to put her on her back. Pinning her down flat, he rolled on top of her and tightened his grip on her arms.

The thick length of him imprinted itself on her inner thigh, but she didn't want it there, she wanted it to be under her mouth again. "I want to know you," she said. "Like you know me."

"You will, shy," he said. Using one hand, he stroked the hair from her face. "But it's been a long time for me, and there's only one place I want to be when I come inside your warm, willing body."

So he didn't want oral to break his dry spell, Devon wouldn't argue with that. He'd taught her to always comply with him anyway. "Zave," she said in the instant before his lips met hers.

"Hmm?"

"This is going to be amazing."

"It's going to be quick," he said, rubbing himself on her leg. "You feel fucking incredible."

That was his opinion already, and he wasn't inside her yet. "I wasn't talking about the sex," she said, running her fingers through his hair. "It's a given that you'll blow my mind. I'm talking about us."

Lifting his lips further from hers, he met her eye. "You've made a dangerous decision, shy, asking for this. Once we do it, there's no backing out. There's one thing you've missed in all your talk of me punishing myself…"

"What?"

"I didn't just dedicate myself to giving up things. I dedicated myself to taking responsibility. After I take you, you'll be my responsibility for the rest of your life."

Pulling him down to kiss him again, she smiled. "I can't wait."

He controlled the next kiss, and his hands were quick to fondle her now that they'd crossed this line. Devon assumed he would be rushed in his caresses, eager to take advantage of the chance to feel the female form again after being starved for so long. But he wasn't.

He was interested in her shoulder, the skin of her arms, the ticklish spot on her ribs. He wasn't racing to any finish line and wasn't caressing her to aid his own desire or even to stimulate hers. He was doing it to learn her every crevice, and he took his time doing it.

He liked her nipples, liked to stimulate them into peaks, to soak them with his mouth and blow cool, circular breaths to strain them further. When he exhaled in her cleavage, she sighed. And when he turned her onto her front and kissed each of her ass cheeks before slowly trailing the tip of his tongue all the way up her spine to the nape of her neck, Devon fell into orgasm and he hadn't penetrated her yet.

Boneless and exhausted while completely enlivened, Devon whimpered. "You're doing it again," she said, struggling to catch her breath when he rolled her onto her back again so he could kiss her mouth. "You're spoiling me and neglecting yourself."

In response, he pulled her legs wide apart and speared the head of his dick between her folds, enveloping himself in her cushioned heat. Yelping, Devon bucked up.

He bit her bottom lip. "Playing with you gets me off," he growled, his voice deeper and huskier than she'd ever heard it. "The power I have over you. I want to know how to use it. I want to know how every inch of your body reacts to me and how you like to be touched. I have to know where you want my tongue to be and when you like a hard press"—pushing himself in deeper, he squashed his flat palm onto her breast—"and when you want it soft." Pulling his hips all the way back until just the tip of himself kissed her threshold, the edge of his fingertip circled her nipple before it ascended to trace the outline of her lips.

"Zave," she exhaled.

"It's not all about you, shy. See, when I touch you, I'm learning how to get you off, how to control your pleasure."

He began to move inside her with more insistence, and the timbre of his voice worked, as it always had, even when he was standing far away from her, stimulating her body with his toys. It had been the caress of his voice drifting over her responsive skin that had heightened the intensity of their connection and her arousal.

"I want to work you in every room we're in," he murmured. "When I know I can look at you and fuck you with my eyes. I want you to feel my hands on you when we're standing a room apart. I want you to remember how my tongue felt right here."

Forcing it between her lips, he occupied her mouth, her pussy, her mind, her soul, all at the same time. His pelvis worked harder. But she couldn't react to the increased friction that made the pressure of orgasm build because she could barely draw breath until he chose to relinquish their kiss.

He wasn't done using his voice to push her deeper into desire. "You're going to know when I do this." He brushed his hand from the side of her neck, over her shoulder, down her arm, all the way to her fingers. "That I possess you. Your body is at the mercy of mine. Your sweet, tight cunt will respond to my training, and when I tell you to come," he growled and licked her lip. "No matter where we are, right there, on the spot, you'll come."

And right there, she did. There was nothing holding her back. Her body went into spasm, her hands gripped for the sheets, hit his shoulders, clutched his ribs, Devon couldn't stop moving or calling out for him. Only when he seized her forearms and slammed them on the bed did she stop the manic movement that had stimulated him into his own growling release.

Tension twisted his expression, and then he was still for half a second before he flipped away from her to land on his back. Separated from her, he lay there, staring straight up with a hand over his heart.

Devon gave him a minute and when she felt that she was able, she kissed his mouth. Out of either exhaustion or reluctance, it took him a minute to respond to her in kind. Eventually, he did and that was when he ran his hand down the back of her hair and gripped the ends to pull her back.

"You made a big mistake."

He could try to warn her all he wanted, she felt like a million bucks. "How did I do that?" she asked.

Zave was still holding her hair when he rolled his head to look at her. "There's nothing stopping me now. I have an appetite for you, one I intend to satisfy whenever I crave you."

"Okay," she said, kissing his shoulder. "You can feast on me any time you want."

He didn't mean what he said as any kind of threat, and he wasn't mocking her. This was his way of letting her know that this was just the beginning, and that was exactly what she wanted to hear.

TWENTY-THREE

SOMETHING BUZZED, and the noise was jarring enough to startle her eyes open. Her body didn't move. She heard the sound again, and she blinked at the vaulted ceiling towering above her, trying to remember where she was.

When she moved her leg, her muscles screamed, and she remembered exactly where she was and who she was with. It took a second for her smile to spread, and she turned her head in time with the shift of the mattress. Zave was on his side on the edge of the bed, his back muscles moved, and she had a great view of his tight ass that almost made her purr.

Before she could reach out for him, he spoke, "What is it, Bess?" he mumbled in a gruff morning voice.

"Oh, it's terrible!" Bess exclaimed, her disembodied voice coming from nowhere Devon could see.

But it was the panic in her tone that made Devon sit up. Anything could've happened, and Bess would know about it first. Maybe it was Jennifer. Could the girl have hurt herself or be sicker than they thought?

"What?" Zave asked.

"What did you do? You have to tell me what happened!" Her quick, worried words made Devon forget about her tired body.

"What are you talking about?" Zave asked, his words slow as he extended a bent arm to rub his eye.

"You didn't bring her back. Devon. Did you? You left her there! What did you do? You chased her off or scared her away!"

"What are you talking about?" Devon liked learning that Zave wasn't quite with it when he first woke up. "What's the problem? Is it the girl or Zara?"

Bess squawked. "No. No. No! It's you!" Bess insisted. "You broke it! That girl was crazy about you, and she hasn't been back to the manor. I know that you left her there in the city! Alone! She hasn't slept in her bed. I went to find her, and she's gone. You have to fix it!"

It was nice that Bess was so worried about her and sort of funny that the woman didn't know Devon could hear every word. Crawling over the bed, she kissed Zave's shoulder then propped her chin on the same spot, draping an arm over him to take her lips to his ear.

"Should we tell her?" Devon whispered so Bess couldn't hear.

A little green light was glowing on the long speaker beneath Zave's alarm clock. Devon had thought it was a radio; apparently, it was an intercom. "You better say fucking something, or I'll never get more sleep," he said.

Picking up her arm, he urged her away so he could lie on his back again, but that put Devon farther away from the speaker and her knees were digging into his ribs in a way that couldn't be comfortable.

Climbing over him, she sat on the edge of the bed. "I'm here," Devon said. Zave moved onto his side again, bringing up his knees to give her a nook to rest in.

He snagged the pillow she'd been using and stuffed it under his head, content to go back to sleep and leave her talking to Bess. "You're there? Wait," Bess said, her initial relief became confusion. "This intercom, it feeds into Zave's bedroom. No one's allowed in Zave's bedroom. No one's ever been allowed in Zave's bedroom."

The compliment from the speaker was joined by another that was making itself known against her ass. Leaning back, Devon laid one arm along his thigh and the other on his ribs. "We had a talk last night," she said, admiring the form of the man who'd agreed to give her everything she wanted.

"You figured it out? You're together?"

"If you want to gossip, go down the stairs," Zave grumbled, thrusting his hips forward as if to nudge her off the bed, but it was a half-hearted attempt that only moved her a couple of inches and she quickly managed to seat herself again.

"No, no, you stay there," Bess said. "I hate to do this, but… Zave, you have business to deal with."

"Tell them to fuck off," he mumbled, punching the pillow between his head and his other crooked arm. "We didn't get back until after dark."

It was late by the time they got back to the manor, but that wasn't why he was tired. He was tired because every time they took a break for long enough that one of them might drift off, the other initiated another session. They'd still been awake when the sun started to rise.

"Not Knight Corp business," Bess said, becoming more solemn. "Kindred business."

Zave swore under his breath, then inhaled. "Give me ten minutes," he said and stretched himself out.

"Devon, dearie," Bess said. "You enjoy being up there. He might never have you back."

Devon knew that the statement was a dig at Zave's fickle and private personality rather than an observation about what Devon's skills in the bedroom might match up to. Touching Zave's temple, she twined her fingers in his hair as he yawned.

"I'll do my best," she said, and that was when Zave reached over to press a button on the clock that turned off the green light.

He sat up. "This is going to be one of those fucking days," he said, but she didn't know if he was talking to her or himself.

Shuffling past her, he tossed his legs off the side of the bed and stretched again, then drove his fingers through his hair a few times. Getting up, he began to move to the door, leaving Devon clueless about what she should do.

"Zave?" she asked as he opened the door, because she needed instructions.

For the first time that day, he looked at her. "Sleep as long as you like," he said. "Depends how long this shit takes. If it's quick, I'll come back and join you."

"If it's not?"

"Then you'll be well-rested and won't need to sleep tonight."

That was as much as he said before he went out the door in his naked glory. Devon hadn't explored all the rooms on the stairway. She'd guess there was a bathroom and a closet. If she was going to be spending more time here, she would learn. But, if Bess was right and she was going to be kicked out, she wouldn't get the chance.

Zave telling her to stay and sleep and that he might come back for another round, made her confident that he hadn't changed his mind about them. He'd been right when he implied the day hadn't started on great footing, and she hoped this Kindred call wasn't a bad omen.

Knight Corp business could be ignored in deference to sleep, but he dropped everything for the Kindred, and from her point of view, the Kindred was the thing that could get him killed. So Devon would always be nervous when she heard that word.

But she was proud too. It was important to him, he was loyal, and his integrity was an admirable quality that she wouldn't, as his girlfriend, take for granted.

***

OVER AN HOUR later, she woke up alone. She guessed that meant Zave wasn't coming back to her. Leaving his bed, against her instinct to stay, she didn't go snooping, but picked up his discarded shirt and buttoned it up before leaving his lab to seek him out.

Modesty had been lost when she admitted to Bess through the intercom where she'd spent the night. Kindred business was conducted "downstairs" in a place she hadn't been yet. So she walked into the dining room expecting to find it empty or at the most to see Bess. Instead, she walked into what looked like a full-blown conference.

Bess was here, so was Thad. But they had been joined by Brodie, Zara, and another couple that she didn't know.

Tugging down her shirt, Devon crossed one leg behind the other. "Oops," she said.

"I didn't know this meeting was clothes optional," Thad grinned, and Zara threw a grape at him.

"Devon didn't know we had company," Bess said. "Can I get you something to eat, dearie? Maybe a milkshake?"

Her face had to be aflame. "No, I'm going to my room."

"Didn't she just come from there?" the man with the blonde-tipped hair asked the female next to him, which earned him a pinch on the arm that he rubbed after an, "ouch."

To avoid a recurrence of this situation, Devon would need to find a quicker, more discreet route from Zave's room to hers if she was going to be waking up there more often. She'd always reached it through this room. Well, except once. When he'd come back from the auction with Jennifer, Zave had taken her a different way, but she'd been too busy kissing him to take notes about the route.

Diverting focus from her state of undress, she changed the subject. "How is Jennifer today?" she asked Bess while trying to quell her urge to flee.

Devon wasn't ashamed of what she'd done with Zave and wouldn't let him think she was by running off. Because he was at the head of the table, he was blocked from her view. He wouldn't make a show of welcoming or reassuring her, he was too reserved for that. Devon could only hope that he wasn't angry or embarrassed that she'd inadvertently announced to everyone what they'd done together last night.

Picking up her cue, Bess answered, "Still eating, more relaxed. She might be the quickest recovery yet."

"Good," Devon said. "Excuse me."

She had to cut across the room in a diagonal to get to the hallway door. When she was halfway there, Zara stood up. "These guys are the ones making plans, we're just window dressing," Zara said, tugging the unknown woman's shirt at her shoulder to encourage her onto her feet. "Why don't we have coffee in the kitchen?"

Devon saw Zara eye Bess, too, so the older woman stood up as well. Zara had sway with more than just her man. "Thanks," Devon said. "But I should probably get dressed."

Zara laughed. "Kindred women have to get used to being naked in front of the group. I wouldn't worry about it."

Bess gestured her over and Devon couldn't say no, except she did take advantage of the opportunity to glance at Zave, who crooked a brow and nodded once. Okay, so she had his consent to bond with the other Kindred women. She was curious about what was going on and Zara had always been supportive, and there was a new woman in the room that she wanted to get to know.

Now that she and Zave had made the decision to be together, these people were going to be a regular feature in her life. Devon would rather put clothes on before bonding, but the trio was waiting for her by the door to the back kitchen, giving her little choice except to go with them now.

The men wouldn't speak again until she was gone, so side-lining inhibition, she went to join her new clique.

***

"SO, MISS DEVON, what's Zave like in the sack?"

This was Zara's first question when Bess brought the coffee pot over to the kitchen island they were seated around. Bess clucked at her. "Devon is shy, Zara, don't you get your sass all over her."

Zara laughed and stood on the crossbar of her stool to take a cookie from the tray that Bess had put out before the coffee.

"He's dynamite, how's Brodie?" Devon said in a hurry.

Bess' mouth dropped open, but the other women whooped and Kadie laughed. Devon had been introduced to Swift's woman as they were sitting down. It turned out that unknown guy at the table was Tucker Holt, also known as Swift, the Kindred computer genius.

"That tells you, Bessie," Zara said. "Something weird happens to a woman when she joins the Kindred. I'm sure it's the fault of the guys."

"Yeah, let's blame them," Kadie said, snagging her own cookie.

Zara licked the edge of her cookie. "And Brodie has his off days, but, you know, he tries to keep up with me."

Kadie swayed over the island on her elbows. "Don't get her started on talking about Brodie in bed. I swear the pair of them still do it ten times a night."

Zara scoffed. "Oh, yeah, and how long have you been with Tuck now, Kade?" she asked, nibbling her cookie. "It's been like seven years or something."

"Not quite," Kadie said. "You make us sound so old and boring! We've not been back together a full year."

Zara shrugged. "Near enough. It's been nine, ten months, something like that, right?" Kadie tilted her head and lifted one shoulder in agreement. "You guys are the ones who fuck all over the manor... Do you forget there are cameras all over that building? We don't need the constant visual."

Devon was impressed. "You and Tucker have been together for seven years? Are you married?" Kadie shook her head. "So you're married to Brodie?" Devon asked, pointing at Zara. "How long have you been with Brodie?"

"We met about... a year and a half ago, bit more than that. It's April now, we met September before last."

"Kindred men have staying power," Bess said, going to the freezer to pull out the ice-cream. "I'm making milkshakes for everyone."

"I have to say thank you," Zara said, picking a raisin out of her cookie to lay it on her tongue. "I never thought we'd get Zave into the boardroom. I spent months wrangling the lawyers, getting the contracts signed to get the merger to go ahead. Now it's happening, and we have to get the companies to play nice. Brodie's been going insane at the amount of time I've spent on this."

Kadie explained. "Zara's supposed to be the defacto

Kindred Chief," she said, stirring sweetener into her coffee.

"Defacto?" Devon asked.

"The job is Brodie's, but the circle would've fallen apart by now if Zara wasn't dealing with the details," Bess said, scooping ice-cream.

"Is that why you give out the names?"

"Finch!" Zara declared, perking up. "Do you like it?"

She hadn't had much chance to use it. "I've never had an alias before."

"You'll get used to it."

Devon guessed the women had to transition to a new way of life when getting with their men. "How did you become Swallow?"

Zara rolled her eyes and tossed her cookie onto the counter. "That's a long story, one I'll tell you another time. We came here for a reason."

"I figured that," Devon said, looking at Kadie who'd become solemn.

Bess licked ice-cream from her fingertips. "Be gentle, Zar."

"This is about the meet," Devon said. "You know when it's going to be?"

"Tuck put it all together," Kadie said. "It's happening this weekend."

She'd thought she would have more time to prepare herself. "This weekend?" The ease of bonding with her could-be girlfriends and her anticipation for milkshake disappeared in light of this news. "What happens next?"

Zara was pragmatic. "Next we pack supplies, get the hell off this island, stock the jet, and go to Mexico."

"The jet? I didn't know there was one."

"It's Zave's, it's new," Kadie said, glittering with excitement.

Zara took Devon's hand. "Apparently, they always had jets until a couple of years ago when there was some sort of incident and the old one was left floating somewhere in the North China Sea. I don't know the details. But they've been waiting for this one to be built for them… now it's ready."

Impressed, Devon didn't know how to respond to

this news. "It's a private plane?"

"Don't worry, both Zave and Thad can fly it. We'll be in, we'll be out."

Zave had said the helicopter was tiring to fly, which was why he and Thad took turns at the helm. They wouldn't need to stop to refuel so many times if they were in a jet and it would be a much more comfortable ride.

"We're all going?" she asked.

"You can stay here. You don't need to be there," Zara said.

Devon wasn't going to sit this one out. "I want to be. Shouldn't I be talking to Zave about it?"

"Everything Kindred goes through Zara," Kadie said. "We take all developments to her, she processes them through Brodie, they share their opinions, consult the group, and then we come to a decision."

"Is that what you were doing this morning?" Devon asked Kadie, who nodded. "Okay. And that's why you're the one talking to me about this?"

"It gets complicated," Zara said, squinting as she went back to her coffee.

Bess slid a milkshake in front of her, and her focus switched to the cherry on the whipped cream. Plucking it from its dairy cloud, Zara bit down to the pit and sucked the fruit from the seed.

Devon didn't mind her taking her time to enjoy it, she'd savored Bess' milkshakes too. But she was frustrated at the delay because she wanted to learn more about what was going to happen. When Zara was finished with the berry, she tossed the stalk onto the cookie plate and twisted to face her.

"It gets complicated?" Devon asked, reminding Zara of the last thing she'd said.

"Zave is a complicated guy, you don't need me to tell you that.

Devon didn't like this. Bess came around to finish handing out the milkshakes and then took a seat next to Kadie on the opposite side of the island from where Devon sat with Zara. "He told you to talk to me," Devon said.

Zara shook her head. "No, Zave doesn't tell me

anything. He talks to Brodie. Since you came on the scene, he's been easier to be around, we all have to thank you for what you've done for him. But I'll be honest, I don't know you."

There was a wariness coming from Zara. "And that makes you nervous?" Devon asked.

"I know what it's like to have a score to settle," Zara said. "How the need for revenge can blind a person… And the first time I met your brother he won me in a poker game, then shot at me… I don't know your morals."

Zara knew Rig. Devon had no idea women were bartered in the games he played or that he would fire a gun at anyone. Except, she tried not to think too hard about what her brother got up to. "I love my brother, but we're not the same."

"Brodie says that if Zave trusts you then we trust you too. I understand that. But Kade and I have experience with being shut out, and I don't intend to coddle you. If you want to be there, you can be there. But you have to let us do our thing, and you can't get in the way."

"Zara," Bess murmured, scolding her niece-in-law with a sigh. "Devon is good people. You've been spending too much time with my cynical nephew."

The serious expression melted from Zara's face to be replaced by joy. "I love Devon," Zara said, leaping up to give her a hug. "Don't think I'm being a bitch. I try to do that as little as possible. But I think it's easier when everybody knows where they stand."

Zara was scarier than Devon had initially thought, but she could understand the need to be clear. "Can you tell me the plan?" Devon asked after Zara sat back down and stuck her straw through the cream into the milkshake.

"It's simple," Zara said, taking a long slurp of milkshake. "What do you know about a device called Game Time?"

Devon had no idea what she was talking about, though the other women in the room clearly did. "Nothing. Should I?"

"No," Zara said. "I just don't know how chatty Zave

is when he's naked."

Zave wasn't chatty full stop. "What kind of a device is it?"

Zara crossed her legs. "There's a long, complicated backstory," she said. "Suffice to say, we can use it to take down the men that hurt you. We know when the meet is taking place, and it's too enclosed for Rave to get a clear shot. We don't know exactly how many men will be there either. Could be five, fifteen, or fifty. So a direct assault is too dangerous. Game Time can distribute any gas without being detected."

Something so shocking had to belong to the military. "Where did you get it?"

"Again, that's another complicated story," Kadie said. "The Kindred have a lot of those. Not so long ago, a bunch of terrorists wanted to use it to spread disease."

"But we're not going to do that," Zara said. "We discussed the possibility of dosing these guys and sending them back to their nests. But if we do that, we risk harming the women they've kidnapped, and we can't do that to them. So we're going to go with a good old-fashioned poison gas and take them out on the spot."

She tried not to be shocked but failed. "You're going to poison them? With what?" The what was less important than the idea of killing a group of men. She'd known Zave was skilled but hadn't realized how committed this group was.

"Thad will help us with that. He'll tell us what will work best and quickest, what will be the safest to transport, and the easiest to get our hands on. We have viruses back at my manor, but we can't use them. We have to work fast, we don't have much time, and we don't know when we'll get this chance again."

Devon understood, but she'd never considered that she might be party to mass murder. But if there was ever a group of men who deserved to be taken out, it was this one. "So this device, you'll load it up and...? What? Hide it somewhere in the meeting room?"

Zara was nodding. "Before they get there, yes. We'll set up one, maybe two of the devices. The guys will be the ones to go in and do it, they're planning the op. Zave can make any engineering adjustments, and Tuck will program the thing. Thad will load it up with whatever gas we're using, and Brodie will probably be the one to plant it."

"What happens if he's caught?" Devon asked. "If these guys find him snooping around…"

Zara smiled. "That's why we send Brodie," she said, exuding nothing but pride. "If anyone gets in his way, he'll deal with them."

Zave had said that he wasn't the killer in the family; now it was clear to Devon who was. "Everyone has their role."

"That's right," Bess said. "I'll stay here and look after Jennifer."

Devon's focus moved to Kadie. "I'll come on the trip, but I won't be in the field," Kadie said. "I like to keep an eye on Tuck, but I don't distract him when he's out there doing his thing. I'm more of an extra pair of hands than anything else."

"An extra pair of hands I couldn't live without," Zara said. "Especially with all this merger crap going on. Kadie's my right-hand girl now, she picks up all the slack and is the only one who can keep the guys in line with the same finesse that I do."

The two women shared a look, and Devon could tell that they were close. "Life is so much easier with another woman around the manor," Kadie said. "I'll bet that's one of the reasons that Bess loves having you here." Kadie put her arms around Bess and rested her head on her shoulder. "Now we'll have an extra voice on our video chats. Two women here. Two women there. Our guys don't stand a chance."

"Next, we just need to get Thad set up," Zara said. "Who'd have thought Zave would hook up before he did?"

Kadie laughed, and although Bess was amused, she didn't share the hilarity. "You leave my boy alone. He's been through enough. And the boy has plenty of girlfriends at his hospital. He'll settle down when he's ready."

Devon was caught up in her thoughts about going back to the country she'd been traumatized in and about being part of an op that could end with loss of life on one, or both, sides. "Don't worry about it," Zara said. Devon had been staring at the cherry in her drink, and her silence must have been noticed. "We do this kind of thing all the time, and we're all still here."

"Says the woman at the table who died," Kadie said, scooping cream onto her finger.

"Shh," Zara said and laughed with her friend again before reaching over to pat Devon's knee. "You don't have to come if you don't want to. You can stay here with Bess or you can come for the trip and stay with Kade."

"What about you?" Devon asked. "Where will you be?"

"Zara's always in the field. It focuses Brodie," Bess muttered in her usual maternal way. "Can't keep that girl away from the action. She's usually jumping in before the boys get a chance to think."

Zara shrugged. "Brodie loves bailing me out," she said, sealing her lips around her straw. "He can't get enough of it." After her drink, she sat up. "It will be useful to have you around to translate."

"I can't believe Brodie doesn't speak Spanish," Kadie said.

"Some of the Arabic dialects, French, Italian," Zara said, growling at the last one. "And Russian too… no Spanish."

"I'll be happy to help," Devon said. Having a job would give her something to think about other than being an accessory to murder. "I can shorthand it… something I learned in one of my many jobs."

"Now you and I can write each other in code," Zara said. "That's another language Brodie doesn't understand. The Kindred have their own shorthand."

"Speaking of the men," Kadie said, bouncing off her stool and picking up her glass. "You and I should check in, make sure those boys are on topic and not planning some poker night or Vegas weekend or something."

"More likely they're planning a full-out assault," Zara said, going after her friend and taking her milkshake with her.

"Brodie keeps talking about the explosives he has stored. He's just looking for an excuse to blow something up."

"He's just jealous that you were responsible for the last epic explosion," Kadie said, pushing the door with her ass to grant her and Zara's exit.

The idea that Zave would go gallivanting to Vegas was ridiculous. Devon hadn't been invited to the meeting in the first place, so she wasn't going to stalk after Zara and Kadie and force herself into the room. Bess was happy to sit and drink milkshake with her.

"I think I'll talk to Jennifer again before we go," Devon said.

"You should. She would like that," Bess said. "But you might want to put some clothes on first."

TWENTY-FOUR

DEVON WENT TO her room to shower and change. After that, she went over to Jennifer's room to talk with the woman for a while, giving their victim a chance to talk about what she'd been through. Hearing another woman's tale helped her to put her own in perspective, and while she didn't give Jennifer any details, she was reflecting on her own past when she went back to her room.

She was sitting on the floor cross-legged, leaning against the seat of the armchair working with charcoals that she had spread out on the low coffee table that had been put in here for her to work on. Devon liked sitting on the floor, feeling the soft pile of the carpet beneath her bare thighs, which was why she chose to wear denim cutoffs and keep her feet bare.

The charcoals tended to make a mess when she worked with them, and they washed from skin easier than they did from fabric, so she'd elected to wear a tank top with narrow straps. The wind was howling outside suggesting it was cold, but in here it was toasty warm. It had to cost a fortune to keep such a huge place with its high ceilings warm all the time. She'd have to ask Zave about that, maybe there was a secret to it.

Bess had offered her lunch a while ago, and she'd refused because she wasn't hungry and was desperate to finish her piece. Engrossing herself in art focused her mind, and Devon needed this time to herself to consider how she felt about what she might have to do this weekend.

She didn't hear the door open or know Zave had entered until he was leaning on the back of the armchair perpendicular to the one she was propped against. He cleared his throat and her eyes darted up.

Lifting her blackened fingers from the page, she used the back of her wrist to push her hair from her eyes. "Busy?" he asked.

"I didn't expect to see you today," she said, placing her charcoal back into its slot in the box it came from. Picking up her cloth, she wiped the excess dust from her hands. "These charcoals are amazing, the best I've ever used."

"You have access to the best now, shy. You can have anything you want."

He'd said that to her before, and even though she'd shared his bed, the strength of her desire for him hadn't lessened. "You are an incredible man," she muttered, looking at the page she'd been working on.

"Zara said she spoke to you."

"She did," Devon said, pushing her shoulders into the seat of the armchair.

"You don't have to go."

"No more than you do."

"It's my mission," Zave said. "This corner of the Kindred belongs to Thad and me. Brodie and Zara are along for the ride, we need everyone's skills on this."

Devon tilted her head. "But not mine?" she asked. "Is that why you're telling me to stay?"

"I'm not telling you to stay. You can come and you'll be safe. We'll all look after you. But if it's going to be too much…"

Pasting a smile on her face after he trailed off, Devon put the heels of her hands on the table to push onto her feet. "Are you kidding? I'd miss the chance to ride in a private jet! There's no way I'm giving that up."

Springing toward him, she kissed him quickly as she passed on her way to the bathroom where she washed her hands. Devon was drying up when he came into the doorway. "The jet will always be there, and it will take you anywhere you ever want to go. It's at your disposal. Don't let that be the reason—"

"It's not, I was kidding. I'm not that shallow," she said, straightening the towel on the rail again. "I mean, yeah, it will be hot watching you at the controls." Crossing, she walked her fingers up his chest. "I've never had sex with a pilot before."

He closed one eye. "You did last night."

She laughed and straightened her arms to hook them around his neck. "I guess you got me there."

"And there won't be time for that, the flight deck is cramped. The jet will be full, and we'll be talking logistics. There will be equipment around and—"

"It sounds like you're trying to talk me out of being there with you. But I have to be there. I have to watch these fuckers go down. And it's one thing to know you're going to an auction where you don't plan to start a fight and another to know you plan to hurt these guys... If they find that out, they'll hurt you and I... I have to be there, lord."

"Okay," he murmured and lowered to kiss her. "I had to know you were sure. I'll let you get back to your work." He backed away, giving her hips a push to separate their bodies.

She didn't want him to go but couldn't keep him here when he had other things to do. "I'll be here if you want me."

"You should eat something," he called over his shoulder.

"Later," she muttered, for her own ears not his.

Going back into the bedroom, Devon looked at the window she hadn't opened, thinking about if she'd like to go outside to blow away her worries. Whatever she did to prepare for this weekend, it wouldn't be enough, because until she saw those men fall, it wouldn't be real.

"Oh," Zave said. Devon thought he'd already gone, but he was there at the door, half out the room. "Rigor is your only family, right?"

She didn't know why that was relevant. "Yuuuh," she said, perplexed by the peculiar timing of the question.

"So he's the only one you want at the ceremony?"

Confused, she squinted. "What ceremony?" she asked, hoping that animal sacrifice wouldn't be part of her Kindred initiation.

"The wedding."

Zara was already married. Kadie wasn't, but when Devon brought it up this morning, she hadn't hinted that she and Tuck planned to tie the knot. But why would Rigor be at Kadie and Tuck's wedding? Maybe they were friends, but why would that be Zave's problem? He was no wedding planner.

"What wedding?"

He let go of the door he'd been leaning on to stand up straight. "Ours."

Devon had no idea how long she stood there gaping at him, but it was long enough for him to realize that she was surprised because he stepped back inside and closed the door. "Ours?" she said, dipping her head forward. The word was so deep and blunt that it didn't sound like her voice.

"I told you last night," he snapped at her, and his brow clamped down to shade his eyes. "I told you if we had sex you would be my responsibility."

"Yes," she managed to stutter, and her eyes widened because she couldn't bring herself to blink. "Yes, you did say that. But I didn't… I didn't know that meant…"

"What?" Zave had never been a patient man and hadn't had much finesse when it came to expressing himself. "I suggest doing it this weekend on the way there or the way back. If your brother has to be present, I'll have to fly him in. Timing will be crucial. If it's necessary, we'll go to him if you have ideas of a formal affair. But that will mean a significant detour."

Devon had never been one of those women who fantasized about her wedding. She'd always assumed that she would be married at some point, but like a lot of people, she had been too busy dealing with life to ponder specifics.

"You want to get married. Married?" she asked.

Her hands went to her chest as she tried to figure out

who he was talking to. Confirming with a fondle that she was actually her, they went up through her hair in a physical display of her disbelief, and then she covered her mouth and nose with her fingers. Surprise became elation.

If any other guy had tried to rush her into marriage or made assumptions about their future together, Devon would've retreated, pulled away from him. Her fear and inhibitions would've stopped her from leaping in. She'd have made an excuse and run for cover.

"Yes. Now pick, on the way there or on the way back? If you want to make a spectacle later, you and Bess can plan that out. But we get the paperwork done as soon as possible, shy. We only have to wait three days for the license. Pick."

"On the way there," Devon heard herself say. Because if something was to happen while they were away, she wanted him to know that she'd been willing to make the commitment with him. "Rig doesn't need to be there. He won't care."

"You're sure?"

And she was, so she nodded and then had another thought that made her scowl. "I don't want to do it in Vegas."

"God, no, we'll go into the city tomorrow and pick up the license. Everything's been drawn up for us, we just have to show up. Then three days later, we go to the courthouse."

"Three days," she said. The cartel meeting was in four days, so their wedding would be a quick stop enroute to the mission. "I can't believe you want to get married."

"You didn't pick up on that?" he asked.

It was odd, there had been no proposal and they were standing almost a whole room-width apart. "You'll have to talk to your lawyers, there isn't much time. I'll sign whatever you need me to."

"Good," he said. "Because I'm sure there's a line on the marriage certificate for your name."

Obviously, but that wasn't what she'd been talking about. "I mean a pre-nup. A guy like you has to protect himself."

"From what?" he asked, and she was grateful when

he came to meet her. Devon went into his arms when they encircled her. "Nobody here cares about that shit. You can have half of everything now if you want it. There will always be more money to be made. And stuff? It doesn't matter. If you want the house, here, you can keep it. Rave has a spare room or two."

Bess had said that Brodie's place was the same as this one, at least on the exterior. So Brodie had more than a couple of guest rooms. "I only want the island if it comes with the lord of the manor," she said, wearing a grin.

His stony expression was serious and not interested in playing. "It does, and you missed the point. You marry me, you'll belong to me. There is no divorce or division of assets. There's no end. No goodbye. You're mine."

Devon didn't doubt that he meant these words. They'd spent one night together, and he was demanding she stand at the altar with him. Now Devon got why he'd resisted sleeping with her, because he'd known if he did, they would be forever, and those weren't just words to him.

Whether it was because of his vow to himself to remain on the straight and narrow or because he just couldn't bear to live without her, he believed in commitment, responsibility, and taking charge.

"You haven't even told me if you love me," she said.

"Love you?" he said, and his scowl wasn't encouraging. Her concern grew when his arms dropped to his sides. "Love is a word that means nothing. It's thrown around like it's important, but it's not. What matters is our actions. Haven't I shown you how I feel in the way I treat you?"

He'd resisted having a relationship, he'd fought with her. But he'd done it with passion and resolve, not out of indifference. He pampered her and spoiled her and treated her like she was on a pedestal.

"Zave, you know I'm not perfect." A glimmer of reluctance seeped into her. "I don't want to do this because you have an idea in your head of what I am. If I don't live up to that and I disappoint you…"

"You couldn't. I know everything about you," he said. "I knew every fact about your life before I first saw you.

You've been in this house for months, shy. Months. Every chance I get, I watch, I listen, I absorb you. I don't think marriage will be a picnic."

Nothing about their relationship had come without conflict. "We will fight."

Zave wasn't discouraged, he brushed her face with a fingertip. "We always have," he murmured.

When she'd sat down to work, she hadn't considered that she might be affianced just an hour later, but now that he'd put the idea into her head, Devon was beginning to like it. "I might have some new demands," she said, picking up his hand as she sauntered toward the bed.

"What kind of demands?" he asked, wary either of her statement or her playfulness.

Devon took a big breath. "Well, for starters," she said, sitting down while keeping his hands. "We have to get another pillow for your bed."

And it was rare enough that when she saw his smile, she pulled him down onto the bed with her because she couldn't resist kissing him for another half second. "Such high expectations," he said, scooping her hair away from where it had flooded his face when she launched her mouth to his. "Anything else?"

"We need a regular script for my pill," she said, pretending to think hard about what she'd need.

"We have a doctor who comes to the island every week. That's easy."

She threw a leg over him to straddle his abdomen. "You'll need to keep me in milkshakes and art supplies."

"Noted."

Devon didn't want anything from this man except him. "And I might need an account at Victoria's Secret."

His hands ran up and down her back. "I'll put that one to the top of the list," he said.

Devon laughed before bowing to kiss him. When she was thoroughly warmed and ready to strip him bare, she sat up and began to unbutton his shirt. "And what about you, husband?" she asked. "We're equal, remember? What are your demands?"

He took his time to come up with something. "You have to let me move all of your things from this room to mine."

Devon got to the bottom button and opened up his shirt to massage her hands over his torso. "I can start on that today. Next?"

"No skinny-dipping. Ever."

She never had, but he had a real bug up his ass about that ever since it had been suggested. Circling his nipple, she traced a line from his throat to his navel. "You never let me do that in the first place. Next?"

Zave was on a roll. "You can walk around naked in the lab as much as you like, I encourage it, but keep it behind our secure entry. Never leave there nude."

That had to be a nod to this morning. "I didn't know we had company," she said. "And I didn't have anything to wear except the clothes I'd had on in the city all day or the lingerie in the bags scattered in the lab. I didn't think you would appreciate me coming into the dining room in a silk teddy."

He gripped her pelvis and slid her down to rock her hips over the hardness of his cock that was still hidden in his jeans. "You give it up, day or night, when I want it," he said. "Don't forget that you started this when you're telling me I fuck you too much."

She wouldn't forget and she would never complain. Rising high on her knees, Devon unbuttoned her shorts and flopped to her back to wriggle out of them before returning to her previous position on top of him. Loosening his jeans, she pushed them down just enough to let her make wet contact with his solid cock.

"Won't ever happen," she murmured.

His hands slid over her. "And your product testing days aren't over," he said. "I'm still going to play with you. Except when we're married, I can go as far as I like."

That was intriguing enough for her to make eye contact, but she was still enjoying her intimate massage and with his hands now fondling her breasts, she didn't trust her memory for his words.

"I'll do whatever makes you happy."

"Devon," he said when she was pulling off her top.

Doubling over him, she stole his mouth because it was still a novelty that she could touch and play with his body without him putting up a fight. When he turned his head and took hold of her shoulders to force their mouths apart, she worried that she might have assumed her freedom too soon.

"Uh," she panted and tried to seek his mouth, but he was too strong, so she had to stay where she was, farther from his kiss than she wanted to be. "Lord, please."

He considered her for a few seconds. "I do love you," he said. "And if you didn't know that already, I still have work to do."

"No work. No work," she said, shaking her head and pouting to try and reach his lips. "I know it. I knew it. I'd never agree to be your wife if I didn't."

"And you will be?" he asked. "My wife?"

It was amazing how quickly shock could become excitement. People got married on impulse all the time, and although they'd just had sex for the first time last night, they'd been in an undeclared relationship for months now, like he'd said. So it wasn't much of a leap that they would tie the knot.

They just made the decision in an unconventional way, which given how their whole relationship had been so far, shouldn't be a surprise.

If he was doing this to distract her from the horrors that she may see, it worked. He didn't put up a fight and he didn't rush away. In fact, for the rest of the day and the rest of the night, she saw no one but him.

They made love. They made plans. She sketched. He worked. And Devon got insight into how their life together would be. No amount of speculation pre-Zave could have matched up to what she'd found with him.

Their relationship would have bumps, and they did have a tendency to fight. But he made her feel a wider range of emotions than any other person ever had, and while it hadn't occurred to her to think about marriage this early, he had a plan and he'd never steered her wrong, so she'd go with it. If there was one thing she was sure of, it was that she didn't want to lose her lord, the man she loved. The recluse, the genius, the sex-god, the savior. Xavier Knight was hers, and she wouldn't be letting him go.

TWENTY-FIVE

SHE WAS NOW officially Mrs. Devon Knight.

One thing became clear quickly: the Kindred were efficient. With Zara at the helm whispering to Brodie, who in turn whispered with Zave, decisions were made quickly and not a second of time was left idle.

Kadie must have been tasked with keeping Devon busy, because they spent most of their time together when she wasn't with Zave. Kadie would explain what was happening and tell her relevant stories as the others worked. Zara would disappear with the men and come back to give brief updates and advise of any changes.

When it had come time to leave the island, Bess bid them adieu, and Devon didn't know who was more worried, Bess about the Kindred, or the Kindred about the one they were leaving behind. But they'd done this before and Bess knew the contingencies. She knew how to sail, too, so if she had to get off of the island in a hurry, she could use one of the boats moored in the sheltered marina.

They took both helicopters to the mainland and left them on the KC roof. Brodie and Tuck were tasked with moving the gear from the helicopters into the trucks waiting for them in the private parking area of the KC building.

While they were doing that, she and Zave did the deed. Zara, Kadie, and Thad came with them to the courthouse. Before they entered, Zave took her aside to give her a diamond so big, Devon was sure she'd develop carpal tunnel just from holding it up. He insisted it was just right and took her inside before she could put up more of a fight.

The wedding itself was quick, words were said, papers were signed, and Devon didn't have much of a chance to savor it. Zave was more detached than she'd have liked him to be, but she understood that he was getting into a zone for what would happen next.

Going straight to the airport, she got no alone time with her new husband. They were ushered onto a jet, and the staff at the hanger were dismissed by Zave before he and Thad went through a series of checks. Brodie and Tuck transferred everything that was needed from the trucks into the plane.

Having never been on a private plane before, Devon was amazed by how pristine and gleaming everything was. They entered into a kitchen with the cockpit to the left and the cabin to the right. There was seating for fifteen people divided into three separate areas with a bathroom at the back of the plane.

Zara fixed drinks while the men did their work. The three women went to the sofas that faced each other in the farthest aft section of the cabin, giving the men space to talk and plan. Then, without any warning, they began to move, and then they were in the air and there was no going back.

Devon hadn't flown much in her life, and she'd always been nervous when the wheels left the tarmac. This time, though, she didn't feel that same anxiety despite it being a much smaller craft than those she'd traveled in before.

As Kadie and Zara laughed about something, Devon excused herself to give in to her urge to seek out Zave. She went through the cabin where Brodie and Tuck were sitting in facing armchairs. Their expressions were serious enough that she assumed they were discussing the mission. Devon expected one of them to stop and question her, except they didn't even look up.

A great thing, she learned, about a private plane was

that she could do whatever she wanted without cabin crew getting in her way or arguing about regulations. Going through the kitchen, she entered the cockpit where both men turned to look at her. Seeing the man who'd made love to her that morning seated up front with his aviators in place and his headphones over his ears, she forgot about their final destination for a minute.

Reaching for his hair, she had to feel if he was real.

"I'm going to take a break," Thad said, probably reading more into her smile than she meant to reveal.

Thad took off his headphones, squeezed past her, and left. Although she liked being alone with her new husband, Devon didn't want to interrupt what they were doing.

"Am I allowed to be here?" she asked. "He doesn't have to leave if it breaks some rule or—"

"It's fine," Zave said, taking her hand out of his hair. "What do you need?"

"I wanted to see you," she said, trying to absorb all the buttons and screens spread out in front of him. "It's amazing that you know how to do this."

"I know how to do a lot of things."

She didn't need to be reminded of that. His skills were wide-ranging and given some of the other feats he could accomplish, flying a plane probably wasn't a big deal to him. "Are you nervous?" she asked.

He checked something on the dash in front of him. "About what?" he muttered.

There was so much ahead of them, and behind them, that he could take his pick. Nervous about flying a plane when so many people he cared about were entrusting their lives to him? Nervous about the married life they'd just agreed to embark upon? Or nervous about what would happen after they touched down?

Their wedding night would be in Mexico, wherever they were sleeping tonight, although she didn't know where that was. At some point, he would have to leave with Brodie and Tuck to break into the cartels' meeting room. It wasn't exactly romantic, but her suffering was part of the reason they were doing this and she was as proud as she was terrified.

Folding her arms on the back of his chair, she lowered her mouth to his head. "Is your head clear?" she asked. "I should've said after, shouldn't I? I'm an idiot. You shouldn't have been thinking about weddings and marriages and—"

"I'm not," he said. "I'm thinking about altitude and wind speed and—"

"This minute you are, but shouldn't you be focused on what's going to happen south of the border?"

"If you're talking about the wedding night…"

It wasn't like him to joke, so this was probably a sign that he was bored of her ranting. "Xavier!" she exclaimed.

He twisted to examine her and sealed his lips as he inhaled. "Sit down," he said, nodding at the chair Thad had vacated.

"I'm not sitting there. I don't know how any of that stuff works."

He took her hand to guide her away from his chair. "I didn't tell you to fly the plane, I told you to sit down." So she did, with his help. "I'm happy that you said before. I'm not thinking about our marriage. I was more stressed before when you were single than I am now that you officially belong to me. This inspires me." His fingers ran over her diamond.

Mesmerized by its glittering beauty, she held it up. "It's ridiculously huge," she said but was smiling.

"It needs to be."

"Why? It's not like you're compensating." Leaning over the center console, she cupped his groin, but he took her hand away to remove her body from the controls between them. "Sorry."

"It needs to be that big because there's a GPS tracker under it. I chose the thing and picked it up on the morning we got the marriage license because I had to tweak it in the lab."

Devon should've known, and she understood now why she'd been left alone in the back of a limo for a half hour while he ran "errands." He wanted to keep her safe, wanted to secret his tech into her every possession to keep tabs on her, not because he wanted to control her but because he wanted to give her security.

Touching his face, she swooned. "Lord."

"Not here," he almost snickered and kissed her knuckles before giving her back her hand. "You go back there and start planning the reception."

"I can't stay here with you?" she asked, scanning all the bells and whistles around Thad's station while slapping her hands on her knees. "This could be fun."

"I'll teach you to fly when we get home. This isn't the best time to add that stress to my life."

Standing, she clasped his face to kiss him. That was when Thad came back in. She climbed out of his seat and squeezed herself behind Zave's to give him room to return to his post.

"You need more time?" Thad asked.

She shook her head. "The man's not stressed about marrying me or about facing off with a dozen Mexican cartel bosses. But when I ask him what that button does—"

"Say no more," Thad said, laughing and holding up a hand. "The patient control freak isn't the best teacher. No, that's unfair, he's a fantastic teacher as long as you do exactly what you're told, when you're told, how you're told, and don't deviate."

Zave was relaxed and didn't react to the jeering. She patted his shoulder. "I'm going to talk wedding cake. Don't work too hard, you two."

Zave knew what he was doing, Thad did, too, and the plane was big enough that they could take breaks whenever they needed them. She might not have aspired to be Kindred, but now that it was happening, now that she was a part of their crew, Devon embraced their methods. They might not be able to change the whole world overnight, but if this mission was successful, they could save the lives of dozens, maybe hundreds, of women.

While the cartels were in disarray and trying to reform a hierarchy, there wouldn't be women snatched from their lives and sold into slavery. Little by little was better than nothing at all, and Devon was honored to be a part of this team.

***

ZAVE HAD TOLD her to go back to sleep. Devon could tell by the number of orgasms he dished out that he was trying to exhaust her. He'd reassured her that all of the Kindred were bunking together in the next room and that the only reason they had their own was because this was their wedding night.

But it didn't matter how much he tried to soothe her, relax her or reassure her, every time she heard a noise or he moved an inch, she pounced up expecting to see him sneaking out.

Eventually, he did.

Instead of lying in bed alone, listening to nothing, worrying about the man she'd just married, she went to the next room to join Kadie and Zara after she heard them laughing, a sure sign that they weren't sleeping. Devon thought she'd be in for the long haul, she expected to pace and worry for hours. But they weren't gone for more than ninety minutes.

They came back one at a time, Thad first, then Tuck, after him was Brodie. Arriving in a drove may have aroused suspicion. One guy on his own was less conspicuous. Brodie sent her back to her room without any apology for evicting her.

She couldn't tell if he liked her or not, but he endeared himself when he explained that Zave would go crazy if he walked into an empty bedroom. When he put it like that, she couldn't refuse. The last thing she wanted to do was worry her lord.

When he did get back, he didn't answer her questions, just told her they needed to rest and demanded that she sleep. Except she couldn't. Not until he wrapped her in his arms and pulled her body to his. They'd never slept wrapped in each other, and it was a comfort she couldn't have known. With her ear pressed to his chest, she'd fallen asleep.

***

THE NEXT MORNING was regimented. Awoken at a

specific time, everyone was washed and given clothes that would help them blend into the surroundings. Devon was given an earpiece, although from how she understood the plan, the Kindred members wouldn't be separated from each other. The guys had planted a bug in the meeting room, and just as Zara had said, Devon was expected to listen in on the meeting to translate.

Devon refused breakfast, only to then be scolded by her husband in front of everyone. He declared that they had to eat a certain amount of time before an op to ensure they had the energy to carry it through and because no one could anticipate everything that might go wrong. The Kindred had to know when their members had last eaten and drank something, in case they were separated from the group and got into physical trouble.

To her, that meant in case she was kidnapped. Given her past, it was the first place her mind went. It wasn't like she could fall from a plane. If she was in a car wreck, they'd all be in the same predicament because they were planning to travel in one vehicle.

Being tense and edgy already, Devon didn't need to deal with Zave's attitude, as well. Maybe he'd forgotten that she was new to this or was just dealing with his own anxiety. Whatever the reason for his abrupt behavior, she did as she was told and ate something.

Before they left, they had one last briefing in which she was reminded to only use aliases for the duration of their time in this country. The other instruction drummed into her was that she should stick close to a male member of the group. Devon wasn't sure if Thad counted, as he wasn't included much in the men's discussions.

Brodie, Zave, and Tuck would huddle to talk, excluding the others. But they shouldered the greatest responsibility since they all had a female in the mix. Except she was new and Kadie was staying at the motel, so Devon wasn't sure if romantic entanglement was the reason or if this was the way it had always been.

It was hot but still early in the day when they piled into the Jeep and got moving. Last night, the men had unpacked supplies in the spot they'd all be hiding in to watch the day unfold. The meet was taking place at another motel. One that was far away from any town, situated on an abandoned road.

Being in the middle of nowhere was the perfect location for what these men wanted. Surrounded by nothing but dust and cacti, even if there were twenty vehicles parked outside, there would be no one around to notice them.

This was neutral ground, and it was central too. The owner of the motel had been told to bolt a couple of days ago. Devon had wondered if he'd ever return, and it was a shame if he did because he'd be shocked to find what the Kindred left for him.

The shelter of a rocky peak a couple hundred feet away gave them a place to hide themselves and their vehicle. Setting up base under an overhang, they had shade and cover, while the Jeep was in a position behind the outcrop that curled around their base.

Brodie took up position at the forefront, closest to the motel, with a terrifying weapon hidden under camouflage. Watching him set up the rifle, she noted his professional efficiency and didn't know if she should be impressed or horrified.

Thad was there with little to do, he was just a medic, so he sat at the rear with her and waited, which was all they could do until the meeting started. They'd positioned themselves early, giving plenty of time for the dust to settle before any of the cartels would arrive.

Every time a vehicle drove along the road, her heart raced. The first drove straight on by, maybe to check things out or just in coincidence that this long, remote road was someone's route to somewhere. Devon didn't know what was at the end of the straight road, but not many people wanted to go there if the lack of traffic was any indication.

When the first truck pulled into the motel parking lot, she hoped it wasn't filled with innocent passersby looking for a place to spend the night. Two other vehicles weren't far behind, and two mean-looking, tattooed men piled out of both.

Suspicious and arrogant, they gave each other wide berths, preferring to gesture and call out to each other. But she couldn't hear anything specific and wouldn't until they went into the meeting room and the bugs were activated.

Zara gave her paper and a pencil. Devon began taking notes as soon as the voices began to fill her ears. More vehicles showed up and more men trooped into the single-story structure that was surrounded by concrete arches leaving a wide porch all around that made it impossible for Brodie to get a line of sight apparently.

The men in that meeting room spoke to those they arrived, rather than with the others, so she couldn't decipher anything that might be relevant. They were talking over each other, too, which made it difficult to pick out details.

The hall they were in was some kind of game room and the largest space on site. A bedroom wouldn't have been big enough for all the people who came. There was no restaurant or bar. She only knew this from overhearing something Brodie said.

She hadn't seen inside but heard the Kindred men talk about pinball and gambling machines at the back of the room. Two of the Mexicans were playing pool, and someone referenced a table tennis table. If this place was trying to be a family resort, it was in the wrong location.

Someone called order, and there was shouting about who was in charge. Devon guessed that if the meeting was getting started, everyone was present. Taking notes of names and relationships that she could figure out, she got so engrossed with writing everything down, that she paid no attention to what those huddled around her were doing.

Devon had a task, and she had to do it well. This was her first Kindred assignment and she had to prove herself.

It was maybe fifteen minutes later that she realized something was wrong. The Kindred around her were talking to each other and even Brodie took his eye away from his sight.

"It should've happened by now," Zara said, crawling over to sit beside her love. "Shouldn't it?"

"Yes," Tuck said from his position on Brodie's other

side. He looked at his watch, "Finch, any signs of anyone feeling ill?"

Devon shook her head. "They're arguing. Someone wants to join forces and share client lists," she said. "No one's sick or coughing or passing out. They're just as loud as when they got there."

"Then something is wrong," Zara said. "Did you guys get the setup right?"

Tuck dropped onto his belly to pull a laptop from beneath a canvas. He opened it and began to tap away. Zave hunkered down at Tuck's side, blocking most of her view with his back.

Farthest from the group, Devon was propped against a rock that gave her back support. With her knees up, serving as a desk, she propped her paper on her thighs to write on it. While everyone was so caught up in trying to figure out what went wrong, Devon went back to transcribing.

"The tech is good." Devon heard Zave say. "It's responsive. It's working.

"Game Time always works. We tested it," Tuck said, moving onto his elbows. "If the tech works, then it hasn't been discovered, it's been corrupted from the outside… someone knows we're here."

"Someone?" Zara said.

Devon was smart enough to understand the gravity of that and stopped writing.

"You think someone went in after us and sabotaged it?" Brodie asked.

The task at hand wasn't enough to distract her. Fear chilled Devon despite the heat around them. She hadn't asked about enemies. Any Kindred enemy could have told the cartels their plan if they somehow uncovered it.

But who would be watching the Kindred? Who would want to see them fail? Who would have a stake in sabotaging their mission?

Something brushed the side of her head. Thinking it was a bug, Devon turned to swipe it away. When she saw what it actually was, her scream was stifled by the hand that pressed over her mouth. An arm curled around her head, squeezing her skull to pull her onto her feet. Clawing at his arm, her pad and pencil tumbled to the ground, drawing the attention of the others.

Her assailant stayed crouched behind her once they were both on their feet. The barrel he pushed into her ear was his protection against the able people now glaring at them. "What the fuck?" Zara said. "Wren, what are you doing?"

Brodie's arm moved, but Thad pulled back the hammer. "Don't move, cuz, stay where you are."

"What the fuck do you think you're doing?" Brodie asked.

This was Wren, Thad, the good doctor, the man who laughed with ease and had vowed to do no harm. Except now he was holding her tight against him and threatening her life with a gun. Walking backwards to the edge of the rocks that hid their vehicle, his face pressed into the back of her head, so he could only be peeking around her with one eye.

"You guys need to stay where you are. All of you, stay."

"You wouldn't do this," Zara said. "What's going on? If you're in trouble—"

"Stay still," Thad called out and prodded the gun into Devon so hard, her head tilted.

Her frantic eyes landed on Zave's. She'd just married him, and now she was going to lose him.

"Put the fucking gun down, Wren," Swift said.

"It was you," Zave said in a cool, slow voice. "You sabotaged Game Time."

Wren's view couldn't be great, but he'd be terrified that one of his relatives would get their hands on a weapon and take him out. Except he was blood, he was Kindred, would they shoot him to protect her: the newbie?

"It's loaded with air," Thad barked, lifting his mouth a fraction higher in her hair.

"Think about this," Zara said. "Whatever you're planning to do—"

"I'm planning to get the fuck out of here," he said. "I'm taking Devon with me, and you all are staying here."

"You're a dead man," Zave said in that same chilling

tone.

"We're all headed for one day, Falc, don't tell me you forgot."

He got them around the edge of the ridge, grabbed a handful of her hair and bolted, forcing her to run with him. Thad stuffed her into the car and gunned the engine. But instead of heading toward the road, he drove around the back of the ridge through a crevasse in the rocks and out cross-country.

Devon didn't see if anyone tried to follow and couldn't hear if there were gunshots. She was still face down on the seat beside him, trying to right herself.

"The earpiece, give me the earpiece," he demanded, and she twisted to see his open, expectant hand.

Complying, Devon pulled it out and put it in his hand beside his own. He tossed both out the window and secured his hands on the wheel. Wherever they were going, he had something in his sights. He'd betrayed his kin, sabotaged their mission, and stolen her.

This wasn't how Devon had planned to spend her honeymoon, but she had a feeling this situation was about to get a whole lot worse.

TO BE CONTINUED...

Thank you for reading this tale!
If you can, please take the time to review.

~

**Ask your local library for more Scarlett Finn
novels!**

~

**For all things Scarlett Finn
check out:**

www.scarlettfinn.com

BOOK SIX

Who will survive the final chapter?

FINCH

Kindred Book Six

SCARLETT FINN

OUT NOW!